POWER PLAY

JASMINE WINTERSON

Camerado Books

This is a work of fiction. Names, characters, places, and incidents are either the product of the author's imagination or are used fictitiously, and any resemblance to actual persons, living or dead, business establishments, events, or locales is entirely coincidental. The publisher does not have any control over and does not assume any responsibility for author or third-party websites or their content.

ISBN 978-0-9882208-4-3

Books by Jasmine Winterson

Climbing to Freedom

*****

The *Uncertain Ground* Series

Roost

Power Play

*****

To Caroline and Rose,
My loves, my heart, my home

~

Part I

~

Changing the Game

By the time he looked up, the kid was halfway across the floor. Snow cascading off boots. Wedges of mud and gravel sludge marking his progress. Fortinbras put down his pen, pushed back from his desk. He stared past the hands struggling with a tightly bound roll of papers, studied the wind howling at the trailer door. He gave it a long ten count. "You have my attention," he said finally. At least the kid had been around long enough to know that much. Interrupting silence was rarely worth it.

"Sir, there may be a problem." The kid leaned in to speak, whispering the words as if that might help.

"Stand up straight. Spit it out," Fortinbras barked. "You made it this far." The kid was no more than a year or two out of school, tall and lanky with a blond crew cut. What he wouldn't have given for those genes. Out here for the adventure like so many of them, if he had to guess. Until whatever romantic ideas of frontier life gave way to fleeting, fly-swarmed summers and soul-crushing winters. A gold rush in the Klondike he could understand. The twenty-first century version, not so much. They kept coming though. That was all that mattered.

The kid straightened up. "It's the heat pipes in the column mounts, sir…" he began. The rubber bands finally yielded. Smudged blueprints unfurled in front of Fortinbras. An engineer, he thought. This would be tedious at best. "Let me stop you there," he cut in. "You know I'm the vision guy. Sometimes I'm the money guy. I'm never this guy. Why didn't you bring this to the others?"

"I did, sir. They said to forget about it."

Fortinbras sat back, mildly amused. His crew liked the kid then. They didn't go out of their way often. To hell with red meat or liquor or smoking, he thought. Recognizing good advice is most of what it takes to make it to a ripe old age. He decided to soften his tone. It was the least he could do given where this was heading. He nodded at the blueprints and settled in. "Go ahead," he grunted. "Surprise me."

The kid looked at him warily, waiting for some hidden trap to spring shut. When only silence and raised eyebrows followed, he started in again, haltingly. "So…the column mounts…their efficiencies are the inverse of what you would expect," he said. "It's a tiny thing. Barely noticeable day to day." The blueprints danced and the words sped up. By the end, the kid had hit his stride. It was a strong performance. "Over time I think the new equipment may actually thaw the permafrost," he concluded. "It could destabilize entire sections of the pipeline."

Exactly, Fortinbras thought. Too bad this was not an open

audition. The world needed to change. People talked about tipping points as if they magically appeared. Sometimes there needed to be a big behind-the-scenes shove in the mix. Fossil fuels needed a helping hand out the door. The natives in this neck of the woods had it right the first time. You don't crap where you sleep. Carving off mountain tops. Fracking backyards. Fighting in foreign lands. Polluting the air, water, and land every step of the way. All while a giant flaming orb lights the sky, winds and water push tirelessly forward, and the Earth's own heat surges underfoot. He wasn't about to explain it to the kid, but saw no need to apologize for his fate either. You couldn't put a price on what they were trying to do. "That's good work," he said. He stared at the blueprints. "I'm going to want to spend some time with these. Mind if I hold onto them?"

His words sent the kid into a defensive crouch. "Of course sir," he replied nervously. "Did you have any questions?" Fortinbras ignored him. He took a moment longer to consider the situation, as it deserved. He decided his initial assessment stood. There were no other good options – the way forward was clear. "We'll need to meet again," he said eventually. "What's your name?"

"Ben, sir."

"Okay, Ben. Stick around at the end of the week. We'll talk more then," he replied. "You've got a bright future in energy ahead of you." He specialized in dark humor, even when no one was there to appreciate it. A good thing in this case, he thought. If the kid had picked up on it, he would have been scrambling for the door and screaming for help. Instead he blinked quickly a few times, murmured a thank you and headed out. This one would go quietly.

Fortinbras grabbed his phone and made the situation clear to the crew. The kid would need a minder, something low key until the camp cleared out for the usual end-of-week debauchery. It was standard procedure – damage control to make sure no one else went down with him. He sighed, disappointed. He had long been resigned to people's limitations. He exploited them every day. But still, the kid was a letdown. A quick compliment and feigned interest was all it took. *Really?* To be so insightful on paper and so blind on the ground. If there was a God he seemed to have a real thing for setting his creations up to fail. People so trusting shouldn't be let out of the lower forty-eight. There were still wild animals in this part of the world.

The pace the rest of the week was frenetic. He sat in on meetings and conference calls, reviewed cost estimates and timeframes. It was the usual show of engagement. As the days slid by, the end of the week nagged at him like a sore tooth. The visit was no longer a victory lap. More review and more refinements would be necessary. Gazinsky and Harper nodded grimly at the news, sitting silently as he throttled the blueprints and threw them to the floor. The process was working. Keeping the plans hidden in plain sight was harder. They had been through a lot to get here – every inch of the damn pipeline had been tailored to local conditions. They had painstakingly put together a dozen teams dedicated to imperceptibly taking down the marvel of modern engineering. They were close – but being almost invisible was not good enough.

As the third day of meetings dragged on, he was unable to keep up the facade any longer. He stepped outside, leaving them to wonder what had gone wrong. He was grateful for the arctic blast that tore at his cold weather gear, forcing him to wake up. He huddled against a small storage shed, cupped his hands and vaped on an e-cigarette, surveying the temporary city that packed up and moved along as pipeline testing and maintenance progressed. Basic was a kind word for it. Several dozen trailers were scattered in uneven rows across the landscape, each sun bleached, grime covered and dented, dorms and offices and supply rooms tethered to generators. Separate from them in the distance, the mess hall stood alone. The bright red building was the beacon for the only beer and warm food for miles. Rome wasn't built in a day, he reminded himself. So what if it was an ugly-as-all-hell foundation for an empire. It was a lot easier to hide than the last place, and that had not worked out so well.

A generator nearby kicked up a notch – rigged lights overhead flickered to life. He checked his watch and shook his head. Days and nights up here were thrown in a blender and poured out across the calendar. It was two in the afternoon and the sun was almost down. Shimmering pinks and reds across the horizon announced the end of the Alaskan day, painting the tops of the evergreens edging the camp with a cold fire. Fortinbras shuddered. He and the forest did not get along. Back east, the forest knew its place. The warm green abundance of summer pulled back in the fall, opening views and exposing ridgelines. Up here it loomed, dark, and impenetrable, waiting to reclaim what had been lost. He would have clear-cut it for miles on either side of the pipeline if he could. Keeping a clean house did not mean letting the wilderness take over. It all came down to balance.

More lights flickered on. As if on cue, people started to appear – a few at first and then a steady stream. A setting sun meant dinner, no matter what the clock said. Fortinbras was about to go back inside when the kid walked by with some friends. He watched the group as they headed for the mess hall. Not too far away, the kid's minder followed discreetly. They would move sooner if they needed to; losing one was bad enough.

Almost invisible. Fortinbras gritted his teeth in frustration. The kid was like a nail pop in a building that should have settled by now. He didn't want to come back – it was Gazinsky's gig from here on out. Three years of bush planes barely clearing the tree lines was more than enough. The crisscrossing vapor trails overhead from oil executives jetting between Anchorage and the North Slope were an endless reminder of how the world currently worked. He had not even seen a bald eagle. The payoff is all that matters, he told himself when new delays surfaced. He believed it sometimes. This was just the beginning. They had to get it right up here. And then some – they had cover in Alaska. This was all going squarely on the shoulders of climate change. Once they got the contracts and started work on crude oil and refined petroleum pipelines in the lower forty-eight, the rapid collapse of the aging systems had to be untraceable. His fondest hope was that the fight over the nation's newest pipeline would continue long after its approval. They could work quietly in each state while the Keystone extension sucked away everyone's attention. By the time the fuss died down, he was confident they would be ready to take it on. Alaska was the practice test. The lower forty-eight systems were the final exam. The Keystone Pipeline was the doctoral review board.

Fortinbras looked down at his hands. They were tensed, as if ready to ward off blows. He could feel his pulse racing. He couldn't deny it – the situation was weighing on him. The mood in camp was not helping. People cut each other off during meetings. Doors no longer swung closed. The crews had hit the end of a long smooth stretch, working their way across the Yukon Basin. Soon Fairbanks would no longer be in range for downtime. *Everyone needs a release.* Most people in camp would get it at the weekend. Even the kid, in a manner of speaking. Fortinbras smiled grimly. His own would come with breaking news reports of several million barrels of tar sands oil spilling across the nation's heartland. He could almost hear the garbled communications. He had imagined the scene a thousand times – the operators perched on their high-tech thrones, frantically trying to restart inert electronics, unable to stanch the flow across a dozen break points from Alberta to Texas. Delayed gratification was not a problem. He had waited this long and finally understood. The Exxon Valdez and the oil spill in the Gulf did not turn heads for more than a few months. All they left behind was lawsuits and more business as usual. Lasting, meaningful change was painful. It took decades. He was playing for keeps this time.

At last. It was Friday. He looked around the trailer for what should be the last time. He threw on the previous day's clothes and grabbed his bag and winter gear. Harper was waiting for him outside. "Are we good?" he asked. The company buses idling nearby tempered his expectations.

"Give it an hour." Harper shrugged. "The kid's still running scenarios in the modeling lab like you asked." They might as well get everything they could out of him, Fortinbras figured. It wasn't like they could hire an outside auditor. Still, he hoped the kid did not come up with much. Too much more and he would have to contemplate another trip. Which was simply unacceptable. He had bigger fish to fry.

"Just you and me today?"

"Yes sir. We're not expecting any trouble." Fortinbras had never seen either of his lieutenants look even slightly troubled. With their backgrounds, he figured they could handle a room full of angry ninjas. The kid was a walk in the park. His stomach growled. "Come get me when it's time," he muttered. He wasn't about to do this without food in his belly.

"Yes, Mr. Fortinbras."

There. Fortinbras allowed himself a slight smile as he walked away. *See.* The words were living proof this was possible. He had pulled it off himself. *I am invisible.* It was the one reason all those years had been worth it. He had designed the escape hatches for all of the elites in case everything ever went south. It seemed like an exercise in waste and extravagance at the time. What could possibly go wrong? The law firm had been one of the most powerful organizations in the world. Its tentacles reached into parliaments, embassies, executive offices, and company suites. It did not distinguish between those who held elected office and those who came to power by force. Its own survival – and the obscene prosperity of those at the top – was its mission.

Now changing the world, *that* was a mission. Fortinbras walked into the mess hall. A few stragglers were still coming round from a rough Thursday night. Everyone else had been able to hold on and was sitting on those buses, ready to cut loose. He slid a tray through the food line, found an empty table and washed down some oversalted eggs and burnt toast with a cup of scalding black coffee. In the back, the kitchen staff was already running the dishwashers. Out front, they were mopping the floors – they would be on the last bus, count on it. You would have to heat up a can of beans yourself if you wanted to eat in camp this weekend.

Fortinbras shook his head. Even now, with everything rolling, the price had been so high. Almost too high. Being Stanley Richards' lackey at the law firm, putting up with that senior buffoon's constant demands and whale-sized ego, had been unbearable. The years had not softened the sharp edges. There were no good memories. Every detail from that time still grated. Weekends packed with overtime. No respect. Humiliation in endless competitions – biking, racquetball, poker, it didn't matter. Outside the office, Richards seduced his girlfriends, then had him bed others when it suited the firm's needs. For a man ungraciously nicknamed "bowling ball" – "bb" – by the firm's elite, he had gotten a lot of tail for a short, fat, bald man. A small saving grace that Richards lorded over him every chance he got.

Once upon a time, everyone knew me as the up-and-coming antitrust attorney in the country, he thought. *They had no idea.* Following the debacle in the desert and the feds rolling up everyone else back east, he was the only one left to use the escape hatches. The old man was dead. *I should have been too.* All because of a woman. *Richards' woman. Katherine Jordan.* If then were now, Richards would not have lasted a week. He would have taken care of the situation long before that fool's lapse of judgment, long before it led to a bunch of mountain biking, organic co-op managing greenhorns bringing the whole thing down. He was in charge now. Which was to say…it was time to deal with the kid.

His phone buzzed as he finished his coffee. He looked down at the text. *About time.* As the kitchen staff headed out the front doors, he headed out a side exit. He heard the buses pulling away as he made his way around the back of the research trailers. Harper's hulking presence made clear where he was headed. He walked over and punched through the trailer door – the kid was working in the back, next to the plotters. "Let's get this show on the road, Ben," he called out. He dragged a chair over and sat down next to the kid. "What have you got?"

"I gave it my best shot, sir," the kid replied. "If we make the adjustments I suggested, the system should be fine. The tensile strength of all materials in this section should be within acceptable parameters." The young man shook his fist in quiet victory. He also looked exhausted. The cans of Red Bull underfoot had not pulled him through as they used to.

Fortinbras realized he had been this young when he came under Richards' wing. He hated to admit it. *I was probably this green back then as well.* Eager to please, an empty vessel ready to be filled with someone else's plans and priorities. He finished law school on the firm's dime after an internship. A summer of excess and delight followed by a decade of hell. There was one difference, though. The kid had a conscience. Curiosity. Creativity. Technical expertise. None of those things mattered if they came with a moral barometer attached. The crew was in the business of creating problems. Solutions would come later.

"I guess that's good news," he said finally. "You're sure? Nothing else?"

The kid shook his head.

"What about recommendations? Can we optimize the pumping stations? Work on the pipeline pigs?"

"Sir?" The kid stared at him, unsure once again how to proceed. "I'm a risk management specialist. I –"

Fortinbras cut him off with a glare. "I understand that. I was just curious." He couldn't hide his disappointment. *Where is the vision?* He marveled regularly at the number of engineers who could not see six inches past technical specifications. "Walk with me," he said finally, pushing back his chair. The exit interview was over. "There's something I'd like you to see."

The kid followed meekly behind. They met up with Harper outside and set off, cutting across the cleared-out camp. The wind howled between the trailers, meeting them head on. The men – even Harper with his massive stride – stumbled frequently; the gravel, mud, and ice underfoot had long since frozen into jagged tire ruts and the uneven patina of a thousand overlapping footprints. A dirty rime clung to every inch of chain-link fence.

Fortinbras raised a hand as they approached the entrance station. The guards' nods made him turn around – the kid was no longer right behind them. He had stayed put twenty yards back. He was walking in a small circle, looking in all directions…a man looking for options. About time, Fortinbras thought. *The kid is spooked.* "Let's hoof it," he shouted. "We have a ways to go."

"Go where, sir?" The earlier tentativeness was gone. The kid's question was a demand – the firm tone clear even in the howling wind. The unspoken subtext infused each word. *There's nothing out there but forest and miles of pipeline.*

"Trust me. I'm not going to feed you to a grizzly," Fortinbras replied. "Plus, I'm paying you, remember?"

The kid started to move, reluctantly. He hesitated once more as he sidestepped the entrance gate. Fortinbras understood. There were no footprints out here. And his boss was leading them down into a boulder-strewn gulley. Having Harper hogtie the kid and carry him down there would save time. But the kid had to want this. Choice was important. Even when things were out of your control. Fortinbras signaled to Harper to hold tight and stomped back up to the road.

"We've built something you're going to want to see," he said, putting a hand on the kid's shoulder. He tried to make his voice sound warm and reassuring. It was not his strength. "There's a prototype. Okay?"

The kid stood still, hands on hips, unconvinced. "Why me? Why now?"

"You've earned the right to see it," he replied. "And now is the only time possible. Very few people know about this. If you want to be part of the future, it's half a mile that way." He watched as the combustible elements – curiosity, drive, ego – ignited in the kid's eyes. *They rarely fail to deliver.* He and Harper had a willing hiking partner.

They made it down the gulley and through the boulder field without any twisted ankles, a minor miracle given the ice. Fortinbras sneered at the trees as they entered the darkness waiting beyond. Short stubby pines in the understory poked and prodded as they passed. Towering hemlocks creaking overhead quietly threatened, holding huge loads of snow on their straining branches. Barely enough light filtered through the canopy. Thankfully, Harper could negotiate the camouflaged marker poles blindfolded; Fortinbras followed his lieutenant's boots as they strode through the forbidding forest. When they stopped, he looked up to see they were only a few feet from the giant silver snake. Thrumming through the wilderness, carrying its thunderous load, the pipeline sounded like a living thing; thousands of gallons of hot oil were pulsing overhead, sidetracked briefly before continuing on their eight-hundred-mile journey south.

Fortinbras turned to find the kid staring at what looked like a giant, seedpod-shaped rock attached to the pipeline. "Where are we?" he asked. "And what's going on with the pipeline? Where is the maintenance road? The grade is clearly not optimal. Where are the heat fins? This looks like —"

"Like it was built in a hurry," Fortinbras snapped. "It isn't perfect and it definitely isn't by the book. The building is not on any map. Neither is the interceptor loop. The only thing that matters is what's inside."

The kid's jaw dropped. "The state and the feds may feel differently."

Fortinbras laughed. The kid was a fish out of water. Too late, he had found his voice and his calling. A born regulator. "You think Tesla and Marconi followed the rulebook?" he asked. "What about Steve Jobs?"

The kid gave him a skeptical glance. "That's some company we're keeping."

"You haven't gone inside yet. Any other questions?"

"About a thousand," the kid replied without missing a beat. "Maybe more."

"Being part of the system should help," Fortinbras replied. He walked over to the base of the rock. *You'll be able to share them with all of eternity.* A recessed camera scanned his retina and a hidden sliding door hissed open. They stepped into a large oval chamber – smooth square panels backlit by tiny beads of white LEDs curved together around them. They were standing on a suspended metal walkway; stairs nearby disappeared into darkness. Straight ahead, beyond a safety railing, the outlines of a huge orb were barely visible. A closer look revealed thick pipes connected to its base. Everything was shades of gray and black.

Harper brushed past them and leapt up the staircase, metal grating clanking underfoot. Moments later, lights and banks of monitors on a platform above them flickered to life. A low vibrating roar surged out of the orb. "We're hoping to eliminate the noise and vibrations in later refinements," Fortinbras said. He savored the astonishment on the kid's face.

"Isn't he security?" the kid asked, gesturing at Harper as he continued bringing the facility to life.

"Harper? Yeah, Russian special forces – SPETSNAZ – for more than a decade. He also holds a double doctorate in engineering and industrial applied mathematics. A gift from the Cold War, you might say."

The kid shook his head. "Can I go up there?" he asked.

"Knock yourself out," Fortinbras replied. He walked over to the edge of the darkness and rested his arms on the railing. Steam was now pouring out of vents in the orb. Turbines somewhere overhead pulled the vapor trails up to the ceiling, where they vanished. He loved how the orb looked like a planet and a witch's cauldron, ready to transform base materials and make the world new again. He gave the kid a couple more minutes to take it all in. "Go ahead. Ask the question," he said finally.

The kid did not hesitate. "What is this place?" he asked. He was staring at the orb, transfixed.

"The future," Fortinbras replied. "I've had time to think about where we're headed. My future. Everyone else's. The planet's." Two years, six months, and fourteen days to be exact. Living in exile. Not that all of it had been spent in contemplation. The first few days had been spent getting there – ditching the jeep and stealing a car, driving through the night to a safe house in El Paso, getting packed in a box with crackers and water, and unpacked days later in Caracas. Then there were the surgeries in another city. Nothing went as planned after that. Days blurred as the pain meds soaked in. He remembered a small square room, a chamber pot in one corner, a stack of sheets and medical supplies scattered across the cool tile floor next to an upturned cart. He lay on a filthy mattress. Someone – he remembered a face, a woman's face – changed his dressings. Food, water, and pills appeared on a tray. Afterward, waiting for sweet oblivion to return, he would stare at the yellow curtains fluttering in front of an open window above him.

"It started with dreams," he continued. The sounds of the city filtered in as he drifted off – scooters buzzing, bus honks, crowd shouts, rodents scratching in the walls, birdsong. "I dreamt of waves of energy, pouring forth from every life form on the planet. I dreamt of surges of power, circling up from the ocean floor and pouring down from the skies. And each time, it all came together in a swirling, sparking electric mass that looked like the shape in front of you." He had barely remembered his dreams before then. For weeks, he lived only to return to them, while his body began to consume itself, and his skin yellowed and bedsores spread and deepened.

All until the door crashed in and the woman flew across the room, screaming at him to get up. "Avíspate! The men are coming! Los hombres vienen, *señor*! Leave now…leave!" Even in his stupor, he knew. Someone had sold him. The manhunt stateside was massive, the reward ever greater as time passed. No one could have traced him here. But someone could have taken a guess at the identity of the Americano drugging himself to death in a back-alley hospital…some army lackey had sent it up the food chain, maybe even to the top. The law firm had laundered tens of millions of el presidente's petrodollars over the years. But times change. He was easy money, even a hedge against sanctions.

The woman dressed him and helped him stumble down a hallway. They burst out a door onto an ancient wooden fire escape. "You are free," she hissed in his ear, as if such a thing was possible, and ran back inside. The door slammed shut. He reached out to steady himself as the world – market stalls, a donkey, and people, so many people – seesawed back and forth below. He looked around for a dry rattling sound nearby before realizing it was his own breathing. He had no idea what to do next. His thoughts were muddled and confused. Moving at all seemed like an insurmountable obstacle, so unnecessary, when lying down here would be such a simple relief, such a –

"We need to go." A firm hand took his elbow. He turned to find the old man standing behind him, gaunt but otherwise unchanged. *Not possible.* He was dead, blown to pieces in the desert along with everyone else. "Stop looking at me and get moving," he growled. "You saved my ass once. I'm returning the favor." He was pissed. They clambered down the fire escape and weaved through the crowded market. Everyone was staring. "Ignore them," the old man whispered. "Any street that leads to the river, take it."

Those streets would fall into his dreams as well. "The spindles are hollow," he said to the kid, pointing to a network of barely visible metal tubes that connected the orb to the walls of the chamber. "They carry a fluid matrix back and forth. Behind these shielded walls, we are surrounded by wafer-thin layers of water. That pressurized chamber can turn any waste material into energy. Or it can churn out other raw materials. It'll make coal. At the moment, the output is sweet crude. The only waste product is water vapor."

The kid looked skeptical, then confused, then astonished. "If that's true, this machine would change everything. But…why do this out here, and with oil?" he asked, barely able to contain his excitement. "There's a million gallons a day pouring by out there. It's old news."

Fortinbras sighed. *Too little, too late*. He made his way up to the platform to join the kid and Harper. "Oil is what worked first," he said. "We're taking our time – to make sure we get it right. The scientists are fine-tuning the systems now, so the orbs can recycle everything. Modern-day alchemy – turning any material into an energy source." While he was speaking, Harper hit several switches. A panel in the floor slid open. A conveyor belt silently rose up between Fortinbras and the kid. Harper hit more switches and it locked in place against the side of the orb. "There," he said. "it's ready to receive material now."

The layers of water joined Fortinbras' dreams last of all – the river, or a series of rivers, as he figured out later. Somehow he and the old man made it down to the water. His feet were cut up and bleeding, sweat stung his eyes. Every bone in his body ached. "What now?" he asked, afraid to mention his meds. Withdrawal was already starting to wrap its long, anxious fingers around his chest. "Now you take your life back," the old man replied and shoved him off the dock. He fell back onto the front deck of a sailboat. The old man worked quickly, tugging ropes free from their moorings. As he realized what the old man was doing, Fortinbras struggled to find his feet, horrified. "What the hell?" he shouted. "You can't cut me loose out here. I'll die. I know who we can call. They can be here in a few hours." He took a step, slipped and fell back on the deck. The old man pushed the boat out into the fast-flowing water. "If you die out there, I'll see you soon," he called after him. "If not, you'll know what to do. Get that poison out of your system and get to work."

From then to now seemed like several lifetimes. In front of him, the kid was checking out the conveyor belt, leaning over to examine the ball bearings. "So how does it help the pipeline?" he asked. "It doesn't," Fortinbras replied. He nodded at Harper, who had quietly made his way down to join them. He moved behind where the kid was standing. "It's been serving another purpose," he continued. "Mostly convenience. It takes care of any problems that come up. Roadkill. Unwanted visitors. People asking the wrong questions."

The kid looked sideways at him, his brow furrowing as he tried to make sense of the words. His eyes went wide when he saw Harper emerge from the shadows. He tried to turn away. Harper caught and pinned him against the conveyor belt, easily deflecting his flailing arms. "I wanted you to know what you have been part of," Fortinbras said. "Phase one is the messy part. You were right. We *are* destabilizing the pipeline. We have other teams working on the grid. Phase one is getting people to change and change quickly, as they must if we're to keep our planet alive. Phase two is making the world a better place. But we have to get there first." It was not the Gettysburg address, he thought, but Mr. Lincoln would have understood. Difficult decisions in tough times were the hallmark of great leadership. Fortinbras straightened up for the final goodbye. The kid had stopped struggling. His eyes begged for mercy. "I also wanted to thank you for your service, even now," he concluded. "The system needs to be calibrated. You're helping us do that."

Harper maneuvered his prey closer to the belt. He took the kid's neck in his hands and twisted it sharply to one side. It snapped like a twig; his body went limp and fell to the floor. Harper bent down and heaved it onto the conveyor. He looked at Fortinbras. "Good to go, sir?" he asked. Fortinbras nodded. Harper brushed past him. He watched the belt come to life, pulling the kid's body toward an opening in the orb. The final stage of his own journey had been so much longer, and a good deal more painful. The river had been in full flood, tearing and pulling at the boat, lapping hungrily at the gunwales. When dawn broke, he realized the sailboat was the only thing on the water. Morning passed. Cities were replaced by villages and then settlements and then mile after mile of forest. There was no one to signal for help. He could not have rigged a sail to save his life. The baking afternoon sun eventually drove him inside the cabin. He found a bed, a bathroom, and a tiny galley kitchen below deck. He tore apart the cabinets, suddenly consumed by hunger. There were stacks of canned goods and several jugs of water. He scrabbled around for an opener and cranked several cans open, gulping down tuna and kidney beans so fast he almost choked. He lay back on the bed, his belly swollen, exhausted.

Rest was not in the cards. With immediate survival taken care of, his mind shifted back to the main event. *Where are the meds?* His skin started to itch and he was soon soaked in sweat. He tore at his dressings; his bedsores were weeping pus and blood. *There must be something on this boat. Find it!* The voice was demanding, insistent, relentless. There was nothing behind the food and plates and paper towels and silverware in the cabinets. *Try the bathroom. Find a first aid kit. There has to be something!* He scanned the medicine cabinet, sweeping aside toiletries. A small bottle of aspirin caught his eye – he downed the pills and moved on. He found the first aid kit on a wall behind a life preserver. *More fucking aspirin!* He fell to the floor and started to shake. Sweat was pouring off his body. He looked around the cabin. *Nothing.* After a brief pause, mania took over. *They must have stashed the good stuff. Find it!* He grabbed a knife from the kitchen and ripped apart the mattress and chair cushions. He smashed picture frames and threw them aside. He kicked in the heating and cooling unit and pulled out the electronics. He jumped to his feet in a rage, tore the kitchen table from its base pole and threw it aside. As he did so, its heaviness took him by surprise and he slipped. His head caught a corner of the table as he fell. The world – mercifully – went black.

In front of him, blackness swallowed up the kid. The conveyor stopped moving, pulled back, and descended back into the floor. Twenty minutes inside the orb and the young engineer would be indistinguishable from the ancient black gold pouring through the pipeline outside. There would be few questions in camp – people came and went all the time. There might be a missing persons report. A family member might even make the trek to ask questions. The front office would take care of it. "He was a nice young man. Smart. A hard worker with a promising future," they would say, welcoming any visitors into a quiet back room. "But he never seemed happy. He was restless, lonely. It's a hard life out here, not for everyone. He was here one day and then gone the next. His bunk was cleared out. No note. Nothing. That's all we know. Now…can we get you something? Coffee? A soda?"

On the boat, that realization helped him hit bottom. If he died, no one would come looking for him. The few people who cared already assumed he was dead. He had nothing to show for his time on Earth but some degrees, a trail of failed relationships, and tenure as a partner at one of the most corrupt organizations on the planet. Whether headed to heaven or hell, they were not credentials that would impress angels or devils. He was small potatoes, a nothing, part of the anonymous mass of humanity marching endlessly into eternity. When he awoke, he was staring at a thick, drying pool of his own blood. His fever had cooled but now his head throbbed; his fingers probed a sticky, matted mess. The gash was nasty but he would survive – a small victory. He tried to haul himself up but did not have the strength. Eventually he managed to slide over to the kitchen cabinets and sit up. Across the cabin, a sliver of a broken mirror told the tale. There was a naked, filthy, blood-smeared animal on the boat.

The breather lasted all of a few minutes. His skin started to itch once again and the cabin walls started closing in. He made it up the ladder and out onto the deck – it was nighttime and the boat was bobbing along in a calmer stretch of water. Overhead, skeins of stars knit together the night sky in a dazzling display. The breeze and open space brought blessed relief for a moment, but then the stars began to pulse and the sky began to bend and bow. He closed his eyes and felt around for a length of rope. He tied himself to the mast. He grabbed a loose bolt lying nearby and sat there, waiting for the voice of addiction to return. Each time it did, he jammed the bolt deep into his cuts, sores, and bruises. The wind carried away his screams. The miles flowed past.

Fortinbras put on a shielded suit and waited until the kid's processing was finished. He could not just walk away. Death would be an inevitable part of their work for years to come. It was an integral part of any great project. He thought of the day laborers lost and buried in the nation's railroad beds more than a century ago. The bodies of hapless medieval workers shoveled in with the rubble into the recesses of castle walls. Divers pounded into the foundations of the Golden Gate Bridge. Witnessing the consequences was part of the price to pay for thinking big. He was more than willing to pay the bill. His own survival had been in question for days – perhaps weeks – as storms raged on the river and delirium ravaged his body. He rationed remaining food and water. During lucid moments, he watched the riverbanks for any signs of settlements. Mostly, he drifted in and out of consciousness, fighting the voice that sought to claim his soul.

Life began again on a hot, humid day. He startled awake, jolted by a foul stench. What's going on, he wondered, pulling back violently. *Where am I?* A second later...*Who are they?* A group of Indians stood around him in a circle, talking excitedly. One man, some kind of shaman – rustling shell necklaces, red-and-black body paint, elaborate facial piercings, white-feathered headdress – was much closer to him. Gasping for air, Fortinbras struggled to take it all in. The carved bowl the shaman had held under his nose had fallen to the floor, its dark paste spattered across several logs. He was sitting in a large round shelter with an open center. The air was thick with smoke from several small fires, but he could still make out glimpses of blue sky and forest. Thatched palm leaves overhead formed the roof. He was sitting on animal skins, his back propped against a post. He looked down – he was naked except for a pair of tattered gray shorts. His wounds were bound up in poultices of dark leaves and some kind of sticky resin. He flexed his arms and legs gingerly. There were no ripping bolts of pain, no thought-shattering moments of pure agony. Even his throbbing headache was gone. I feel pretty close to normal, he thought, amazed. *How long have I been here?*

He smiled reassuringly at the group and tried to get up. The shaman pulled back and the group fell silent. He could not move. He was lashed to the pole with a heavy rope. "Can someone help me?" he asked. "Help? Anyone? Ayudarme?" He made hand gestures when none of them responded. His heart sank when several of them smiled. These were not the smiling brown natives of a thousand National Geographic specials. They all had rotting teeth and shredded gums. He saw clearly now the sunken eyes, the torn-up skin and acne-laced faces. Meth had made it into the Amazon. He did not know if he should laugh or cry. There was good news – the stuff was getting in here somehow. But it meant the natives were going to do anything to get more. He had traveled countless miles and not gone anywhere. A white man washing up on the shore had to be worth something to someone, somewhere. He tried not to panic. It could be days or a matter of minutes until someone came for him. *Think.* He smiled and nodded at other natives as they came and stared. *I can't do much until they leave me alone.* Children brought him bowls of food. Some were naked, some wore loincloths, others were wearing faded Yankee shirts and Barcelona soccer jerseys. A bowl of still-wriggling grubs and caterpillars he left untouched. He wolfed down the mangos, bananas, and papayas. He understood. He was worth more healthy. They were fattening him up for market. His teeth crunched down on something hard. He pretended to eat and tongued the material carefully into his palm. It was hard and sharp, wood or bone, he couldn't tell. It was something. He prayed that his novelty would wear off by nightfall. He had work to do. *How am I going to get out of here?* He strained to get a better look outside the shelter, but could not make out much. Maybe there was a road. He listened for the sound of a car or the low roar of traffic. No luck. All he could make out was murmurs of conversation, an occasional fire pop, and the wind rustling tree branches overhead. Surely the river was close by. The thought of getting back out there made him shudder. But it had to be his best chance. If there was a road they would track him easily. In the forest, he would be a snack for a jaguar or a plaything for a boa constrictor. The river it is, he decided. Then what? Even if he could find it, the sailboat was not much of an option – he could not steer it to save his life. *Canoes.* The thought was a revelation. Any indigenous people worth their salt had dugouts. If he could slip away in the dark, he could paddle as well as anyone and maybe even get a few hours' head start.

The afternoon slowly slid into dusk. As the darkness settled, they posted a lone guard – a chain-smoking man who fixed him with a fierce stare. No one else was nearby. Awhile later, the man seemed to lose interest in his assignment and went off to grab a smoke with some friends. He came back every half hour or so. Fortinbras prayed he would not look too closely at the fraying rope. The cutting was slow, tedious, painful work. The rope rubbed his fingers raw and then they started to bleed. He hoped the shadows would hide the blood. Thankfully, the night was cloudy and the air was still thick with smoke. He tried moving his shoulders and arms, aiming to create some slack. As he sawed away and kept shifting around, the ropes began to move slowly up his arms. It was enough. He realized he had already made too much progress; he would not be able to hide it. *I have to go now.* The timing seemed fortunate; the guard was in a heated argument with two other men who had just joined his group. Fortinbras awkwardly wriggled his way free. He crept along the edge of the shelter, looking for a way out. He found a small gap in the leaves and slid out onto the ground. He had barely had time to stand when the guard sounded the alarm, shouting at the top of his lungs. There was no cover – everything near the shelter had been cleared. He looked down at the base of the shelter and saw it was a few inches off the ground. He dropped down and squeezed his body into the small space, scratching, pulling, clawing his way in. Feet pattered above him and ran past his hiding place a moment later. He tried to watch where they went, losing sight of them as they crashed through bushes at the far edge of the clearing. Seconds later, he heard the best sounds he could have hoped for – people were splashing around in the river, followed by more shouts. Men burst back out of the bushes and sprinted past, just feet from where he lay. He counted them as best he could. Twelve had run past. Eleven had returned. They had to have posted a sentry. Assuming there was a boat, he liked the odds.

He made for the edge of the clearing. No one called out. He slid quietly into the bushes and crawled down the slope. He almost wasted his chance, coming inches from slamming head first into the sentry's leg in the darkness. He held the cutting fragment tightly in one hand and silently rose up behind the sentry. He clamped his free hand over the man's mouth and drove the fragment deep into the base of his neck. As blood jetted out, he kidney-punched the man several times, driving him to the ground. Only when he rolled the body over did he realize he had killed his guard. He saw now the man was a boy – he had barely hit puberty. *Better you than me, kid.*

He looked up to see six dugout canoes resting high on the riverbank. Next to them, several torches burned in the muggy night air. The future is looking up, he thought. *About time I caught a break.* He headed over to pull one of the boats into the water and push off, then he realized he could buy more time. He turned over the remaining boats, pushed them together, and ran around picking up anything that would burn. He tossed bark, branches, and leaves over the boats and grabbed the torches. "Burn baby burn," he whispered, and threw them in. The wet wood sputtered and hissed but parts of the boats caught fire. It would have to do.

He pushed his boat into the water and jumped in. There was a hand-carved paddle by his feet. *Sweet. I have no idea where I'm going,* he thought. *But I'm going there as fast as this boat will carry me.* The current picked up and soon he was flying down the river. Surely, eventually, the massive water snake would pass a city large enough where he could disappear. If I live, he thought, I will come back and burn this place to the ground.

Much later, he was able to put names on his journey. The Orinoco. The Casiquiare Canal. The Rio Negro. The Yanomami. Manaus. For the energy orb, the names of its parts were not quite as memorable. The mass-spectrum inverter. A cross-catalyzed ion coupling amplifier. He stared at the black sphere as it cooled down. The journey and his addiction-addled dreams led from there to here. From the depths of depravity to the edge of greatness, he reflected. Harper walked over and handed him the diagnostics. Processing time was down to fourteen minutes. Clothing had been vaporized and removed from the system. In total, ninety-five percent of the kid's body mass had been converted into crude oil. They were getting close – bones and teeth remained the biggest challenge. The kid was on his way to Valdez.

"Are we all set, Mr. Fortinbras?"

He looked at his watch. "I believe we are, Sergei. Let's get back to camp." Things were starting to look up. Dealing with the kid had not delayed things. Harper and Gazinsky would be able to take care of final modifications. Now, he could let himself think about the week to come. He could not remember when he had last taken some time out – certainly not a day since returning from Brazil. Operations everywhere were running smoothly enough now. A little R&R lay ahead. There was just the commercial flight to Seattle to suffer through. Still, even that got him out of the wilderness. Then it was onto a private jet and on to all of the delicious details – everything was in place. Best of all, after hitting Aspen's powder, it was time to go back to where it all began. A place where empire building took place in offices and smoke-filled back rooms. A place he knew like the back of his hand. Only this time, he was in charge. There was a bounce in his step as he left the facility. Someone had to be there to pick up the pieces when business as usual fell apart. *Time to come in from the cold.*

Coming to Terms

He was talking faster and getting louder. He was gesturing wildly at the group. He hated himself but could not stop. It had been months and there were no leads.

"What do you want us to do, Ry?" Jackie asked. "I feel like we're harassing the cops as it is."

He sighed. *What about your freaking boyfriend? What good is he?* Andy was sitting quietly beside her, studying his shoelaces intently. A sergeant in the county police department, surely he would have been able to ferret out any scraps from the investigation. But he seemed stuck in rotation between the K-9 unit and traffic duty.

"Yeah bro, all we can do is sit tight," Sam chimed in. "And, you know, try to help Anna through this."

Great, more of the status quo, just what we need, Ry thought. With some cereal box wisdom thrown in.

"Ry, I think we should talk about this some other time." Katherine's eyes bored into him. He could see she was furious. They had talked before everyone came over. People were dealing with everything in different ways. Give them time and space. Try to be a good listener. We will get through this together. The talking points were all well and good. But what about making sense of it all, he wondered. What about justice? The thoughts coursed through his mind unanswered, building into a torrent of anger and frustration that finally tore through any last vestiges of restraint. "This isn't the Game of Life, people!" he shouted. "There's no path to follow, no dice to roll to live happily ever after."

No one answered. He understood. Here they all were, sitting around the deck on a beautiful late spring day, a group of good friends hanging out. Everyone had gotten comfortable. Beyond Sports bike shop was a national mecca and the Bookcliffs Challenge was the hottest ticket on the mountain biking circuit. The co-op had expanded across the southwest. He had done it too. He had buried everything away, just like the others. The weddings helped. Then he and Katherine had Jonah and Nora and moved into a beautiful home in a leafy downtown neighborhood. Everything kept moving forward until that Sunday night phone call forced him to look back. Ever since, sharp shards of the past kept cutting into his days, his relationships, his thoughts.

Ry's anger began to subside, but he knew it was too late. The barbecue was over. The kids were still playing and there was a bunch of meat to throw on the grill, but he knew he had crossed the line. Again. "I'm sorry," he said simply. And he was. Anna was heading inside, her shoulders shaking. She brushed Derek's arm away as she walked past. Now Derek was standing there staring at him, hands on his hips. His expression made his feelings quite clear. *Really, Ry? We had to go there now? Please stop doing this to my wife.* And Derek was the only one who had any time for his theories. There was only one way to make it right. He ran up the back steps and followed Anna inside. She was sitting in their living room, wiping away tears. He paused in the doorway. "I'm sorry, Anna. I –"

"They could still rule his death a suicide, you know," she said quietly. There had been no sign of a break in, no sign of a struggle.

Ry wasn't sure what to do. He wanted more than anything to make things better, to say something that could help. But he couldn't. Her brother was gone.

Anna's voice filled the silence. "It's easy to go the other way, too. There were a thousand people who wanted Luis dead," she continued. "He defended the worst of the worst and lived like a king off their money. You met him – he was prickly, arrogant, unbearable. There were plenty of times I wanted to kill him."

"He's also the reason we're alive." Ry's words hung there, heavy and awkward. Anna looked down at the carpet. He realized he had sidestepped any meaningful conversation with her since it happened. Just quick condolences and passing pleasantries while dropping off meals. He was pretty sure he knew where this was headed. "Anna, I'm sorry for going off like that out there," he offered. "The last thing I want to do is cause you more pain." He could not bring himself to say more. It wasn't fair to her. It sounded crazy even to him. *We are still in a life-or-death struggle with forces beyond our control. We have to accept that our lives may never be normal.* That was a lot to lay on someone who had lost so much, so fast.

Anna shook her head. "You misunderstand me, Ry. Things are complicated. I have to live with that. Now stop pussyfooting around. I don't need your pity. I know it looks like I'm barely holding things together." She paused to grab another tissue. "But I'm going to get through this."

You could be forgiven for falling apart completely, he thought. Her tired, bloodshot eyes told the tale. Her beloved Mami lost her will to live after Luis' death, and passed away a month later. Paul came home for the funerals but had to get back to school in Cali. She and Derek had been struggling with two estates in probate, a mansion with a possible crime scene, and a police investigation that was going nowhere fast.

Anna folded her arms and met his gaze evenly. "I can take it," she said firmly. "*Dígame.* If you've got something to say, I want to hear it."

She has a right to know, Ry thought. And after what the women went through out there in the desert, this was a walk in the park. "I think your brother's death is tied to the Network, to the Otters, to Stanley Richards' law firm," he said. "I think the past has come back and found us again."

Anna looked unimpressed. "Forgive me. I've been there, done that," she said. "They're all gone. No one has come after the rest of us. Wouldn't we all be dead by now?"

"I know," he agreed. "I have the same questions. I don't have answers. But keeping it bottled up inside isn't working out very well – I'm turning into an angry asshole I barely recognize. I'm tense all the time."

"Me too," Anna replied, visibly relieved. "Tense, angry, and confused. What we went through, no one should have to see those things. We're going to carry them with us forever. I've been seeing a shrink. It think it's doing me some good. Have you thought about finding some help?"

Ry gritted his teeth. *She thinks it's all in my head as well.* "I should, I know," he said. "But I think there's more going on here."

Anna shrugged. "Okay. Try me," she replied. "What do you have?"

He walked over and sat down. "It's fragments, really. If Luis was cross-examining me in a courtroom, I would be laughed off the witness stand."

Anna promised she would do no such thing.

"Your brother did more than help us, right?"

Anna nodded.

"He made the difference out there," Ry continued. "The race happened because he cut through the red tape. His security kept us safe. He evened the playing field and no one even knew he was there."

"I'm with you so far," Anna replied.

Ry dreaded sharing the other details, but pushed on. "What if someone had survived out there?" he asked. "Someone who took what happened personally? Very personally?"

Anna looked at him blankly.

"The man in the trailer, Anna," he continued. "I've read the transcripts. You called him a man out of place." Anna's eyes went wide as he spoke. She shuddered. "The man Katherine recognized from back east. He was some hack attorney. He worked with Richards. Not a hired gun, like the rest of those thugs."

Anna looked panicked. "So what?" she asked. "They didn't find his body, but so what? They didn't find much of anything, either. There was a drone strike, remember?"

"I know," Ry replied. "But here's the strange part. When the feds went through the law firm's accounts and employment records, there was no trace of a man by the name of John Wellsey. The firm's associates swore they had never heard of him. But the three of you saw him clear as day."

Anna looked down. She sighed. "He was with the old man," she said quietly. "They were talking business in the middle of all that carnage. Talking about the future as they left us to die." Neither of them spoke for a long time. Finally, Anna looked at him. "They were the ones who hurt Cobie," she said finally, her voice cracking. "You think they —"

"I...Anna...I..." Ry tried to speak but the words would not come. Hot tears filled his eyes and cascaded down his cheeks. I misjudged a man once, he wanted to say. I condemned him, cursed him, wrote him off. *I did nothing for him, and he saved our lives.* Cobie's final selfless act, throwing himself at Derek as bullets kicked up around them, played endlessly in Ry's nightmares. Sometimes, he leapt across the highway dividers to reach them. Other times, he sprinted across the blood-soaked ground. Every time he was too late. Now another man was dead. An irredeemable bastard who also happened to have made their lives possible. *I will never misjudge someone again.* He could have gone to the FBI and DEA with the fragments. They might have offered them protection. Just a precaution, they would have said. They could have a man in a suit with an earpiece and a Glock sitting on their side porch right now, keeping an eye on the street. But Ry knew the man's presence would not be reassuring in the least. He remembered the DEA agents. Jim Layles was a stranger at least. No one – not even his best friend – had seen Jake Lyons' betrayal coming.

"I think they pried your brother's name out of Cobie in that trailer," Ry followed up. "And

all this time later, someone came looking for revenge." Finally, he had told someone. The right person. A heavy load he had not even realized he was carrying suddenly felt a little lighter.

Next to him, Anna was lost in her thoughts. He was surprised to see color returning to her ashen face. "We'd better get up there. To Carbondale," she said matter of factly. "I've got people clearing out the mansion this weekend. I'm not saying I believe you. But I'm not saying I don't, either. All of his files are still there. Maybe they'll tell us something."

"Uh…okay," Ry stammered. It was his turn to be surprised. *She doesn't think I'm completely crazy.*

"Ry, there's one other thing." Anna stood up and came over to hug him. "You're going to need to forgive yourself. We did the best we could. We all wish we could have saved Cobie. We made a brutal choice. It was war."

The tears flowed again.

It was jarring to return. Anna had not planned to go back until there was nothing but freshly turned earth and newly planted grasses and trees. For so long, it had been home to what she held most dear in the world…and everything she wished she could change. Mami had never wanted for anything, but had been a prisoner inside its walls. As her mother's mind betrayed her, Anna's weekly visits became a distraction, an inconvenience, an intrusion into her brother's whitewashed world of perfection. She rolled her eyes. What was I going to do, she wondered. *Sue him?* She took a deep breath. Now it was just…empty. She stepped under the police tape and held it up for Ry. She walked up the perfectly symmetric bluestone pathway to the perfectly tiered stairs, shaded by the perfect stone pillars and exposed beams, fumbling for the keys. No maid opened the vintage art deco glass door. No delicate strains of classical music greeted them. Their footsteps echoed across the perfectly gleaming marble floors. Ry whistled as he walked into the massive entrance hall.

Ballroom staircases swept upstairs to either side. A massive crystal chandelier sparkled overhead. Scattered crates held the paintings and furniture headed for auction. "Quite the place," he said quietly. "It must be worth millions."

Anna nodded.

"And you're knocking it down next week?"

"I'd do it sooner if I could," she replied. "We've got forty-eight hours to look through his stuff. Then this place is history." Nothing should have been built here in the first place. The monstrosities of Sandoval Hills – ten-thousand-square-foot mansions built on the side of one of Colorado's most iconic mountains – were an environmental disaster. Once upon a time, there was only an old fire road that led into a wild, tranquil place of incredible beauty. Money, power, and influence had won out. *Not this time. This hundred acres is going back to how it was.* Auction proceeds would cover demolition costs and fund a foundation to help migrant workers. The conservation easement would make sure none of the neighbors got an itch to build guest cottages, or an airstrip, or whatever else insane billionaires dream up in their spare time. The years of law school had been worth it, she decided. The easement was iron clad.

"Brace yourself," she said, leading Ry down the basement stairs. "Looking for a needle in a haystack comes to mind." She opened the door to her brother's office and ushered him in. She watched as Ry struggled to take it all in. "Wow," was all he could manage. File boxes were everywhere, stacked from floor to ceiling. Luis' many monuments to his own magnificence had been collected and stacked against walls. To one side, a narrow path led to an opening in the center of the room. Ry led the way. Anna pulled the draft investigation findings out of her bag and leafed through it as they made their way through to his desk. "Everything has been photographed, dusted, taken apart, and put back together again," she said. "They found blood, fingerprints, and several hairs that belonged to Luis. That was it." They slowly circled the desk, making their way around to his chair. Next to one of its legs, a ragged circle of plush carpet was stained dark red. Further afield, a fine spray of dried blood flecked a wide swath of the yellow fibers.

She dug deeper into the report. "Forensics indicate conditions are consistent with a self-inflicted gunshot," she noted. "Luis owned the gun found next to his body. A holster and bullets matching the gun were found in a closet safe upstairs. All footprints match his shoes."

Ry looked at her. "Sounds like the crime lab has got it all sewn up," he said. "No sign of forced entry. No sign of a second person in the room. And your brother dead by his own hand."

"You'd make a good attorney, Ry," Anna replied, smiling. "That was a decent closing argument…for the status quo."

"So what did they miss?" Ry asked. "What detail is out of place?"

"This is your wild goose chase, counselor," Anna observed. "Put me to work."

Ry walked over to a stack and squinted at the contents listed on the side of each box. "Let's find the most recent files," he declared. "From the last year? Look for anything out of the ordinary – an angry client, a creditor with a grudge, a large payment or debt."

"Now you're talking." Anna tried to sound enthusiastic, but the words came out flat. She wasn't expecting any revelations, much as she appreciated Ry's energy. They each tackled a stack of boxes and found some space in the back of the room where they could work. They dove in, hauling out files and spreading them across the floor. Ry's first papers were for a yacht magnate in San Diego being sued by his suppliers. Nothing there. Anna came across a stack of unpaid legal bills. Luis had defended a publisher from libel charges. The publisher had responded to his bills with angry handwritten letters, claiming his billing was outrageous and unjustifiable. What makes someone cross the line, Anna wondered. She stared at the emphatic slashes and sharp curves of the publisher's handwriting. Had something finally snapped? Did this guy get on a plane, walk in unannounced, and somehow force Luis to put a bullet in his head? It seemed a stretch. And even if they followed up and started asking questions, there could be hundreds of files crackling with anger, frustration, misunderstandings, and a thousand other possibilities. They could never follow up on all of them, not in a million years. It could even be law enforcement, she realized. It wasn't just the bad guys who might have sought retribution after a blown verdict or an unpredictable jury. Plenty of prosecutors, judges, special agents, and cops would have smiled and moved on without missing a beat after hearing the news.

She watched Ry leaf through another set of folders, lines of frustration deepening on his forehead. *Or maybe there is nothing to find. Maybe the facts speak for themselves.* Her brother had been intensely private. For all she knew, he could have been depressed for years. He came across as cold and distant, but that façade masked a raging cauldron of emotions. She knew he hated getting older, and finding there were things his money could not buy. He hated losing control more than anything. Anything less than perfection was not an option. *Maybe pulling that trigger was the only way he knew how to say goodbye.* She shook her head. She had grown up with her brother and still barely knew him. They had both been headstrong. He wanted to kick the red dirt off his boots and take on the world. She dug in her heels and kept fighting the battles her parents had started. A fair wage. Decent working conditions. A chance to make a good life. They only ever had one thing in common – a love of Grand Valley. And when it mattered, that love had been enough. *He kept us safe.*

The afternoon faded into evening. They spoke little as they sifted and searched. She could not decide if she wanted Ry's idea to be more than a hunch. Growing up in the migrant fields, the child of labor activists who were hunted like animals, she learned early that conspiracy, intrigue, and bloodshed made the world turn all too often. The Network had simply been painting on a larger, global canvas. But there could not be a cloak and dagger behind every door.

People do things we don't understand, she reminded herself. Luis may well have taken his own life.

They finally took a break when Anna's paralegals joined them. It had taken a little arm-twisting, with an evening of overtime and Chinese food thrown in. "Seems pretty far from employment and immigration," Josie said, shrugging. "But who doesn't want to play detective?" She was young and smart as a whip, working her way through school with a young family just like Anna had. Bill just nodded. He had come over from Taiwan with his parents when he was a teenager. Quiet and deferential, he focused ferociously on nailing down the facts. He could build an airtight case and track down any lead, no matter how faint. She knew she could count on both of them, despite the out-of-the-blue request and vague mission. Which was good, because it didn't look like Ry was going to make it much longer.

After the break, Ry lasted another hour. He looked over at them, then stared down at the files he was reviewing. "You know, I'm no good at this. I don't have a clue what I'm looking for," he admitted. He stood up. "Something could be staring me in the face, and I would have no idea." Anna had been formulating some words of consolation – good intentions, noble efforts, best shots, let's go home – and was about to roll them out when his face suddenly lit up. "I know what's staring me in the face!" he cried. "Are you guys okay if I work on something else for a little while?"

Anna sighed, exasperated. Except that this was all your idea, she thought. *Give me a break!* One thing was clear – Ry wasn't waiting around for an answer. "Is there a ladder someplace?" he asked, already halfway across the room. She could not think of a single practical item in the house. "Sorry, Luis had contractors for everything," she called out, unable to stifle a smile. The man may have a lousy attention span, she thought, but his energy is infectious. Ry slapped his hands together in delight and bounded up the stairs. "Even better," he said to no one in particular. "I'll grab my ropes from the truck." Anna exchanged glances with Bill and Josie. She met their puzzled looks with a shrug. "I have no idea what he's talking about," she said. They returned to the search.

Sometime later, they heard several loud thumps overhead. Muffled cries followed. Oh shit, Anna thought. Ry was in trouble. She sprinted up the basement stairs and threw open the front door. Running outside, her panic surged. Light was flickering wildly off a corner of the house and nearby trees. A dark figure clung to the guttering. "Here, under the eaves, Anna, check it out," Ry called down. His tone was normal, casual, like they were meeting up for coffee. "Sorry for the banging. Just trying to get your attention."

Anna laughed. The news headline flew into her mind. Man Hangs Out Under House Gutters to Relax. His bobbing headlamp was creating the crazy light show. "I've been trying to get a closer look at this," Ry said. "It's barely noticeable. I almost missed it."

"What is?"

"This camera. Tiny, wireless, encrypted signal, state of the art.

Did your brother ever mention it?"

"The house has a security system," she replied. "But I didn't know there were cameras." Anna was far past being surprised by her brother. Surely, ten-foot-high property fences, an alarm system, and a manned security gate for a subdivision in the middle of nowhere were enough? How many other secrets had Luis taken to his grave, she wondered. And how many are we going to need to dig up?

"This might be our lucky day," Ry noted. "I'm going to climb down. We should head for the attic. I'm guessing this camera's signal routes to somewhere far away. But you never know. There might be a cable, a backup system, something up there."

Anna's jaw dropped. To hell with dusty files, she thought. Video footage was the equivalent of a smoking gun. Either someone came in the house that night or they didn't. She waited while Ry somehow climbed down the front of the house and jumped easily from a window ledge to the ground. "I told you I was good for something," he said, smiling. "Just nothing legal."

Upstairs, they found the attic hatch in a bedroom hallway. A sharp tug on a hook in the panel overhead and it opened smoothly; a set of wooden stairs extended to the floor. "Ever been up there?" Ry asked. Anna shook her head. "We should take this slowly," he replied. "One of us needs to poke a head up there and look around."

Anna nodded. She took Ry's headlamp and made her way up. The light swept over roof trusses, insulation, floorboards. She coughed. The air was stale and musty. "Nothing to see. It's a finished attic," she called down. "Want to head up?"

"Wait a second!" Ry said sharply. "Turn off your headlamp. Take another look with these on." He handed up a pair of thick black rubber goggles. Anna passed him the headlamp and slipped them on. The blackness sheared away, replaced by a dazzling view of the entire attic bathed in electric green light. She gasped. A network of thin bright lines crisscrossed the room.

"Let me guess," Ry called out. "Lasers?"

Anna nodded. "I think so," she replied. *I guess my brother was even more paranoid than I thought.* "It looks like the web of a very organized spider."

"Are there any gaps?"

She carefully studied the beams of light. Most were along the floorboards. Others were waist and chest high. "It looks like the roof trusses aren't covered," she observed. "And the four corners look like they're safe ground."

She looked down and saw Ry nodding confidently. "We can work with that," he said. "Give me a few minutes and I'll see what I can find." The two of them started to trade places.

"Ry, is this normal?" she asked, stopping halfway down the stairs. "A setup like this?"

He shrugged. "Luis was hard-core serious about security," he replied. "He had the money, so why not? No vulnerabilities. No one was coming in through the roof. And no one was knocking out his security cameras. I'd bet there's a safe room hidden somewhere in this house. All of which makes suicide seem even more unlikely to me. This is a man who wanted to live."

Anna looked away, suddenly moved by his words. "What if we trigger something?" she asked finally, trying to stay focused on details.

"I won't," Ry replied as he climbed further up the ladder. He slipped the goggles over his head. "And to answer your question, I don't want to find out."

Anna watched him reach up and pull himself into the darkness. She paced the hallway as the minutes slowly ticked past. She wore a path in the carpet, but it didn't help; the past kept trying to find a way in. Her brother as a boy, loud and rambunctious, able to turn crates and frayed rope into a compelling adventure. Her brother as a teenager, increasingly moody and distant. By the time he went to college, the transformation was complete. The warm, loving boy had been replaced by a stranger. She looked at her watch. *Come on.* Fifteen minutes had passed. *Surely, he should be coming down soon.* She paced back and forth a few more times, trying to fight off a growing sense of panic. What if he's hurt, she wondered. What if some invisible weapon severed an artery? Katherine would never forgive me. She headed for the attic stairs. *I have to do something.* She made it halfway up when a pair of legs shot out of the darkness, followed by the rest of Ry. They collided, clattered down the stairs, and fell into the hallway in a heap. They looked at each other sheepishly, gingerly testing out their arms and legs. "All limbs are intact," she said, smiling.

"Sorry, Anna," Ry replied. "That took way longer than I expected. The trusses felt like they were closing in on me. But, I did find these." He pointed at several small black squares scattered on the carpet.

Anna picked one up. It was shiny and hard, about the size of a pack of baseball cards. The port on the side gave it away. "Let me guess – four cameras, four hard drives?" she asked.

"Yeah, looks like we may have gotten lucky," Ry replied, barely able to contain his excitement. He leapt to his feet. "We just have to hope these things store a whole lot before overwriting themselves."

Between them, they had four laptops. Bill scrounged around in boxes of wires in the basement for connector cables. "We're in business," he called out finally. They headed upstairs and set up camp in the dining room. A fine layer of dust had settled on the massive mahogany table and high-backed chairs. Looking at their wrinkled clothes and tired faces in the huge mirror on the far wall, Anna realized it had been dark for hours. She glanced at the clock on her laptop screen as it fired up. 2 a.m. "You sure you guys are okay?" she asked. Josie and Bill nodded emphatically. "Damn straight," Ry said. "Let's find that night and see what's there."

When Anna clicked on the hard drive folder, row upon row of files filled the screen. Judging from the dates, there was file for each day. No encryption, thank goodness. She scrolled up until dates from last winter appeared. *Bingo.* Around the table, the others were doing the same thing. She took a deep breath and just sat there, staring at the screen. Talking with Ry and sifting through file boxes had been one thing. She was humoring him, keeping her distance, going through the motions. Since the lasers in the attic, those walls had started to crumble. Now, she felt like she was tumbling toward the edge of a black hole, trying to pull back but finding no way to hold on. Each click of the mouse was bringing her closer to a once-unfathomable reality. What if someone really had killed Luis?

Josie shattered her thoughts. "Here!" she said. "You guys need to see this." Anna scrambled around the table and stared at the fuzzy gray camera footage. A dark figure emerged from the trees in the backyard, crouching as he approached the house. He hugged a stone wall and then stood and sprinted across the rear deck before disappearing from the camera's view.

Ry was saying something urgently and Josie and Bill were somewhere in the background. She did not pay them any attention. She could not take her eyes off the footage looping on the screen, the anonymous figure approaching the house over and over and over again. *This house.* There could be no closure now, no peace. Her brother had been murdered. And the past was no longer past.

Showtime

Derek walked into city council chambers. The room from the public access TV channel sprang to life before him, startling him with its vague familiarity. How many times have I flipped past it, he wondered. How many hundreds of planning commission hearings and council presentations have I missed? The small, cramped auditorium had a central aisle and worn flip-down chairs on either side. The walls were padded with tired orange and yellow panels. A light fixture overhead made a small case for grandeur, but the claim was undercut by its off-kilter angle and several busted bulbs. The cheap drop-ceiling tiles above reminded him of classrooms he had fled long ago. It felt like the nineteen seventies had been held hostage in the room while taxpayer dollars were spent on utility upgrades, neighborhood speed bumps, a green roof three floors up.

Derek noted that some of the people sprinkled across the seats looked like they might have been part of the furniture for a long time as well. They were not here because of the evening's meeting. They were just…here. A large man with serious mutton chops had overflowed several seats in the back. With his black vest, chaps, and

51

shit-kicker boots, he should have been out riding a Harley. A small, elderly lady was perched up front, her knitting needles clacking away. A couple rows back from her, a wiry couple wearing glasses and near-matching outfits – khakis and sweater vests – were lost in a heated debate. These are the regulars, he marveled. Witnesses to history. *Some of the most boring, incremental history ever recorded.*

He made his way down to the front of the auditorium, where councilors and his team were milling around, taking a look at the conceptual plans. John Edwards was a giraffe of a man, tall and lanky, with a thick beard and a warm smile. He was the rare engineer who could translate technical site plans for the general public. Next to him, Vivian Stowe had a similar gift; she could weave stories that turned architectural plans and designs into living, breathing buildings and landscapes for people. Each of them had a couple of the councilors in tow. Derek was profoundly grateful as always. "Not my bag," he muttered as he strode up to join them. *Give me a bike and an open trail any day.*

The meeting started a few minutes later, with the councilors making their way up to the raised platform and their desks at the front of the auditorium. The three of them took seats in the front row, ready to leap to the podium and get started. "This meeting is hereby called to order!" the Mayor shouted with promising energy, rapping his gavel firmly on his desk. Mayor Gambly was something of a local celebrity, owner of a bed and breakfast featured in a celebrity cooking show a couple of years earlier. Gregarious and relentlessly positive, the Mayor had almost singlehandedly put Grand Junction back on the tourism map. He traveled relentlessly, talking up the town to travel associations, business groups, boy scouts, journalists, anyone who might be looking for something new, something different – A warm welcome! Rich history and heritage! Unparalleled natural beauty! Remarkable recreation! Derek found their interactions completely exhausting. But this is not my first time at the rodeo, he thought. *If this thing is going to go anywhere, it has to go through him.*

Tonight, the Mayor took a long look at the evening's agenda, then peered over it at the sparse crowd. "Good to see you, son," he said, nodding at Derek. "We're looking forward to your presentation this evening." The other councilor's heads bobbed slightly in agreement.

Apparently it could wait, however. The officials promptly proceeded to get lost in meeting minutes protocol, then took on a rezoning request. Derek looked at his watch and sighed. They would not be getting out of there for hours. He wondered how everything was going in Carbondale. He was hoping Anna and Ry's trip would help his wife find some peace. Part of him hated Ry for having kept half-baked questions of conspiracy and murder alive. Even without his outbursts and uncertainties, the last few months would have been hell for her. But part of him was strangely grateful. *I asked for honesty out there – no more lies, no more doing what's best in the shadows.* Ry had held nothing back ever since. And slowly, he and Anna were getting to a better place. For a long time, she had cried herself to sleep in his arms. Now, in the quiet moments of their busy days, they talked about visiting that place in a few years' time. When the wildness had returned. When prairie grass had healed the ground and forest had begun to reclaim the manicured lawn. We are all in a similar place, Derek realized. *New days. Second chances. Healthy futures.* Or, he corrected himself, we should be. Hopefully, the elected officials sitting in front of them understood.

For a brief instant, he thought it was time. Council voted to deny the rezoning request and the group looked expectantly at him…before the Mayor rapped his gavel again. "Us old timers need a few minutes to stretch our legs, make sure the blood is flowing," he said with a booming laugh. Derek turned to John and Vivian to review their approach one last time. "This has to be all about our vision," he said. "All about the future. About how we can help get the heart of downtown beating again." He left the rest unsaid. *Otherwise, we will get mired in the acrimony and politics.* The hospital had not done anyone any favors when it moved south of the river to Orchard Mesa. They made polite noises about finding a buyer for the old medical complex, about "partnering with development groups to ensure innovation and remain in the heart of Grand Junction." Time had told the tale. Behind those words, the real message was "we skipped town for lower taxes and wealthier, healthier patients." With the taxes unpaid, the city took over the abandoned buildings in a fit of optimism, flirting with development groups with fancy names, leaping at their grand proposals. Mixed uses. Thriving commercial retail. Thousands of condos. Fully leased office space hosting startups and the innovative juggernauts of tomorrow. Everything had fallen through during the long, lean years of the economic downturn. Proposals came and went and nothing happened, except the neglect deepened. Now, the sprawling complex was completely falling apart. Roofs were caving in. Deer, raccoons, and groundhogs had moved in. Parking lots had become waving fields of grass. All of which suited Derek just fine.

"It's time to see things with fresh eyes," he said, finally opening the presentation after the break. "It's time to picture an urban treasure where recreation, nature, and people come together. Where we create new stories, new adventures, new possibilities." Derek went over to their projector screen and talked through a few slides. "Across the country, this is what we are doing. We are transforming an old paper mill in Michigan into a skate park. We're opening up former military warehouses in Alaska for snowboarding in the winter and speedskating in the summer. We are turning an old gas plant in Texas into an adventure park. But Grand Junction is my hometown. This is where I would like to do something really groundbreaking. We would like to work with the city and the community to pioneer the country's first urban BMX nature area. Grand Junction BMX Park."

"Together, we would do it safely and carefully," John chimed in, taking over the presentation. He walked council through building and engineering surveys as the potential first step. Vivian spent her time talking about threading natural systems throughout, integrating sunlight, water, and soil to create a vibrant park. "It would appeal to all generations, to all walks of life," she said. "Raised beds would turn concrete slabs into a gardening mecca. Walking trails would link with education areas and connect neighborhoods with downtown. A world-class BMX facility in the center would draw visitors and crowds. And it would make our world a better place. Natural systems would filter our air and water. Solar panels would provide clean energy. Any wastes would be composted or recycled."

Ta-dah, thought Derek. You'd have to have your head buried in the sand to turn down an offer this good. *If it was up to me, we would sign the papers tonight and get to work in the morning.* Instead, council members unleashed a torrent of questions.

"How much would this cost the city?"

"What about liability issues? What happens if a building collapses on children?"

"Security worries me. What would you do if squatters or crackheads moved in?"

"Seems like everything we do in this town is for young people. Isn't it time we focused on something for older people?"

Just like old times, Derek thought. The old bats were every bit as tough and narrow-minded as Halderman and the other federal bureaucrats, back when they had fought to get permission for the bike race. What is it about me and bureaucracy, he wondered, trying his best not to look ruffled. Everywhere else, they had been invited in to work on the projects. People bent over backwards to make things work. *I have a track record now, for goodness sake.* The Bookcliffs Challenge brought more people to town than the peach festival, music jams, book fest, and winter carnival combined. It gave Grand Junction massive national exposure on ESPN and other networks. For those few days, a good chunk of the sports world turned its gaze to Colorado's Western Slope.

"We're thinking we could do it in phases," he replied after the questions had finally subsided, papering over his frustration with a broad smile. "Take on a first few acres first, old parking areas and the parts in the worst shape, the intensive care wing and the power plant. If the city could bring in some grant money, we would put up the rest. Then see what happens. If it goes well, we work out a revenue sharing agreement, sign a long-term lease."

Another onslaught followed. John and Vivian took turns at bat. Sitting there listening as the objections, doubts, and random asides mounted, Derek's frustration blossomed into anger. *I need to get out of here. I need to grab a bike and ride.* He was about to walk out – to hell with the consequences – when the Mayor finally reined in the inquisition. "Well, we sure have a lot of interest here, it sounds like," he boomed. "And lots of good questions." Derek had to admit the man was a marvel. He was indefatigable. Three hours in and he still looked as fresh as a daisy. It had to be the key to his success. He could wear people down, talking and smiling and talking some more until trade organizations, politicians, business owners – whoever – agreed to whatever was on the table in return for blessed silence. "We will take your proposal under advisement," the Mayor concluded. "Thank you for your time."

Derek looked at John and Vivian. They looked as confused as he was. *I thought our presentation was unstoppable.* "Thank you, Mr. Mayor," he stammered, trying to think on his feet. *What does taking it under advisement mean?* "Thank you to council as well for its time this evening. Would you like to set up a work group or schedule a follow-up meeting?"

The Mayor slapped on a fresh smile. "It means you have given us a lot to think about," he replied. "We intend to do just that."

Wow. Not even a 'we'll be in touch,' Derek marveled. He mumbled a thank you. The three of them packed up their gear. Outside, he thanked Vivian and John as best he could. They both looked shaken. "Can't win them all," he said, trying to shake it off. "You both did a great job. We'll talk soon." Derek helped them load John's car and said good night. As he turned to walk away, the news headline slid in. Olympic Biking Champion Conquers World, Cannot Get Past City Council. He had to smile. Anna's habit had long since become his own. He grabbed his phone. She picked up on the first ring.

"You were right."

"I'm sorry, babe. No 'I told you so's' here." Her voice was warm and comforting. "How are you feeling?"

"I didn't need them to swoon at our feet. But I needed something, you know? More than a brushoff." He sighed. "At least it's a beautiful night. I'm walking home." A long but comfortable silence followed. Anna's earlier advice filtered into his thoughts. He understood better now what she had been saying...*you need a crowd behind you to make them move...take them in those buildings, let them get a feel for it what could be like...spend time with each one of them. Politics is personal. You are going to have to make them care.* He could not get past that. The project spoke for itself. And the Bookcliffs Challenge was only three months away. *We have revitalization projects going on all over the country now. All I want to do is get out and ride.*

"It doesn't have to be you, you know." Her words startled him. He stopped walking and stared across the street at the city's little league. It was late innings, the infield and outfield erupting from the darkness, floodlit in blazing yellow-orange light. A kid was stepping out from second base, waiting for the pitch. "I'm not bringing someone in," he said finally. "I can't stand marketing people."

He could hear Anna's breathing as she waited for him to follow. *Who then?* Someone people could trust, he reflected, someone who knew the community and the biking scene. It was a pretty tall order. A legal whiz would not hurt, either, he thought. Luis would have made mincemeat of council's concerns. He would have tied up all of their loose ends with a big red bow and laced in some subtle legal threats to get them moving. Sam popped into his mind. Derek grimaced. *In another lifetime, maybe.* His kid brother could get anyone talking, have a person sharing their life story in minutes. He would have council eating out of his hand in no time. But that gift was now his bedside manner. All those years of training and he had never wavered. Derek was beyond proud of his younger brother. *I would never try to hold him back. But I miss him. I miss those days.* Together, he and Sam had taken on the racing world, crisscrossing the country in their custom racing trailer. Now, they lived in the same town and barely saw each other. It was months since they had last gone riding. *Times change...*

"Struggling a little?" Anna asked gently. "I'll give you a clue. He's young, handsome, good with people. He's been your biggest fan since he was a kid. He's living out of state but I happen to know he could take or leave his summer internship. As his mother, I'm probably slightly biased but..." Derek roared with laughter. Across the street, an outfielder leapt forward in surprise. The tall, skinny teenager turned around, squinting into the darkness beyond the left field fence. Sorry kid, he thought. My wife is damn funny as well as beautiful and smart as all get-out. She was also right. *Paul could be a good fit.*

"If you need any other help, don't forget about Jackie," Anna continued. "Remember where she worked. That woman is a sharpshooter, and she's got a monster rolodex if you need to call in the cavalry. From what I've heard, she might be getting a little bored over there at the old desk job."

"Would you please stop it with the mind reading?" he asked,

amazed and slightly exasperated at the same time. "It's spooky. I don't know how you do it. You know me better than I do." All while you keep your own cards so close, he thought. He knew better than to ask how things were going on her end. Anna shared things in her own time. *I can only hope I come close to doing for you what you do for me.*

"Just some food for thought, babe," Anna replied. "Now get home, put your feet up and crack open a beer for both of us. It's going to be a late night here. I'll see you mañana, cariño."

Derek loved when she spoke to him in Spanish. "See you then. Buenas noches," he replied. "Y que duermas bien, mi amor." He heard Anna laughing as they hung up. He had learned just enough Spanish to be dangerous. He practiced only when they were alone. The previous week he had managed to call her a cauliflower by mistake. He walked past the ball field and headed home through the neighborhood streets. A dog barked. Most homes were dark. It was the end of another very long day. A thousand new details awaited tomorrow. At least it would all wrap up with Anna's return from Carbondale and a quiet weekend to come.

He slid the key in the lock. He stood there, motionless, for a good while before pulling it back out. He walked around the side of the house to the garage and pulled up the door. He struggled out of his suit, dug out bike clothes and shoes, grabbed his favorite beater and was gone. He laced between parked cars, popped curbs, leaned into curves and blurred past street signs. The ball field lay ahead; players were walking out to their cars with their parents. The floodlights shut off as he shot past, plunging the road into darkness. He raced into the blackness, tires whispering. Buildings, stop signs and traffic lights gradually fell by the wayside. Thunder rumbled overhead and thick, fat raindrops cascaded down, hissing on the still-warm asphalt. He leaned forward. The tires spoke, faster, faster, faster. The still air became a warm, humid wind. The valley offered up its lightning-shadowed fields and distant mesas. He was gone.

Managing Expectations

Jackie drove slowly into her spot and pulled to a reluctant stop. She left the engine running. She checked her hair in the vanity mirror. She fiddled with the radio presets, settling on a hard-luck country tune. She found a gum wrapper and a pen and wrote down the things she had forgotten to pick up at the store. That left staring out the windshield. So she did that as well. She studied the manicured landscaping masking the base of the building. Behind the nandina fronds and mottled crepe myrtle bark, silver glass and concrete erupted skyward. The greenery could not compete with the attention lavished a few feet away. It had a green roof and recycled wastewater and conserved energy, and did umpteen other green things. It had won many awards. "It may be a smart box," she said to Katherine at the ribbon cutting. "But it's still a box." Then and now, it seemed like a poor trade. Once upon a time, I would have been parking under apple trees, she thought. They would have been in blossom right about now. Kettle Orchards had stretched as far as the eye could see. The first few years, they had come out for summer festivals and fall craft fairs. The first few board meetings had even taken place on picnic blankets here. The cider had packed a punch, making for some lively gatherings. *Not like this funeral.*

Someone walked in front of the car. One of the suits. It was a woman, wrapped up in a tight blue outfit and wearing heels that said *I mean business.* She took the stairs in stride and vanished into the lobby. She had probably flown in with the rest of the corporate clones the night before, made it to the hotel bar, and figured they had a pretty good read on what this place was all about. Then it would be on to Des Moines or Columbus or Hattiesburg, or maybe all of those places. Change a few slides, update regional references, insert appropriately diverse staff. Build some trust and then move in for the kill. Deep Jungle did not mess around.

While the clones were nursing their cocktails, she and Andy had been a thousand miles away. They spent the previous evening out in the hills, sitting on the hood of his muscle car, working on a bucket of fried chicken and watching the sunset. She wanted to be out where everything was still okay, where the valley was still…itself, fields and people laced together by the Colorado River and a vibrant network of family farms. But even that had proved bittersweet. She was going to miss dating a cop. It was hot. Had been hot. Window steaming hot at times, like when they discovered just how good peanut butter could taste…the man was good at what he did. But it felt more and more like she was another job to be taken care of, another item on a list to be checked off. It was time to move on. She slapped her hands on the wheel. *Listen to me. People go hungry and I have more complaints than they do. Snap out of it!* There was nothing for it. Time to face the future. She turned off the engine, grabbed her bag and headed inside. Blessedly, there were no clones waiting for the elevator. She hit the button and waited. What was it about the GVFC, she wondered. Cutting things off with men had never been a problem. And Grand Junction was easy pickings…her neighbor two doors down…the new yoga teacher…that guy in her photography class. But she could not seem to quit the GVFC.

The words waiting on the fifth floor wall reminded her that she likely had it backwards. The Food Connection, she corrected herself, appears to be doing its best to get rid of me. The branding people were sure about the new name and logo. The test groups could not be wrong. It was time to think bigger. Much bigger. You are not just about farms, or Grand Junction, they said confidently. Gone was the picture of the green-and-white barn and farm. Gone was the outrageously chipper tag line – "We Bring Food and People Together in All Weather." Even when she was taking a bath or running, the new corporate-ese would seep into her thoughts. "We are an e-commerce innovator in the commercial retail sector…we are well positioned to increase our market share…integrating value-added solutions into a seamless experience for our customers." *Blah blah blah.* Integrate this, Jackie thought. I want to downsize and move back into our old offices. So what if we had to work around dental chairs and walk past unnerving animal tapestries every day. I want to celebrate farmers. I want to celebrate the valley. I want to celebrate things that are real and local and complicated and surprising and interesting. I've gone along with months of this crap and look at what we have instead, she marveled. A name that makes us sound like a conveyor belt and a logo that looks like dragonflies having sex. *Progress.*

She turned the corner. Her breath caught; the reality of the day swung into sharp focus. Their boardroom took up most of the fifth floor. It was a large rectangle with clear glass walls. Everyone in the surrounding cubicles could look in, and anyone meeting inside could see out. No secrets. Transparency and openness. Core values of the co-op. *Not today.* Today, the clones had taken it over. A couple of them were chatting up the early-arriving board members. One was placing brightly colored handouts at one end of the long slate table. A couple with intense looks stamped on their faces was troubleshooting some kind of presentation glitch. Today there would be nothing but smoke and mirrors in there. *At least it will be on display for the world to see.* She had been planning to make a graceful, silent exit. Follow Anna's example. The facts were simple. The co-op had grown and grown. Now they were in four states, each with offices like this one. All of them filled with strangers happily plugging away, committed to a future of reaching more people with healthy food. Saying anything would be petty and pointless. *It isn't my thing. Fair enough.* She had not gotten there easily. Without talking to Anna, she would not have gotten there at all. They had gotten together for a quick meal after work.

"You've come a long way," Anna said. "I remember when we first met, I couldn't get you to come out on farm visits."

"Yeah, I remember." Jackie blushed a deep crimson. "I thought if we built a fancy website and I held down the fort, people would just call or show up." She felt incredibly guilty about bringing this all up while Anna was dealing with...everything.

"Please." Anna waved her concerns away. "I could use a break."

"I probably should have invited Katherine. But...I guess I need to find out if what I'm thinking is crazy."

"I understand. Shoot."

They ordered food and then Jackie went for it. Anna nodded and listened. When it was finally Anna's turn to speak, Jackie felt like she had been doused with a bucket of cold water. "I don't doubt you love the valley," Anna started out. "You're right. It is an amazing place, with an incredible history. So many people have worked so hard to restore the valley's farms, to fight off the people who keep showing up with big plans. Drilling. Drug cartels. The Network. More will come, I don't doubt." She paused. "I think it's also easy to look at the valley through rose-colored glasses. There is so much beauty. But those pretty views mask a lot of pain. Those fields have held workers down in poverty. For decades, syndicates controlled everything. Prices were the least of it. They were paying people pennies and charging them dollars to sleep in lice-ridden camps and eat slaughterhouse scraps. Then when commodity prices fell, the syndicates pulled out and people moved on or starved. Nothing grew in those fields for years. Then the oil companies swept in with big promises and ninety-nine-year leases to get at the oil shale under our feet. They paid pennies on the dollar too. Then they moved on. But those mineral right leases are still there. Locked away in company safes from Dallas to Dubai like slowly ticking time bombs, waiting for the days of cheap energy to pass…so when I hear about the co-op growing, I think of people finding more good-paying jobs, jobs that bring them closer to other people in the valley. Jobs that mean people can work in farming without having to work in the fields. And I think of that happening other places, in other valleys…but also in urban areas and suburbs. I think of there being a little more muscle on the other side of the equation, so that maybe when another syndicate pushes its way in one day, we'll be able to push back."

Jackie had just sat there, stunned, before finally managing a quiet 'thank you.' Anna's compelling picture helped her let go, helped her prepare to walk out the door and wish The Food Connection well without her. But that was two weeks ago. It might as well have been a lifetime. That was before Deep Jungle changed the equation. Until seventy-two hours earlier, Jackie bought books and gifts and appliances and shoes from them like everyone else. Then the buyout offer came in the door, reams of fine print dolled up with sweet talk and dollar signs on the front page. The Food Connection may no longer be my thing, she decided, but it sure as hell was not going to be theirs, either. Her reaction had been immediate and visceral, straight from the gut.

A quick glance at Katherine's face and her hopes fell.

They took a day to read through the buyout offer. "Imagine what we could do. Think of how many people we could reach," her friend said when they got back together. They found a quiet corner of the building's cafeteria to talk. "How many people we could help. We would be working nationwide. This could put healthy food and America's farmers back on the map. Knock the multinational food conglomerates down a peg or two. We would be starting a new conversation." Jackie stared into her coffee. "But it wouldn't be a 'we' anymore. You know that, right?" she asked. "It would be a 'they' from here on out."

Katherine shrugged. "But we would still be here. The board would stay on. We –"

"Page three, Katherine," Jackie cut in. "Deep Jungle assumes responsibility for all employment decisions. And that's just the beginning of the fine print." She was amazed. "Keeping people around is pure window dressing. Assets. Staff. Strategic direction. It all goes into a black box." *Haven't we been here before? Don't we know how this movie ends?* Things get big and then you have to feed the beast. Time passes and one day you realize the beast is all that matters. It makes its own rules, follows its own paths, and corruption and greed are among its most indispensable tools. *We have not lived through everything to end up in another desert in another time. Or worse. This time we would be on the outside looking in, while new faces create the tragedy.*

"I'm not saying we just up and sign the offer," Katherine replied.

Her face was a smooth mask. "But let's hear them out. I'm not sure we have much of a choice anyway. This is up to the board."

She was right about that at least. Deep Jungle would be coming to town to make its smooth, silky pitch. The board might be our saving grace, Jackie thought. Christa, Mac, Jill and the others were not going to roll over. She was confident they would resist the siren song that apparently had Katherine in its thrall. *But they can't fix this.* She looked at her friend and had no idea what to say. She and Katherine had not been on opposite sides of anything since they were in college. And that was just over men. This was new ground. Uncertain, broken ground.

"Fine," she said eventually. "But we're going in with our eyes open." Over Katherine's objections, they flew in a contracts specialist from Luis' old outfit in Chicago the following day. Lucille did not disappoint. She was an older black lady with the no-nonsense, lay-it-bare delivery of Aretha Franklin back in her prime. "Picture an iceberg. There's what's on top. That's the nice stuff," she said, tapping her pen on her chair as they worked through the offer. "They want to buy all of your hard work and leapfrog ahead of everybody else. If that's what your company wants, they're willing to pay a premium."

"We're not a company," Jackie interjected. "We're a co-op. That's the whole point."

"That's not relevant," Katherine responded. "We're still structured like a business." Her tone was harsh and dismissive.

Lucille looked at them in turn, noting the tension. "Let's get back to the iceberg," she said. "Everything under the water. The stuff that can sink your boat. Deep Jungle does not mess around. If you and the board do not want to negotiate with them, maybe they sweeten the deal. More likely, they play hardball. Plan on them having other options lined up. Another group of players they can work with and throw their weight around. Shutting you out. Or they make a run at this themselves. Goodness knows they've got the warehouse space."

It was not a pretty picture. Looking at the Katherine's tight smile, Jackie knew the same set of facts had led them both to opposite conclusions. At least she knew her own bottom line now. I might lose my best friend, she thought, but we can steer the ship around the iceberg. They cannot force us to tear a hole in the hull. Even if they start filling the ocean with icebergs, we would still be afloat. *And I'm not going anywhere until we're back in open water.*

Now, days had passed like minutes and Deep Jungle was here. Jackie swallowed hard. She was about to make her way over to the boardroom when Katherine walked up. "I hope we can both keep open minds in there." The same tight smile was plastered on her face. Jackie managed to nod. She was afraid of what she might say if she opened her mouth. It's the board I need to reach, she thought. If Katherine and I can make it through this without scorching the earth, maybe we can find our way back to solid ground.

They walked over to the boardroom together in a show of solidarity. Jackie suffered through handshakes and pleasantries with the clones while they waited for the other board members. They were so young, so enthusiastic, so well dressed, so...bland. If she asked one of them a personal question, Jackie imagined the eyes glossing over, the words slurring, a cardboard cutout falling to the floor. Six more would probably pile in the door to take its place.

Enough with the sci-fi visions, she thought. Reality is bad enough. She sought out Christa for a brief respite. "Don't vorry," their old compatriot said quietly as she approached. "Vee have seen volves before, yes? And vee kept zem out of zee henhouse."

"Thank you, Christa." It was the first time Jackie had smiled in days. Tears pricked the corner of her eyes. "It is so good to see you." While they hugged, Lucille walked in behind them. The attorney put down her briefcase and pulled a chair back from the table. At least we have a witness, Jackie thought. To whatever is about to unfold.

A few minutes later, after the rest of the board had arrived, everything started to roll. Katherine opened the meeting with a brief welcome. "The past few days have been a whirlwind. I would like to thank everyone for making time to be here today," she started out. "We are of course flattered by Deep Jungle's interest, and excited to hear what you have to say." Next to her, Jackie bit her tongue and did her best to keep a neutral expression. Now was not the time to give anything away.

The lead clone, a tall, muscled woman named Erin, took it from there. She prowled back and forth at the front of the room, tossing her long blonde mane around as if she was starring in a beauty products commercial. "Thank you for hosting us," she said. Her voice was warm and a little husky. "We hope today is the start of new relationships, new possibilities." Jackie realized Erin was selling more than a buyout offer. She had to give it to her – the woman was physically captivating. Judging from her perfectly toned body – the tight blouse and short skirt left little to the imagination – she was a serious athlete. The men in the room were mesmerized.

Then came the music – a happy, bright pop vibe – and the valley sprang to life on the screen behind her. Jackie's jaw dropped. She had been expecting stock photos. Instead, she was looking at Flying Turtle Dairy. Nice sunrise shots of Swansong Farm and Westbrook Nurseries followed. When 145 Riverside flashed up, Jackie realized this was no casual tour through the valley. Christa's industrial sculptures were well off the beaten path. Someone had *really* done their homework. These were all shots of board members' farms. The last one stung. Kettle Orchards slid into view, then dissolved into their offices and The Farm Connection's new logo.

"The Food Connection's track record has been remarkable," Erin was saying. Bar charts and pie wedges sprang to life behind her. "Top line revenue and margins trending upward month-over-month. Gross and net margins improving dramatically as…"

Jackie tuned back out. She stared at the blue and red lines and shaded shapes. It was one way of measuring what they had accomplished. She and Katherine knew the data backwards and forwards. She also knew what the charts left out. How do you calculate what it meant for farmers to be respected and valued in the community? How do you measure delight on children's faces as they bite into the juicy flesh of a just-picked peach? How do you gauge people learning about where their food comes from? Their most important work was not to be found in any annual report or presentation. It was out there, happening every day, in thousands of conversations, farmers markets, and farm visits.

As if reading her thoughts, Erin suddenly stopped pacing. She reached out to the group. "At Deep Jungle, we believe in the triple bottom line. A healthy environment, healthy communities, and a healthy economy." Her tone was urgent now, rising for the closing pitch. "Where they come together, you have an opportunity to make a difference, to do something special, to make the world a more sustainable place. That is why you're here. And that's why we are here."

Bullshit, Jackie thought. The window dressing is nice, but we could not be more different. We are here to help people and you're here to separate them from their money. We are just another fruit tree in another orchard. Tomorrow, you will be over the horizon taking over someone else's business. *You have to feed the beast.*

Another one of them stood up. "Thank you, Erin," the man said. He walked over to join her. "I'm sure everyone must have lots of questions. Let's get started." Jackie noticed he was different than the others – older, well-dressed, elegant. His salt-and-pepper hair was slicked back into a ponytail, his tailored suit tapered to a pair of

74

crimson cowboy boots. The clothes could not hide the years of tough living. His skin was leathery and weatherbeaten, his cheeks and forehead creased by deep lines. So much for the pretty face, Jackie thought. This guy is their closer.

Silence fell. Katherine and Jackie looked around the room expectantly. They had agreed to let the board take the lead. Eventually, Mac Birnum shifted forward in his chair. "I'll get us started," he said in his low drawl. "Tell us more about why Deep Jungle is interested in us. Where you see this thing going in the future."

"Yes, absolutely," the man replied. He brought his hands together carefully as he spoke. Long fingers tapped against each other. "Our whole focus is getting people what they want and need as fast as possible, at a great price. We thought long and hard about food and groceries. Why should they be any different? People need to eat, and we can save them time and money. They can come home from work and have it all waiting. We're aiming to be everyone's online grocery." The man paused, looking around the room for dramatic effect. Jackie did not like what she saw in those pale blue eyes. She had seen predators before. "Been to a video store lately?" he asked finally. Everyone around the table shook their heads. "One day, maybe grocery stores will follow them into the history books," he continued. "We think there's a better way."

"I'll have to think on that," Mac murmured. "Thank you." Next to him, Jill Gibson did not hesitate to jump in. "I'm all for saving time and money," she said. "But I think food is different from toaster ovens and razor blades and books. Food is local, or it should be. Food is about people coming together, or it should be. Food is about understanding a place and its history, or it should be."

"Well said, Ms. Gibson," the man replied. He smiled blandly. "You know, I've been a rancher much of my life. Over Nebraska way. Some people want to know about the Sandhills and my seven thousand acres. Some people care about our land stewardship, or the diverse grasses and forbs my cows graze on – the bluestem, buffalo, reed canary, brome, et cetera. Some people care about those stories. For others, maybe other things are more important. Some just want a steak that tastes good. I sell my beef to everyone."

How did you get from there to here, Jackie wondered. Sounds like you're a hired hand, brought on whenever Deep Jungle needs some authenticity, the salt of the earth brought to life. "So…that sounds like you've still got your own thing going," she said, struggling to understand the man's metaphor. To hell with staying silent. Someone needed to pull apart what he was actually saying. "Would we be like that, a separate entity, doing what we do?"

"You would keep on doing what you've been doing," the man replied. Jackie found it to be a strange, partial answer. "Always?" she pressed. He looked slightly uncomfortable for the first time, shifting his weight from one foot to the other. "Always is a word I try to stay away from…but like I said, you would keep doing what you've been doing. With an eye to doing it in other places in the future."

Across the table, Jill slid her chair forward. "But you were talking about online groceries earlier," she said, rejoining the discussion. "So there is something larger here, some bigger plan, that we would be a part of?" There we go, Jackie thought. We need to keep digging and pushing, getting past all of this vagueness. I don't care about his cows.

"There would need to be some integration, yes," the man replied. "We would be looking at systems and how to bring everything together."

"And would we be a part of that...integration?" Jackie looked to her right in surprise. Katherine had asked the question.

All of the clones frowned. "The board and executive directors would be advisors throughout the process, as stipulated in the offer," the man replied stiffly.

"Advisors to who, exactly?" Katherine followed up.

"Our teams," the man replied, perhaps a little too quickly. "They are hard at work on the business ecosystems we will need for the transition."

Katherine leaned over. "Business ecosystems ... transition ... integration ... what does that all even mean?" she whispered in Jackie's ear. "I'm thinking maybe this is not the greatest idea. I'm thinking we –"

"Vell, I have heard enough," Christa said loudly, interrupting their brief huddle. She folded her arms tightly across her chest. "Zee Food Connection does vat it does, and it does it vell. It eez eet's own zing, not whatever zees people vant it to be. Vee should valk avay from zee offer." An awkward silence descended. Board members stared down at the carpet. The clones' faces were blank masks. Apparently, they had gone into standby mode. Jackie and Katherine talked quietly and quickly, trying to come up with a carefully worded response. On the far side of the room, Lucille stood up. "If the board and its executive directors were to decline Deep Jungle's buyout offer," she asked, "what might be the consequences of such action?"

The man and Erin both returned to life, flashing bright smiles at the group. "Good question. Simple answer," the man replied. "We would respect their wishes and walk away." Jackie looked at Lucille, flummoxed. The attorney's eyes narrowed. "But perhaps we would ask the group to take some more time to consider the offer," Erin chimed in. "To make sure everyone is on the same page."

"I don't think that will be necessary," Katherine said forcefully.

"Could we go around the table?" the man asked. "To make sure we have heard from all board members?" Was that a glint of anger in his eyes, Jackie wondered. Everything seemed to be moving very fast now.

"I don't have a problem with that," Katherine replied. Jackie looked at Lucille for a long moment before responding, trying to read the tension on the attorney's face. Things could not be this simple. But Jackie couldn't see the tripwire either. "Fine with me," she said finally.

"I would also like to say that we hope the board and the

executive directors have found our offer more than generous," the man said. A thin smile split his lips. "The offer reflects The Food Connection's impressive accomplishments. Either today or at a later date, we hope that you will accept the terms and join us."

"Duly noted," Katherine replied. "Now let's go around the room. I would like to ask our board members if they have any thoughts to share before we vote on tabling Deep Jungle's buyout offer."

Mac, Jill, and Christa shook their heads. The five other board members looked at each other before following suit. "Something is wrong," Jackie whispered to Katherine. "Why did they just do that?"

"I don't know," Katherine replied. "Let's get this vote taken care of and get these people out of here. Then we can figure out this mess." "Thank you, everyone," she said to the group. "I would like to propose –"

Joan Strahan cut her off. "Point of order!" she shouted. "The executive directors are non-voting members of the board. Per board guidelines, only voting members may bring motions to the floor." Jackie sensed wheels starting to turn, things once hidden finding their way into the light. The Kettle Orchards heir rarely spoke at board meetings. She never raised her voice. But now this diminutive business leader was standing up and banging her fist on the table. *What is going on?* "In the best interests of this organization and the community," Joan continued, "I would like to bring a motion that the board accept Deep Jungle's offer. Today. Right now."

"Seconded," said Bill and Susan Edgars in unison. The owners of Flying Turtle Dairy were both stone-faced, sitting ramrod straight in their chairs.

"All in favor, please raise your hands," Joan said. She was leaning over the table, her body tense with nervous excitement.

Five hands shot up.

"Motion passed."

Jackie felt faint. She tried to sit down. A firm hand at her elbow kept her on her feet – she found a smiling clone by her side. Others were already escorting Lucille and the others to the door. They bought the board, she realized. Or enough of it to matter. There was no Plan B. This had been the plan the entire time. She stumbled past Erin's vacant smile, locked eyes with the man. Those pale blue pools were no longer distant and remote; huge, black pupils glared back at her now. "I'm sorry you had to see that," he snapped. "If everyone had just gone along, it would have been much more pleasant." She couldn't remember what she said in response. She remembered a stunned elevator ride. Someone was crying. She remembered Katherine next to her as she walked out into bright sunlight. Mostly, she remembered feeling numb, sitting down on the building's front steps and staring up at the blue sky arching overhead until building security came out and asked them to leave the premises. *It was not supposed to be like this.*

~

Part II

~

Making a Statement

No one paid any attention to the tall Russian walking the Kennedy Center galleries. Around him, furs and tuxedo jackets fluttered past. The grand crystal chandeliers overhead dimmed several times. He ignored the signal, watched people gathering outside the concert hall. Painted faces searched in evening bags. Fingers swiped smartphones for final microhits. Heads bobbed in recognition. Both sides of the aisle were here tonight. He checked his watch. If he was lucky, he might hear the orchestra tuning. He imagined the conductor stepping up, his musicians before him, the bows poised, all eyes tracking the hovering baton, the tension marred only by an occasional cough or late arrival. Then, finally, the sweet blessed release, the river of notes offering salvation to those who could hear them. At least that was how it had always been for him. He had loved classical music since he was a boy, entranced by the sonic stories and conflicts, the mountains and valleys, the waves, clouds, and storms conjured by vibrating strings, slides, valves, keys, reeds, and mouthpieces. It was a world he had never been invited into but instinctively understood. Life was a short, dirty mess. Religion masked that reality. Art was the only way to transcend it.

But not tonight. He was too keyed up to go in. He looked out at the few stragglers huddled on the terrace. He watched as they headed inside; they brushed past him without a glance. Smoke from their final drags swirled in the air. It was still snowing out there. Just enough to add a veil of quiet beauty to the evening. He turned back to survey the swelling crowd. The turnout was impressive, he thought, given the town usually shut down for a half-inch of ice. Tonight was the culmination of a week of symposiums, galas, and receptions honoring U.S. ties with Hungary, Brazil, and Russia. The world premiere of a lost Bartók concerto no less. All sponsored by Aponix. Things were going to move fast now. He turned away and stepped out onto the terrace. He headed for the far side and stood by the railing. Below, the crests of some small waves caught splashes of light from Rosslyn to the west and Georgetown to the north. The rest of the river was dark and sluggish, its dirty white riverbanks spider-webbed by oak and sycamore branches. A DC-10 hooked down out of the clouds and rumbled south along its flight path. Even in the depths of winter, it was one of his favorite places in the city. Part of the nation's capital and yet cut off, doing its own thing, a temple to the arts in a country that no longer cared, if it ever had. People had come out tonight. The boss had seen to that. But most nights there were few footsteps on the plush red carpets, few hurried glances at the evening's program notes.

Harper looked back at the immaculate white building. The

marble was starting to crack. Mesh wrap held parts of the pillars in place. Paving stones underfoot were chipped and uneven. Even Kennedy looked haggard. Backlit in one of the huge rectangular windows, the huge bronze tilted to one side, his expression unreadable. The world turns and then one day it changes, Harper thought. A summer day in Dallas. Then another day comes to pass, and it changes again. This time, they were the ones taking a swing at history. He walked back over to the terrace doors, watching for any signs of activity through the dirty, smudged glass. Nothing yet. He badly wanted a beer. He wanted to stand there and knock one back as the doors opened, savoring what they had worked so hard for. Being a witness would have to suffice. Soon, people would be asking questions and looking for answers. Sticking your head up when everyone else was headed in the opposite direction was a sure way to find trouble. He had thought about the details a thousand times. Senior officials would usually be taken to a secure location, or whisked away in black Suburbans. But this time, there were so many of them…some would have to come out those doors, he was sure of it. Would they try to look calm? I would put money on them running, he thought. The fragmented details, the grim possibilities made it almost a sure thing. A potential attack on the nation's energy infrastructure…terrorists perhaps already on the move to new targets…the nation's fragile sense of safety plunged into uncertainty. Then, days later, tentative relief blossoming as the facts came to light, only to be replaced by new, unprecedented concerns about the planet's health. The President declaring in a special address that "today, our nation faces the first massive casualty of climate change." Experts endlessly cycling across news outlets, explaining how melting permafrost could cause the catastrophic failure of the Trans-Alaska Pipeline. But it was the footage that would make the difference. Video of millions of gallons of oil pouring not only across pristine wilderness, but down the main streets of Fairbanks and Valdez and a hundred other towns. Those images would spur new questions. Those questions would open new doors. And one company was positioned to walk straight through them.

Harper felt little sympathy for the congressmen and women and agency bureaucrats who would shortly find their worlds turned upside down. He looked back at Kennedy's crumbling visage. To hell with the Cold War. The days of governments, of democracies, socialist states, communist empires, Islamic caliphates, had long since passed. It had just taken longer for Washington to get the message. He knew it as a teenager two decades earlier, felt it deep in his frozen bones. He learned the big picture later. Yeltsin came to power and the oligarchs took over. Everything that had belonged to the people – farmland, rail lines, factories, power plants – belonged to them in name only. What he knew was that one day the technical institute closed and their high-rise lost power in the dead of winter. His father was sent home and his mother scraped together a few kopeks cleaning and taking in laundry. As gangs proliferated, they were forced to choose sides. His father ran errands for them, came home wide-eyed and strung out, bought for a couple of cheap scores. His mother whispered to unseen voices, barricaded herself in their bedroom. From a hallway shelf, behind brittle glass, the worn peasant faces of his long-dead grandparents stood grim vigil over the family's disintegration. Harper stared at the fading farm fields and draft horses, trying to make out the tools in their hands.

He left before they came for him. The only government organ still functioning in Volgograd was the army. He walked into the recruiting station, an abandoned butcher shop that smelled of garbage and piss. "Does your mother know you are here?" the soldier on duty asked, stepping out from behind the shattered glass cases. His too-big uniform flapped against thin arms and legs. Harper said nothing. "Never mind." The soldier spat out the words, sized him up with a laugh. He placed a filthy, threadbare green jacket on his shoulders. The man stank of gin. "You will do fine. Mother Russia is your family now."

Harper shrugged off the jacket and the soldier's lurching come on. He survived basic training and learned in Chechnya that he was good at something other than schoolwork. He would have fought and died there if it had not been for a passing encounter with a three-star general touring the front line. He jerry-rigged the front end of a jeep after a mortar round took out most of the man's entourage and drove him to safety. Serving on the general's staff, an improvised workaround for missile batteries got him into postgraduate work at Moscow State University. Before finishing, he took the train back to

Volgograd. He found the district almost unrecognizable, the high-rises razed and replaced by a sprawling casino and racetrack. He took the train back to Moscow that night, sold his services through his faculty advisor to a Brazilian conglomerate when he graduated. The way forward was clear. Structures and systems fell apart. Nation states were dinosaurs. Overlapping interests, partnerships of shared opportunity, and money were what remained. Meeting Mr. Fortinbras had been a breath of fresh air.

He turned back to the concert hall, startled. Pleasure surged through him as an oversight became clear. The orchestra might still be playing when the doors flew open. The muffled glory might be unleashed as the incoming news drove people from their seats. And so it was. He closed his eyes. For a long moment, he kept them closed, lost in the transcendence. Then he did his job. With a quick series of blinks, the camera in his contact lens began recording. After thirty seconds, he had what they needed. Then he did what everyone else was doing. He ran.

Harper hastily swallowed a puddle of watery oatmeal and took the elevator down. Fortinbras looked up briefly as he stepped into the waiting town car. "Not much in the press," he said, settling in. He scowled. He realized he had left his mug of coffee by the kitchen sink. Someone was drilling away inside his skull. Fortinbras grunted, returned to scrolling on his phone.

Good morning to you too, Harper thought. *No news is good news.* The previous day's hearing had been another marathon, almost ten hours of senators' posturing, bickering, speechifying, and occasionally asking them a question. He knew it was all part of the game, but he did not have to like it. It was a twisted game of cat and mouse, everyone waiting to pounce on a bad word choice, a poor turn of phrase. Every member of the committee was looking for a chance to preen for the cameras, to string together some choice quotes to share with constituents back home. He and Fortinbras were simply there as props for most of the day. *Without a cup of something strong, I won't even be able to do that.*

When they were on stage, he thought Fortinbras handled the big picture well. "Aponix is a global provider of energy infrastructure support services," his prepared notes read. "We maintain and service oil pipelines in thirty-six states, including the Trans-Alaskan Pipeline. We are the primary support contractor to the Alyuska Pipeline Service Company. We grieve with the nation during this time of unspeakable tragedy." Fortinbras spoke the words quietly, emotion tugging at each word. Harper had memorized the whole thing, just in case. "Like everyone," the remarks continued, "we are looking for answers. We have been on the ground since those dreadful early hours, working alongside emergency responders and the military." Here, Fortinbras' voice cracked. A nice touch, Harper thought. Acting was never my thing.

"We have seen what this has done to so many communities, to

so many families," Fortinbras continued. "*I have seen the devastation stretching mile after mile across the Alaskan wilderness. This must never happen again. We must work together to make sure...*" Here comes the pivot, Harper thought. *Laying the groundwork.* It was his favorite part. "We must move away from business as usual," his boss continued. "We must all ask, what can we, as a nation, do differently? How can we learn from this and become stronger, as we have always done in challenging times? We must not falter. The world has changed, and so must we." They waited for the committee to respond. Camera flashes cascaded. Aides scurried. Papers shuffled. Harper felt like they were miles above the ground, two men gingerly balancing on a rope that extended into darkness. Then they were excused. Relief washed over him as they left Capitol Hill.

Today was round two. The car turned off the Ninth Street Expressway. Pennsylvania Avenue was quiet, the asphalt dark from the early morning rain. The drilling in his head intensified. A few sharp turns and they were soon underground, pulling through checkpoints staffed by exceedingly well-armed guards. Another day deep in the bowels of the U.S. government, Harper thought. They had done one-on-ones, task force meetings, subcommittee meetings, zipping back and forth on the congressional subway system, all building up to the big show. Time was blending into a bureaucratic blur of office buildings and endless discussions.

The previous day, when the chairwoman had finally gotten around to speaking, Harper was on the edge of his seat. He could not help it. He and Fortinbras were up there, alone, exposed. So much work, years of it, was on the line. He felt the darkness drawing in close around them. Dianne Gladenton had built her career on skewering corporate and labor bigwigs alike. There was not a deep pocket she had not gone after at some point. He looked over at Fortinbras. If he felt the rope underfoot starting to sway, he gave no sign.

Then it was time. The senior senator from Alaska thanked them by name and turned to her notes. "The committee would first like to recognize the tireless efforts of all the men and women of our armed forces who have joined with Alaskans in responding so heroically to this tragedy," she said solemnly. "For every aid delivery that is helping communities rebuild, for every moment you have taken to help a family in need, we say thank you." More camera flashes. More aides scurrying. More paper shuffling. The senator reached for a pair of glasses and pulled over a large binder. "I would like to enter the National Transportation and Safety Board's preliminary findings into the record," she said. "I would also like to take a moment to read some of its findings aloud. It reads in part, 'All evidence indicates that the catastrophic failure of the Trans-Alaskan Pipeline was caused by rapid, uniform melting of permafrost. We have been unable to find any evidence of negligence or malfeasance. The safety and backup systems put in place by Aponix exceeded design specifications. We are left to conclude that the failure of the pipeline system could in fact have been much worse. Further study will be needed to understand the impacts of global temperature rise on Alaska's..."

The senator's words faded into the background. Harper sat back in his chair, deeply relieved. The NTSB's findings had been closely guarded; they had been unable to get any advance word. The day's hearing could have turned into accusations, persecution, a Congressional lynch mob. Instead, they were on solid ground. All of the preparation had been worth it. *We are invisible.* He looked over at Fortinbras again. Was that a slight smile on his lips?

The chairwoman removed her glasses and peered over her microphone at them. "Do either of you gentlemen have any recommendations you would like to share with the committee?" she asked. "Please speak freely. We are here to fact find and learn from this catastrophe, not to assign blame."

Bullshit, he thought. That is exactly why you are here. Having the NTSB blame Mother Nature is not going to cut it. U.S. crude oil supplies are down fourteen percent. The Middle East is in flames again. Global energy markets are in turmoil. Someone needs to be seen doing something. The NTSB report leaves the United States government searching for someone, anyone, to own this...tragedy. He and Fortinbras politely demurred. "Thank you for this opportunity, Madame Chairwoman," his boss replied. "Aponix will continue our efforts to support the cleanup and restoration of Alaska's communities and wilderness as best we can. If there is anything more we can do to assist the committee in its work, please let us know." Harper did the heavy lifting the rest of the day, walking the committee through the company's pipeline safety and maintenance procedures. If Fortinbras was the shine and polish, he was the nuts and bolts. He made sure the mundanity of the information shone through. By the time the chairwoman gaveled the hearing to a close, there were no more camera flashes. Aides were slumped in chairs around the room. Papers had metastasized into uneven mountains and drifting piles of binders and folders.

Now, yesterday felt like a week ago and they were heading back into the same room. He was relieved to find a coffee urn near the entrance and made a brief pit stop. He tossed back a couple of aspirin and took a gulp of the steaming liquid. The drilling in his head seemed to step down a notch. Better, he thought. Not great, but better. He couldn't help smiling as they walked in. It was like a bowling alley where all the pins had been reset. Everyone and everything was back in position. Except for the two of them. He and Fortinbras headed for anonymity in the rows of chairs behind the witness tables. After they found their seats – reserved center aisle, third row, a promising sign, he thought – he took a good look at the day's victims. There was barely any room to move up there. The heads of five major oil companies, each accompanied by an attorney, were crammed around the table. Fortinbras had been adamant on that point. "No counsel," he shouted during one of the planning sessions. "It looks like you have something to hide. It's like dangling fresh meat in front of a hungry lion." All of them were dressed impeccably in tailored suits. All of them were staring straight ahead, trying to look solemn and relaxed at the same time. Beads of sweat on several brows gave the game away.

Harper realized his own shirt was soaked through. He took another gulp of coffee, hoping the drilling would ramp down a little more. It had been a long time since he had struggled through a hangover. The previous day had demanded nothing less. The town car dropped them off at a bar in Fairfax, a solid hour away from the eyes and ears of the Hill. The place was owned by an old friend of the boss. Safe ground. The rounds went down easily and Harper felt increasingly warm and relaxed. Beer mixed with liquor. He heard words coming out of his mouth. It felt so good to talk after using shorthand code for weeks. The boss came out from behind his usual grunts to caricature the committee. Fortinbras even laughed. It quickly became clear, however, that the chip on his shoulder was going nowhere.

"We're the support staff, the backstage crew, the cleaners," Fortinbras hissed. "We do what people tell us to do. So they think...what do they know? Imagine what we could tell them...imagine the looks on their faces if we peeled back the layers! Up is down and left is right. Everything they know is wrong. Fools! We are going to lead those mules by the nose. They just don't know it yet." Harper understood. Taking the long view was one thing. Living it was another. "Hiding in plain sight is hard work," he replied. He shook his head, trying to chase away the descending fog.

Fortinbras did not hear him. He was on a roll. Spittle flew from his lips as he pounded on the table with a fist. "Now they call for the big boys. They will share their bright ideas. We will all bask in their glory. Or maybe not! Surely one day we will tire of bowing and scrape to those bloated whales." A sly smile spread across his face.

We can only hope, Harper thought, that that day is tomorrow. Some things are out of our control.

There was no sign of fireworks before the lunch recess. The morning was taken up entirely with the companies' opening statements and committee members' fawning over the executives. "Bought lock, stock, and barrel," Fortinbras whispered. "Every one of them." Harper noticed the chairwoman was the only one not to speak at length. He was unsure how to interpret her silence. Fortinbras seemed unperturbed. "Patience," was all he said on the subject. "Hungry?"

Harper realized he was starving. Several platefuls of food in the Senate cafeteria put a dent in the gaping hole. More aspirin left him with only a dull headache. They headed back and found their seats. As other people were still filtering back into the chamber, the chairwoman gaveled the hearing back into session with surprising energy. A small, knowing smile flittered across Fortinbras' lips. "Gentlemen, we have been exploring the pipeline, past and present," she said, peering past the edge of the committee table at the group.

Her eyes narrowed. "I wonder if you might share some thoughts on its future?"

The executives and their attorneys were still finding their seats as she spoke. One of them managed to get near a microphone. "I think we all can agree on the pipeline's importance, Madame Chairwoman, both for our national security and for Alaska's economy," he began, leaning over the table. He reached back awkwardly to drag a chair over as he spoke. "At the same time, we must recognize the pipeline is not an infinite resource. It operates at about twenty-five percent of its full capacity, down from two million barrels a day when it was built."

"And what conclusion should we draw from this…fact?" the senator asked.

The executive looked at his colleagues for a long moment before responding. All of their attorneys were poised to interject. "That, uh, to maintain the nation's energy independence and strengthen Alaska's economy, uh, we may need to look at new options, uh, at diversifying our portfolios," he said finally.

"I see," the senator replied. "That does sound important. What are you actually suggesting?"

"That we take a fresh look –" the executive paused to clear his throat. He gulped down some water – "at Alaska. That we think about boosting production. That we not let this tragedy define us."

The chairwoman was clearly irritated. "For goodness sake," she replied, shaking her head. "Say the words. Where would this boosting happen?"

The executive looked miserable. The others stared straight ahead. "We would need to work with our local and state partners before we could commit to specific locations," he said finally. The chairwoman threw up her hands, exasperated. "Fine. I'll say them for you. The Arctic National Wildlife Refuge for one. The National Petroleum Reserve for another."

The attorneys whispered furiously in their clients' ears. The executives shifted uncomfortably in their chairs. None of them spoke. Their heads did not move. After a long silence, one of them finally broke. "Look, this could be a time of real opportunity, a time to do something new," he said. "I'm not sure why this committee sees fit to go after –"

The senator did not let him get any further. She smelled blood. "A time of opportunity? Doing something new?" she asked rhetorically. "You're trotting out some very old ideas. New drilling would mean new pipelines, or new rail lines. New infrastructure facing the same challenges that just wrecked one of the world's largest energy systems, in the depths of winter no less. Climate change is going to change our world."

More furious whispering followed. But the senator was far from finished. "Tell us, what are your companies doing to address climate change?" she asked. An executive in the middle of the pack looked relieved. "All of our companies are conducting global operations reviews for exposure to climate liabilities," he responded confidently.

"You're doing that now? Wow, that's good news," she noted dryly. "It's good to hear you're changing gears." The executive nodded warily. His confidence had vanished. "Changing gears after spending two decades fighting climate change science," she continued. "After two decades spending countless millions on lobbying and public relations to hide the facts and confuse people. Tell me, do you have any findings yet from these reviews?" The executive shook his head. Good plan, Harper thought. Keep those lips buttoned. You're not going to convince this lady of anything. She has been three steps ahead of you since the gavel came down.

The senator was not finished, either. "Hmm. Well, you will excuse me if I don't hold my breath," she said. "Let me recap. Your recommendation – at all times, under all conditions – remains more drilling, which means more infrastructure. You have no systems in place to account for the impacts of climate change on that infrastructure. You will get back to us on that." Waves of camera flashes lit up the executives as the senator spoke. I would be surprised if they said another word, Harper thought. They would have been better off taking the fifth.

Meantime, the senator kept rolling. "You see what happened in Alaska as an 'opportunity.' An opportunity for new business," she noted, "just as soon as we can clean up the world's biggest oil spill. All this while you sell off your wind and solar farms and spend pennies on R&D for new technologies. Mining oil, gas, and coal is making your industry rich while cooking the planet. The bills from the global damage you cause are coming due. Make no mistake, *that* is the story of the tragedy in Alaska. It is time to end business as usual. It's killing our planet."

Harper realized in a flash what she was doing. Writing the headline, drafting the talking points, providing the quotes. Packaging everything up with a cherry on top. All while using very familiar language. The media was going to have a field day. He looked over at Fortinbras. The smile was now a mile wide. "I told you they were all bought," he whispered, leaning over. "The oil companies own the rest of the committee. We own her."

After that, doors opened for them all over Capitol Hill. There was a problem. A massive problem. And Aponix was the only game in town. They hinted at a game-changer, at innovation just over the horizon. "Our system will take transportation out of the equation," Harper explained patiently to groups of lawmakers. He found most of their questions off target; they were out of their depth. "Local energy generation is the future," he continued. "We are looking at a limitless supply of cheap domestic energy. Period." In other meetings, he watched as Fortinbras played the big-picture game like a grandmaster. "People don't want to be handed things," he said. "They want to feel like they've earned them. And they want them yesterday. We are just giving them what they want."

In return, the two men got what they needed. "We're not

looking for subsidies. We are not the oil companies," Fortinbras said a thousand times, in a thousand places. "We need protection from the oil companies." They got everything – federal distribution agreements, intellectual property assurances, pricing guarantees. "You guys deliver on this, the courts will not touch you," the Speaker of the House said over dinner. The Wagyu steaks were almost raw, their plates red and bloody. Harper smiled. Apparently, there were still smoke-filled back rooms in Washington. He found the lawmakers' attempts to apply pressure pathetic. There was no mistaking who was in the driver's seat. "We're like bookends," Fortinbras said. The town car was on its way to the airport. "If you look forward, we're there. If you look backward, we are there too. We were there before things fell apart."

Harper thought back to the Kennedy Center. The man was a genius. The company's name had been everywhere, from the programs to the banners overhead. A year ago, the name Aponix meant little. Just another special interest currying favor. A new player in town, joining the age-old game. Not anymore. He could almost reach out and touch those final perfect moments. The snowflakes falling. The silence. A sudden lurching stop brought him back to the present. "That is why they are so comfortable with us," Fortinbras was saying. He stared at the driver, irritated, before continuing. "They think we are the ones who can get them back to a safe place." Back to when the post-9/11 world had finally begun to settle, Harper thought. When the doors had not yet opened. The new musicians had not yet come on stage. The music remained unheard. When a thousand details of people's old lives still mattered. The car glided to a stop outside the Departures Hall. Harper smiled as he got out. Even then, the future had been waiting. Stacked in warehouse rows, ready for delivery. Ready for the rest of the world to catch up.

Going Down the Rabbit Hole

The trail went cold and stayed that way. The flickering, grainy video played endlessly in her thoughts. The figure was a phantom, untraceable. The cops said they needed something more to go on. Another sweep of the house and yard yielded nothing – not a hair, not a footprint, nothing. They all went about their lives as best they could – another Bookcliffs Challenge came and went, bigger and better than ever. She did her best not to let the mounting dead ends drive her crazy. Months later, the wildflower meadows at 9656 Sandoval Hills Drive were blooming for the second time.

The flowers would wilt and die in this blast furnace, Anna thought. She had never been to a place so hot. The valley in August did not come close. She and Ry stepped to the curb and waited for the next taxi to pull up. Ry fumbled in his pocket for the piece of paper with the address on it. He thrust it at the driver. Anna was relieved to see the man nod. They left him standing by the open trunk. "No luggage," she said, shrugging. "Visita rápida."

Nothing for months, and then...they were here. Everything changed in two instants. A brief stop at the Carbondale police department led to a passing conversation with a tech-obsessed police sergeant. That turned up a detail the police chief had neglected to mention to detectives. The entire town was wired, courtesy of a huge homeland security grant. Apparently, the police department kept most of the cameras turned off, in deference to local billionaires irate about unrequested government surveillance. One on Main Street turned up car plates from that night, including a set from a single out-of-town visitor, a rental from Denver airport. There was no name, just a registration. Aponix. The name meant nothing to her. A quick search online yielded a headquarters address in Manaus, Brazil. The next day, follow-up digging online turned up months-old footage of the head of the company testifying on Capitol Hill. They shared it with Katherine that night.

"That's John Wellsey," she said simply.

"Whaa?" was all Ry could manage. Anna tried to pick her jaw up off the floor. She had been in the trailer, had seen the man who passed through the carnage unscathed. She could see no resemblance.

"He has a new name, but that's definitely him," Katherine continued. She stared at the laptop screen, mesmerized. "Fortinbras, huh? He's had a lot of work done, but some things you can't hide. The way he hunches over the table. That sneer before he answers a question. His voice is exactly the same. Looks like he's doing all right for himself. Send the link to Jackie."

They did, without comment. Anna's phone rang moments later. "I don't know how you found him," Jackie said quietly. "What now?" Anna had no answer. Jackie's question echoed uneasily in her thoughts as days passed. They shared everything with local and state police. She was amazed at their response. "There's no sign of any vehicle at the scene," said the detective assigned to their case. "No record of the individual in the video in Colorado. He was in Alaska at the time. And as you know, we have no record anywhere of a John Wellsey with the background you describe."

"Isn't it your job to make those connections?" she wanted to shout. "Do we have to do your jobs for you?" It was unbelievable. They had turned up fresh leads, and their reward was more questions and more dead ends. Screw the cops, she thought. One path was open now, even if the authorities couldn't see it. Someone associated with Aponix had driven up to Sandoval Hills and killed Luis. Was it this Fortinbras guy? It was impossible to tell if he was about the same size as the nimble phantom caught on the security camera footage. Regardless, if Fortinbras was Wellsey, Anna was sure only one thing mattered. A clock was ticking. She and Ry heard it more clearly than the others. Katherine and Jackie remembered a junior attorney with an ugly temper who would do anything to get ahead. A short, stocky bull of man, bald headed, sleeves rolled up, sweating profusely through a tailored shirt. "He was Stanley Richards' right-hand man. He was the mind behind the firm's muscle," Katherine said. "You didn't mess with John Wellsey." Ry's face darkened as they talked about him. "We have to get out in front of this," was all he said. Anna remembered the pleasure that flickered across the man's face when he saw her bleeding on the floor of the trailer. Whatever he had been, he had clearly switched masks and built a new life. *A life that includes wiping out inconvenient reminders of his past.*

All of which led to a place she had never heard of two weeks ago. Flying into Manaus, she had been amazed at the size of the city. The street grid stretched in all directions, hemmed in only by dark ribbons of blue. Seen from the sky, the Negro and Solimões rivers were enormous. Flotillas of cargo ships, ferryboats, and canoes dotted the water. Now, on the ground, a couple million people were going about their business all around them. Trucks laden with fruit, panels of glass, and lumber barreled past. Motorcycles swerved through the heavy traffic. As the miles passed by, fields and industrial parks near the airport gave way to shining office towers and faded condo towers downtown. The driver pulled abruptly off the highway, crossed a bridge, and plunged down a hill into dense neighborhoods. "Las favelas," he called out. "Shanty town." Anna watched in amazement as the modern city vanished behind them, crowded out by tangles of overhead wires and strings of small fluttering flags. They roared down narrow muddy streets, bouncing through potholes as they made their way past broken-down market stalls. She looked out at toothless old men hawking tobacco and tired, leather-skinned women casting sidelong glances for customers. Straight in front, posses of small brown children chased hula hoops with sticks and kicked at dirt-gray balls made of rubber bands. In the background on either side, faded wooden shacks leaned together for support. Doors hung loosely on worn hinges. Tired paint peeled from windowsills holding shattered flowerpots and scorched soil. Angry green and red scrawls of graffiti raced across rows of political posters and advertisements on the fronts of shuttered businesses.

A moped suddenly shot out of a side alley, narrowly missing the front of the taxi. "Merda!" the driver shouted. He raised his arms in disgust, then slammed his hands back down on the wheel. "Estúpido!" he muttered under his breath. Anna put out an arm to steady herself as they lurched through junctions barely wider than the cab. She started to cough as the air soured further, the unmistakable odor of human waste mixing with a sharp chemical smell and burning charcoal.

Ahead, the way forward did not look good. The road narrowed further. Slow-moving crowds blocked their path. Two-story shacks crowded out the daylight. The day's heat pressed in. Anna felt sure she was about to faint when the driver spun the wheel sharply with one hand and gunned the engine. The taxi rumbled over cobblestones, flew over a small ditch and skidded out into a wide-open space. Anna took a deep breath. All limbs intact, she thought. *Vomiting seems like a good next step.* She and Ry squinted in the bright light, trying to make any sense of where they were. A breeze poured in the windows, carrying new smells – rotting fish, diesel fuel – that told her they were near water. The driver flipped a red flag to stop the ticking meter and looked back expectantly. "GPS say is there," he said, pointing through the windshield. Still blinded, Anna could make out the outlines of a tall fence and little else. Ry fumbled in his pocket and fished out several real notes. The driver offered a curt "obrigado" but no change. Fair enough, Anna thought as they got out. Driving like that, he was not going to live much longer. Might as well make the most of it.

They found a dusty park bench and sat down to get their bearings. Anna saw the open space was actually a large cobblestone square that led down to a dingy-looking ferry terminal. A small crowd had gathered near the entrance; a boat was pulling in. Voices called out, hands fluttered as passengers disembarked. A chorus of angry horns erupted. Anna saw their driver had jumped the taxi stand line and was shoveling a startled family into his back seat. She smiled. The guy had a pair. She checked out the rest of the square. The slums they had driven through ringed the area, the tidal wave of poverty pulling up just a few feet from the curb. Trash littered the broken chunks of sidewalk nearby. The sound of several generators clanking along led her to several food trucks nearby. She realized she was seriously hungry. They walked over to one of them, pointed at the menu board and hoped for the best. She unwrapped a foil square to find chicken, caramelized onions, sweet peppers, and a side of electric orange mango. She plucked at the meat with her fingers – it was steaming hot. It also smelled incredible, crowding out the stench of decay pervading the area. When they were finally able to taste the food, the contrasting flavors and textures – spicy, sweet, tangy, mild, wet, dry – came together in a heart-stoppingly good combination. This must be how people get by, she thought. Overwhelming the senses seems like a daily requirement for survival.

Anna crushed up the foil and balanced it on top of an overflowing trashcan. She looked at her watch. "Let's do this," she said. Ry nodded. They pulled their caps down low over their faces and moved into the crowd of people and animals – ragged dogs, caged chickens, goats on leashes – moving ceaselessly along the riverfront. They had twelve hours until they caught the redeye back to Miami. That had been part of the agreement. The absurd disguises – a wig and dark sunglasses for her, and a pornstache and John Deere ball cap for Ry – were another. None of the others had thought it was a good idea. "We don't have any better ones," Ry pointed out. They could see the terror in Katherine's eyes. Anna spoke more softly. "We'll be careful," she said. "They'll never know we were there." That was one thing they all agreed on. Poking a monster without a plan was suicide. But they needed more information. "We have no idea why Anna's brother was killed and we are still alive. But it's not just about us, or Luis," Ry argued. "Fortinbras is bad news. You think he's out there spreading happiness and goodwill? It looks to me like he's building a new empire. God only knows what's behind that corporate front."

So now we're here, Anna marveled. Thousands of miles from home. People spilled around them as they stopped walking and stared across the street. They had not bothered to look up the address online; Anna figured they would end up outside a sleek office tower. Instead, the city's skyline lay in the hazy distance. Across the traffic-filled road, there was nothing but overgrown fields and forest. Anna could make out a crumbling house and a collapsed silo. A rusted-out hay bailer and other pieces of farm equipment were strewn across the land like discarded toys. A small numbered sign with a company logo on a call box told her they were in the right place. The gate behind it was the only break in the tall silver fence that curved away in both directions. The landscape tells one story, she noted. Nothing to see here. Move along. The coils of fence-topping barbed wire and cameras posted every few feet tell another.

They started moving again, shuffling along with the crowd. The sun was overhead now and the day's heat was even more stifling. Wherever she looked, the air shimmered. If anyone else noticed the sauna, they gave no sign. She and Ry were the only ones sweating like pigs. To their left, barefoot boys and men with bloodshot eyes tended long fishing poles resting on the river wall. Occasional breaks in the wall led to gasoline-stained sand and wooden wharves packed with small boats. Overconfident seagulls skimmed the sky and strutted underfoot. Across the road, the fence curved and curved. The fields were about to give way to forest when she noticed something else, set way back on the property. Almost hidden by a slight rise, a long, low warehouse stretched into the trees. A massive solar array twinkled on its roof. Storage means transportation, she thought. The farm road at the entrance would not cut it. There had to be another entrance. A few hundred yards further on, she found her answer. The sidewalks and rundown road gave way to a gleaming two-lane drawbridge. Through the black metal gratings underfoot, she could see the river making its way to a huge pair of closed steel doors. The canal lock at the property boundary was enormous, big enough to berth a container ship, as if someone had moved a chunk of the Panama Canal a thousand miles south. Further on, steel trestles supported an elevated rail spur that disappeared through another gate. Between the canal lock and the rail line, a trickle of water dripped from a huge outflow pipe at the water's edge. That has to be over-engineered, she thought. You could fit a tank in there.

On the far side, the road reverted to dirt potholes and uneven sidewalks. A hundred yards ahead, it plunged back into the favelas. She studied the bridge, trying to make sense of the infrastructure. The place had its own port, its own rail line, its own energy source. It didn't need a road. She was reminded of a line from one of her favorite childhood books. *"You see, nobody ever goes in...and nobody ever comes out."* In that case, we are in good company, she thought. Charlie Bucket found his way into the chocolate factory. *Now we just need to find our golden ticket.*

By the time their second flight touched down in Denver, they thought they had a decent plan. Far fetched, perhaps, but solid. First, however, they had to lay the groundwork. Ry invited the group over for beers the next night. "I'm just glad you're okay," Katherine said as they headed out on the back deck. The kids were in bed. "I still think the trip was way too risky."

"You're sure you weren't tailed or caught on camera?" Derek asked. "No security guards taking an interest?"

"The cab rides were the most dangerous part," Anna joked, trying to cut the tension. "We kept our distance. We kept our caps pulled down low. We weren't there more than a few hours." She saw Ry holding Katherine's hand. *I wish that would work with Derek,* she thought. Both she and Ry had been doing their best to calm their jittery spouses. She knew Derek and Katherine had full plates without their wife and husband jetting off to South America to play spy games. *Which is why I think our plan may work.* Anna grabbed her laptop and got straight to the point. "We didn't find a smoking gun," she said. "But it was a pretty strange place. Some kind of storage or manufacturing building, or both, right there in the poorest part of the city." She talked about the massive amount of infrastructure connected to the property. "And everything inside the fence line is a different story," she said. "You'll see what I mean." She brought the city up on a digital map and zoomed in on the property. The farm fields were zigzags of light green. The forest looked like dense clusters of broccoli. The warehouse was a long, squat rectangle. The solar panels were visible. The aerial also clearly showed a good-size helipad on the roof.

"Here's where it goes from strange to downright weird," Ry said. "The canal berth is massive, and the rail spur is big too. But there is no sign of either from above. You hit the fence and there's nothing but trees."

"Meaning what?" Sam asked. "The gates are a bunch of stage props?"

"Or they've gone underground." Jackie chimed in, "in a complex big enough to swallow a container ship."

"Exactly!" Ry replied. "I think we're looking at a massive facility, hidden in plain sight." The group fell silent. Everyone stared at the screen. Paul finally broke the silence. "Maybe Aponix is just a front for the Brazilian military, or their government," he offered. "I mean, who else could build something like that?" There was no denying it. Front or no, the company had serious money and power at its disposal.

Anna looked to Jackie and Katherine for more information. "Has Lucille turned up anything?" she asked.

Jackie held up a folder. "So far, not much. Just a bunch of boilerplate language in their U.S. registration documents," she replied. "They're all about energy...green energy. Transforming the way we live our lives. Creating a more sustainable future. Et cetera. All big-picture stuff, no details. Maintaining energy infrastructure seems to be their bread and butter."

"That part makes sense at least," Anna replied. "Manaus is the world's most sustainable city. Green roofs, walkable neighborhoods, public transit, parks, renewables – you name it, they're on the cutting edge. But it doesn't look like Aponix is part of the scene. They are not low profile. They're no profile. We need to find out more."

Katherine sighed and rolled her eyes. "Yeah, great. Another mystery to explore…fantastic," she said sarcastically. "Roswell…the Kennedy assassination…both small potatoes compared to our conspiracy theories. The Network is done, finished, rolled up. So what if John Wellsey is still out there? So what if he has a new name and a new face? Why would we go and kick that hornet's nest?"

"I know none of us want to be here, talking about this," Anna replied, choosing her words carefully. "I get it. But this is something I have to do. My brother is dead. This guy Wellsey, he's connected to it somehow. And it's bigger than that. You think he's out there spreading happiness and goodwill? He's got a good cover, I'll give him that. But God only knows what he's up to. We have to stop him. No one else is going to." She sat back, exhausted. Talking about Luis was like ripping open a wound. Healing was no longer an option. *Not now.* Next to her, Derek said nothing, but his body language – arms folded across his chest, jaw tightly set – was not promising. Katherine and Jackie were staring at the ground. Only Sam and Paul looked interested. "Ry and I aren't stupid," she continued. "This is dangerous business. Which is why we think we have a plan that will keep us safe." She looked over at Ry. *Here goes nothing.*

Ry jumped in. "Imagine a Broadway show," he began. "Or better yet, improv. We are the creative team in the background. We provide the stage directions for the actors, maybe even some of their lines. And then we sit in the audience and see what happens."

"Enough with the metaphors," Katherine said caustically. "Cut to the chase."

Ry nodded. "Fair enough," he replied. "The actors are the muckety-mucks of our own fair town. Grand Junction does not have an international sister city. Manaus does not have one in the United States. We convince the Mayor that the two places should link up, in the name of fostering world peace, global harmony, linking hands with our South American brothers and sisters. He'll hear the bottom-line possibilities – good press, business development, international travel on the community's dime. For town twinning to happen, delegations need to visit. We help the Mayor put one together. Make sure Aponix is approached as a partner. Line up a visit to learn more about what they do. We watch how they respond. Delegation returns home. We learn what is behind that fence, safely and secretly." They both looked around at the group. "That's it. What do you think?" Ry asked.

Sam and Paul were on board, as she knew they would be. "Just keep me out of it," was Katherine's response. "I can't speak for Jackie, but I've got my very own conspiracy to deal with, right here at home. It seems like a long shot, and a lot of work. But do what you want. As long as we're hidden, that's what I care about." Jackie nodded. "Katherine's right. The litigation with Deep Jungle has taken over our lives," she said. "We can't back down, can't dial it back. Not at the moment. If you want to try this, I'm fine with that…so long as you're sure we're not exposed."

That left Derek. He sighed and tapped his foot for a while. "This would be on me, wouldn't it?" he asked eventually. "You're asking me to take this to council?"

"You're our best shot," Anna admitted. "You've got the star power. The Mayor likes you."

"I don't know that I have much pull," he replied. "Our plans for the old hospital have been mired in committee hell since forever."

"Maybe this would help," Paul offered. "We've tried pushing, cajoling, sweet talking, standing back. I'm out of ideas. This might lead to something. At least we would be talking with them again." Anna still could not believe that her son was back in town. He was the lead for most of the revitalization projects now. Despite his best efforts, however, the Grand Junction proposal remained a high-profile train wreck, going nowhere fast.

"What it won't do is get us killed," Sam followed up. "It's something rather than nothing. I'm pretty sure the hospital would be on board. I say we go for it."

Anna studied her husband's handsome face. She knew that look. He was usually incredibly relaxed and easygoing, able to put people at ease with an offhand compliment or funny story. But when things got serious, when things mattered, his face changed. The smile vanished and his eyebrows formed a stern, focused ridge. A vein pulsed down one side of his forehead. He rubbed his jaw vigorously. When things were on the line, there was no one else she would rather have in her corner.

"I'll do it," he said simply.

Hallelujah, she thought. I prefer Plan A. Plan B had some rough edges. Get on a plane to Washington. Find Wellsey. Strap him to a chair, beat the truth out of him, get him to turn himself in. Playing the long game is not my strong suit. *If this doesn't work, everyone's getting in a bunker while I go after that bastard with my bare hands.*

Paul was enthusiastic going into the second council meeting. "This might just break the whole thing loose," he said to Derek at the bike shop. "Something has to change. You said yourself that the Mayor is all about economic development. This is all about connecting Grand Junction with new markets, right? Twinning with Manaus is just good business. How could they possibly turn this down?"

Derek shrugged and grabbed his keys. Council's earlier reaction weighed heavily on his mind. "I hope you're right," was all he could think of to say. He appreciated Paul's unflagging enthusiasm but did not share it. He had lost count of the number of planning meetings and visioning sessions. The one-on-ones with councilors had gone nowhere. He had answered the same questions, over and over again, on a dozen site tours. Paul's energy and dedication had not changed the situation. After almost two years, a small but vocal group of area business owners was now pushing the city to bulldoze the crumbling hospital complex. Derek was strangely certain the Mayor had wanted that outcome all along. He could not shake the feeling that something else was going on. *This has never been about the BMX park.* That the twinning idea was still even under discussion was a miracle. "Man-what?" had been the Mayor's first reaction, a week earlier. Council's was not much better. "How about somewhere that speaks English?" one asked. Another offered that she had Scottish roots and had always wanted to trace them, as if this could be the basis of an international partnership. Do any of you think before you open your mouths, he wondered. *Silence is golden.*

Paul fielded the big picture well. "Why Manaus? Well, it's a global center for green initiatives and sustainability," he pointed out. "We could learn a lot from them. But because it was hidden away in the Amazon, no one knew about it. That all changed with the World Cup being held in Brazil. Manaus is now on the world stage. Twinning with them would mean we would be punching well above our weight class. Our reputation as a tourist and recreation destination should appeal to them. We are a gateway to North America. It could be a golden opportunity for us and for them." That got the heads nodding. Regardless, Derek was dreading the obvious follow up. Eventually, even council was able to get around to it. "How would we go about doing this?" one of them asked. He sighed. The honest answer was a simple one. None of us is sure what to do next, he thought. *I'm not a diplomat.* "The city could reach out directly," he offered, stepping into the discussion. "Sending a delegation to Manaus would be a good early step." The heads stopped nodding; eyes glazed over. What am I, chopped liver, he marveled. He could guess what they were thinking – *sounds like work…we've got plenty on our plates…why won't these two just go away?* As usual, the Mayor had the final word. "Thank you both for sharing another idea with council," he said curtly. "We will discuss it further."

Derek kicked at the carpet in frustration as they left the chambers. "Another wasted evening," he muttered to Paul. *How are we ever going to get close to Aponix?* They were standing in the parking lot talking when the Mayor's chief of staff caught up with them. "I think I can work on them," he said breathlessly. "We need something like this. My brother-in-law is Brazilian. He's a civil servant in Rio. I'll see what he can find out." Incredibly, a week later, the wheels started rolling. "The Mayor of Manaus is a huge fan of BMX racing," the chief of staff explained in a brief, out-of-the-blue call. "He wants to meet you. We need to get council together on this and strike while the iron is hot. Are you available this afternoon? Council has a working session scheduled." Derek's mind raced. There would be no time for the group to talk this through. They were just going to have to go for it. "We'll be there. Thanks Eric," he replied. He hung up and looked at Paul, stunned. "Manaus is on," he said simply.

Now they were back. Paul pushed open the doors. They both looked around, surprised. The chambers were empty. "Get in here," a voice growled. The Mayor appeared from a side entrance and strode up the aisle to meet them. "How dare you go behind my back!" he hissed as they approached. His face was beet red. The tendons and veins in his neck stood out in thick, tight cords. "Some guy calls from the Brazilian embassy and he can't stop talking about *you*, Olympic champion this and X-games that. I can barely make out what he's saying, the damn idiot is talking so fast."

"We had no –" Paul tried and failed to jump into a brief pause in the diatribe.

"Shut up, kid," the Mayor replied. "Council's all excited, and they've leaked it to the media. I can't stop this now, but I'm sure as hell not doing you any favors. We'll take a delegation down there, but you won't be a part of it. I do not care one bit how much their Mayor likes BMX. He can wait to meet you here, during your oh-so-big-and-mighty race."

Derek tried his best to look disappointed. He could not believe what he was hearing. *Our stage production could actually get off the ground.*

"One other thing," the Mayor continued, jabbing his finger at both men. "I can't believe I'm saying this. You can have your BMX park…so long as your friends stop holding up the takeover bid for their food co-op."

Derek's brief moment of relief vanished. "That's my line, Mr. Mayor," he replied, as the scales fell from his eyes. *I don't believe this.* "All this time, we've been a bargaining chip?" He saw Gambly now for what he really was. A puppet. A bought marionette. "You *let* the complex become an urgent public safety hazard, didn't you?" he asked. "To justify spending taxpayer dollars on cleaning it up. And then what, Deep Jungle sweeps in as the savior in a sweetheart deal? Another corporate feather in your cap. Let me guess. Their plans changed and now you're singing a new tune."

The Mayor shook his head vehemently and got right up in Derek's face. "I don't know what you're talking about," he replied, spitting out the words. "But if I did, I would strongly advise you to stay focused on the offer. You will not see another one. Who knows what might happen in the future?"

Derek stepped back and turned to Paul. "Time to go," he said quietly. "I've had enough of our fearless leader and his noble ways."

"I heard that. Get out of here!" the Mayor shouted. "If I never see the two of you in here again, it'll be too soon."

Derek wanted nothing more than to turn around and punch the duplicitous snake. Instead, they headed for the doors.

"Where did all of his anger come from?" Paul asked afterwards. "It was like watching a volcano erupt."

"It was something to watch," Derek agreed. "Best I can tell, his handlers were playing him. He's a man used to being in control. It must be pretty disturbing when you realize you've just been borrowing your power." He checked his phone and nearly dropped it. Katherine had tried to reach him more than a dozen times in the last half-hour – *what else was going on?* He realized they were not the only ones trying to start a new show on Broadway. *I need to get home. We need to call the others.*

Katherine stared at the open binder. Words blurred. Lines of black ink swam in front of her eyes. Spreadsheets honeycombed page after page after page. Her hands were shaking as she turned them. Next to her, Jackie was walking everyone through the legal bombshell express-delivered the day before. "Lucille said we were making it difficult for them in arbitration," she was saying. Her tone was flat and resigned. "It looks like she was right. Deep Jungle just rolled out a game changer. Either we accept the buyout's original terms, or they will introduce a thicket of new motions. At best, this would drag everything out for months, possibly years, while we run out of money. At worst, this information could allow them to renegotiate the buyout on radically different terms."

"How is that even possible?" Paul asked. "Did they find some kind of smoking gun?"

"Not exactly," Katherine replied. She saw the young man's face was still ashen. She had never seen him look so shaken. Staring brazen corruption in the face will do that, she thought. *It's not going to be the last time, either.* She rolled out Anna's old map of the valley so everyone could understand. She remembered when Anna had first used it to walk them through the area's history, desperately trying to help two ignorant newcomers before their business crashed and burned. Seeing it again, remembering those early days of promise, made her want to cry. Back then, the map was a confusing mess of property boundaries and topography lines. Now, she knew every inch of Grand Valley like the back of her hand. "It's all about these gray lines that crisscross the map," she started out. "Those are mineral rights. The valley's farmers may own the soil, but oil companies own everything under the ground. Those leases have never gone away. And Deep Jungle is arguing their development could one day wipe out the value of Grand Valley's farmland."

"Based on what evidence?" Sam asked, leaning in for a closer look. "They've been in place for years, right? Getting the oil out costs too much."

Katherine shrugged. "Conveniently, companies have started buying up some of the valley's leases. Same goes for other leases across our coverage areas in other states. We think Deep Jungle has set up shell companies to do it. They're doing enough to suggest the co-op's assets are overvalued."

"Phase one was divide and conquer," Jackie pointed out. "Phase two is revaluing and buying out the co-op at a fire-sale price."

"What do you make of the timing?" Paul asked. "Derek and I are at city hall at the same time this bomb goes off?"

Katherine sighed. She and Ry had tried to pull the previous day's events apart, looking at it from every possible angle. Neither felt like they had come close to cracking it. The corporate behemoth was toying with them, pulling levers, staying several steps ahead. All so that we can go online and buy cheap books, diapers and, now, food, she thought. "Lucille's take was that Deep Jungle decided they weren't going to take the city's sweetheart deal, for whatever reason," she replied. "And they wanted to use the BMX park as leverage before they lost it."

"It's all guesswork," Derek followed up. "They've been playing the city like a violin. Our twinning idea only got legs because the Mayor's chief of staff went behind Gambly's back."

"But it's definitely on, right?" Ry asked urgently. "We're sending a city delegation to Manaus?"

"It looks like it," Derek replied. "At the end of the month."

Katherine watched her husband for a long moment. She knew he had tuned out for most of the discussion. He thought only about one thing. He was constantly on edge, quick to anger, easily startled. His foot tapped the floor constantly. He had lost weight. At work, she heard he had stopped taking out bike tours. He spent most of his time at the shop trolling the Internet for Aponix news. At home, he was distant and distracted. The gentle, thoughtful man she had married had gone into hibernation. She listened patiently while Ry followed up with a flurry of questions. "Any thoughts on who could be our man on the inside?" he asked. "Someone we can trust? Do you think we could get a camera in there?"

Katherine saw the concern written on Derek's face when he responded. "Sam is confident the hospital will be asked to send someone," he said. "They're the largest employer in Grand Junction. A hospital rep. could be our best option, possibly our only one."

"I do have someone in mind," Sam revealed. "The new head of our research and development team. Liz Conway is razor sharp. I trust her. She would have good cover for requesting a tour of the Aponix facility. Medical applications for innovative technologies, something like that."

Ry was nodding emphatically, looking pleased, but Katherine's blood ran cold all the same. There was always going to be a price to pay. Their plan might keep them hidden, but there were still people up there on the stage. Innocent people with no clue about the play's backstory. *And then what?* All Ry thinks about is the next step, she thought. All I can see is a staircase descending into darkness. We have our children to think about. Eventually, something we do will kick the hornet's nest. We have to be prepared.

No one said anything for a while. Katherine watched their faces as they tried to make sense of the day's events. She found Anna was the only person who did not look angry or confused. She was sitting in an armchair on the right side of their living room, lost in thought. The two of them had never been close. Katherine wished she knew how to help a woman in so much pain. Meals for her freezer just did not cut it.

There was one more item of business. Katherine looked at Jackie. "Should we tell them?" she asked. Jackie nodded. Katherine stepped back from the map. "Jackie and I have made a decision. We are going to stop fighting Deep Jungle's takeover," she said. "It split our partnerships. It has decimated our customers. And as you know too well, it has made our lives miserable for more than a year." The words tasted bitter on her tongue. They had created something special, something that made people's lives better, and soon it would belong to a faceless corporate machine. What might come next did not bear thinking about. Visions of factory farms haunted her dreams.

The group looked stunned. Even Anna was surprised. "You mean, you're giving up?" she asked, startled out of her thoughts. "To make the BMX park possible?"

"*No.*" Katherine and Jackie replied in unison. They both smiled. "This is not about the park," Katherine continued. "And we're not giving up. We're doing things differently." She had not felt so sure about something in months.

A night ago, she had left Ry to his conspiracy theories. She drove out of town to see the valley and catch up with her dad and Jill to get some perspective. She took the small, winding roads slowly, looking west as the sun cast the patchwork of fields and farms in a deep purple haze. She pulled up at Christa's place to see her latest sculptures. In the distance, the warm red desert rock of the Bookcliffs and the Grand Mesa provided a gentle reminder of the landscape's ancient history. Katherine's heart caught in her throat. They had helped people believe in farming and themselves again. Together, they had shown that this beautiful, sun-dappled valley could put food on everyone's plates, support a living wage, and help restore the scarred earth.

Driving through the gates of Bunscombe Ranch brought it all home. They had even managed to bring around the valley's long-time ranchers. She had to smile. In Jill's case, maybe falling in love with her dad had something to do with it as well. Maybe everything can still work out, somehow, she told herself.

Her moment of optimism did not last long. Jill threw a bucket of cold water on her hopes during dinner. She was sympathetic, but did not mince words after Katherine brought them up to speed. "You're playing by their rules, in their world," she declared. "You've fought hard, but they'll wear you down. You will not beat them at their own game." She reached for the green beans.

"So what, we're supposed to roll over?" Katherine asked. "Deep Jungle just…wins?" She fought back tears, determined not to show how much Jill's words hurt.

"No, my girl, you misunderstand me," Jill replied, patting her hand. "I'm saying you're making the same mistake you made when you first arrived. This is not about you. You don't have to 'save' anything, or anybody. Your co-op has helped all of us rediscover who *we* are."

Katherine blushed deep red. *I am still making rookie mistakes.*

"People are dazzled by dollar signs when they shouldn't be," Jill continued. "Sometimes they don't know their own best interests, even if you hit them over the head with them. A little time will tell, I think. Give us a chance to show you what we're made of."

"But how can we do that?" Katherine asked. "Deep Jungle will mandate long-term contracts for all producers. Everyone's hands will be tied."

"Only if you say so," Jill replied. "You're giving up a lot. Tell those scavengers they need to give up something too. You agree to stop contesting the buyout. They agree to offer shorter-term contracts with opt-out clauses for current producers. At the very least, it will keep them honest. Deep Jungle will only stay in the valley if they are making money. Profit margins dip, and you see if they don't head for greener pastures."

Katherine laughed. "Jill, I didn't know you were such a strategy guru!" For a second, the weight of the world lifted from her shoulders. Then she looked at her watch and it descended once again; another clock was ticking. She and Jackie needed to respond to Deep Jungle's latest motions, they still needed to talk to the group, and this was a radical departure from where they had left things. "I hope you don't mind, but I've got to go," she said quickly. "Jackie and I need to talk. The original game plan was to keep on fighting." She walked around the table to hug both of them.

"Love you, dad."

"Call us, honey," he replied. "Let us know how it all goes down. We're right behind you."

Katherine lingered, taking in her dad's transformation one more time. He remained as quiet spoken as ever. Otherwise, the thin, wiry, leather-skinned man in front of her was nearly unrecognizable. His hair had disappeared under a worn blue Carhartt cap. Only his warm smile and bushy salt-and-pepper mustache remained. This place has been so good for both of us, she thought. *My mother turned him into a mouse. Now he's a cowboy.* Decades after he had worked as an errand boy for the stewards and jockeys at Belmont Park, her dad had returned to his true calling. *I had no idea.* Jill said he was the closest thing to a horse whisperer she had ever seen. "Carl is simply a natural," she said to Katherine early on. "From the first time he stepped out there, it was plain as day."

He started with troubled yearlings. The horses had the breeding to be champions, but things were not working out. Some would fade early. Others would bolt late. Some wanted to bite, or fight, or mount anything that moved. Others did not want to set foot on a racetrack. "A few are anxious. A few are angry. Some need more help than others," he explained. "Every horse has a story, just like people."

Co-op deliveries and pickups originally brought Katherine out to the ranch. Over time, the real reason for her visits changed. This was personal. She and Jill stood in the shadow of the ranch's main horse barn, watching her dad work. "Carl's like a horse magnet," Jill said. "Keep an eye over there." Sure enough, while her dad worked with a yearling named Sidelong, the horses in the other paddocks nearby looked up and trotted over to watch. When they were finished, the other horses whinnied and pawed the ground. Her dad walked over and talked in a quiet, firm voice to each of them in turn. Then he came over to join them. Katherine could see the sparkle in Jill's eyes. She heard the excitement in her dad's voice. The early blush of new love remained in bloom.

The horses and Jill know what I know, Katherine thought. She had always drawn a huge amount of strength from her dad. Now, she could rely on him and the love of his life. Jill was one of the strongest women she had ever met, running a huge ranch that bred, trained, and delivered world-class racehorses all over the world. For his part, her dad had become the go-to guy in Colorado for dealing with troubled horses. He was on the ground during the state's annual mustang roundups, helping the feds make sure herds were healthy and sustainable. "There's a hard way and there's a right way – horses remember how they're treated," he pointed out. "We have to make sure the roundups don't interfere with mustang's strong family bands." The work took him to the remotest parts of state. Ry and Derek were after him to help them expand the region's network of mountain bike trails on public lands. "We'll just need a helicopter to get there," Ry joked. Katherine gave her dad and Jill both another hug and headed out. A late-night powwow at Jackie's place followed. They drank strong black coffee in her kitchen and finally fell asleep at the table, exhausted and on the same page.

No wonder I'm yawning, she thought. I'm running on fumes. The group's meeting was winding down. They had told Lucille of their decision first thing. Now, everyone knew. That felt good. Her and Jackie's phones both buzzed at the same time. This had to be it. She reached over to swipe the touchscreen and there was the text. Months of legal wrangling and heartache, and it all came down to a few words. "Deep Jungle has agreed to the terms," Lucille wrote. "Final papers will be ready in the next couple of days. Congratulations."

Katherine stared at the words. This time they did not float or blur. The black lines and curves stayed firmly fixed in place, daring her to look away. Is this what winning looks like, she wondered. The terms did not seem that way – they were harsh and unforgiving. She and Jackie could not step foot in the co-op's offices. They could not initiate contact with its employees or the board. A non-compete clause meant she and Jackie could not do anything even slightly connected to food or farming for the next nine months. Strangest of all, they would be surrounded by daily reminders – delivery trucks, commercials, mailings – of the co-op rolling on without them. Still, we are free, she noted, out from under Deep Jungle's thumb. Her heart fluttered at the idea. It had been so long since she had done anything – taking the kids to school, hitting the town for a date with Ry – without clouds of uncertainty hanging over her. *Now...*

"What happens next?" Anna asked, reading her mind. The hard part, Katherine thought. Following Jill's advice. *I'm not good at being patient, or stepping aside when it's time for others to lead the way.* She was grateful when Jackie answered Anna's question. "We wait," her friend replied. "We've put our trust in the valley's producers. In six months' time, we see how many of them walk away."

"And then what...back to the good old days?" Anna asked. "You and Jackie renting out-of-the-way office space and tooling around town in a barely running pickup?"

Katherine laughed. "For the record, that was *your* truck," she replied, smiling. "It might look a little like that, staying local, focusing on the city and the valley," she conceded. "Without all of the mistakes, without feeling like we had to save the world. Something comfortable. Something we all help create this time around." Yeah, she thought, that does sound like something to celebrate. *New possibilities. The Grand Valley Food Connection, Version 2.0.*

Getting in Touch

Even he had to admit things were going their way. First, the twinning idea had gotten off the ground. Now, within days of the announcement that a city-led delegation would be visiting Manaus, an eight-hundred-pound gorilla had muscled its way in. "Grand Junction Now Part of Mile-High Initiative," read the headline. "Denver Mayor to Lead Regional Effort." Ry put down his tablet. He looked over at Katherine. "That's putting it politely," he said, shaking his head. "Can you imagine?"

"Hey I'll take it," she replied, smiling. She finished making coffee and walked over to the table with the mugs. "It's about time we caught a break." Pulling out of arbitration with Deep Jungle…and now this. Ry could see how much it all meant to her. His wife looked relaxed. She was smiling. Her body language had changed completely. And it *was* good news, he reminded himself. Our fingerprints are nowhere to be found on this whole thing. But —

"Can you remember the last time we did this?" Katherine asked, interrupting his thoughts. "Just sat and talked?"

Ry drank some coffee and thought back. It had been months since they had done much of anything, just the two of them. Date nights were a distant memory. Even pillow talk had been a casualty of exhaustion. They had been lost in their own worlds, and trying to be decent parents in the meantime. "Katherine, I'm sorry," he replied. "I know I haven't been giving you what you need. I know I –"

Katherine ignored him. "You know, after I drop the kids at school, I have nowhere to be…" she purred playfully, leaning over. She locked eyes with him, and slid her hand along the inside of his thigh. "Maybe we could, you know…"

"Man that sounds good," he replied. Making love would be so nice…but the voice in his head was having none of it. You can't let down your guard after some good news, it raged. *This is war. You think they take a day off?* He frowned and looked away. Can't you take a day off, he wondered. I'm the one sailing the ship here. When he met Katherine's gaze again, he was horrified to see the sparkle in her eyes had dimmed. She pulled away. "No," she said simply. "Whatever you're dreaming up, the answer is no."

"Katherine, please…" He reached for her but it was too late. She left the table and called for the kids to come down for breakfast.

It's not like that, he wanted to say. But then you would be lying, the voice pointed out, taunting him. It *is* like that. Admit it. You are obsessed. That is why I'm here. You're doing this for her. For all of them. You are the sentry on the tower, keeping watch. You're the one keeping them safe. Am I, he wondered. *At what price?*

Katherine stayed away after that and he did not reach out. Days and then weeks rolled by. He put in his time at the bike shop, but his mind was constantly churning. How would Fortinbras come after them? How could they protect themselves? Sitting still was infuriating. The investigation into Luis' death had bogged down, with the feds showing no interest in pursuing their leads. Anna had warned him off any action for the time being. "If we stick our heads up he'll cut them off," she said succinctly. "We need something first. Some point of leverage, no matter how small. The Manaus delegation is our best hope."

There was little he could do on that front, either. He had met Liz Conway. She seemed cool. But as the visit approached, he grew more concerned that her participation was not going to cut it. The visit to the Aponix facility was officially on the itinerary. She would get inside those walls. But they had no way of coaching her, no way of pushing boundaries without raising the stakes. "We can't do it, Ry," Derek warned. "We can't break cover. I don't like it either. It's bad enough we're sending her undercover on a two-thousand-mile journey. Putting her at risk would be unforgivable."

"So we wait and hope she comes back with something we can use…" Ry's voice trailed off. "That's the best option we've got?"

"It's the *only* option we've got…for now. You know it is."

He did. It was. If there was another way, he had not found it. Even we're not sure what we're looking for, he thought. But without getting off the official tour, without slipping away to open doors and poke around, Liz Conway was only going to see what Aponix wanted her to see. The thought of getting so close and walking away with nothing drove him crazy, kept him awake at night. Katherine had stopped asking what was wrong. "Tell me when the fever breaks," she said in the darkness.

One idea took root in his thoughts and grew. He could go back to Manaus. "Like a one-man advance team," he said to Derek. "I could get down there undetected. I could watch the place to see –"

His friend was having none of it. "Man, you just don't know when to take no for an answer!" he replied, slamming down his repair wrench. "Any whiff of us near this trip and we're done. You don't think Aponix can access flight manifests? You don't think they're monitoring the delegation? *Count on it."*

Ry stepped away. He left the bike shop to walk off the surging anger. In his mind's eye, his dreams sprang to life. A lone sentry on an ancient castle wall, shivering in the cold. In the distance, raw pink shards of dawn bled the horizon. Dry grasses waved in the wind. Trees cast broken silhouettes. A rutted horse track curved into the distance. Yesterday, there had been nothing to see. Today, there was nothing out there. But tomorrow? He was losing the group. Katherine, he understood. Now Derek was pushing away. And Anna? They had been on the same page for months. She saw things like he did. They were a team. Now, she wasn't even returning his phone calls. *She's backing off as well?*

The dream rolled on. Days passed. Thick fog curled in. Storms muscled through. The sentry marched back and forth. He lost track of time, his oilskin shedding sheets of water in the darkness. He stumbled and almost fell, surprised, when things changed. Winches groaned. Ropes pulled taut. Below him, guards slowly raised the portcullis. Moments later, gilded carriages set off for the horizon, jouncing behind struggling mares. He peered over the wall for a glimpse of the people inside, but the windows were dark. The soldier watched in horror as massive thunderclouds billowed in the distance, blotting out the sun. Ink-black shadows crept over the fields, seeping ever closer to the churning carriage wheels. He screamed to warn them, but the wind tore at his voice and left him doubled over, fighting for breath. When he stood again, their fates were sealed. The coachmen did not see the danger, did not slow or stop, until it was too late. He saw the animals rear up, kicking at the sky. Spittle and foam flew from their mouths. Wood splintered. Harnesses snapped. One of the horses was catapulted high into the air, flung from its harness as the carriage whipped sideways. The shadows moved as if they were living creatures, pulling and tugging violently at their prey. A door swung open and someone leapt clear, sprawling in the mud. A dark tentacle whipped around their waist, and pulled them effortlessly into the darkness.

Ry sighed. He kicked at a crushed soda can. He did not see the beautiful spring afternoon unfolding around him. He did not smell the trees and flowers bursting into blossom. The dream was always the same. It shattered his sleep and haunted his days. Its message was clear enough, but he fought the powerlessness with every fiber of his being. *It doesn't have to be like this. There has to be something I can do.* He walked on, leaving downtown behind. He made his way through a neighborhood, savoring the midday quiet. Eventually, he found what he was looking for. He stepped through a gap in a fence and headed out into the desert. He hopped from stone to stone across a dry creek bed, headed for a small mesa about a hundred yards away. Scrub brush tugged at his jeans. Overhead, the sun was tracking higher, warming the dusty red landscape. Moments of dry heat hinted at the ferocity of desert summer to come. When he got close, he pulled himself up onto a large flat slab of sandstone at the mesa's base and kept climbing. His muscles were tight but soon relaxed as old habits took over. The handholds were wide and plentiful, and he made fast time. *Too fast.* He slowed down, seeking out the most challenging parts of the face, pulling a couple nifty moves to leap past a section of blank rock and crimping onto a distant ledge. *Better.* Now high above the valley floor, he swung a leg up onto flat tabletop, brushing the rock dust from his clothes. Just a little light bouldering, but it still felt damn good.

Let's push it, he thought, taking in the timeless view. The elevation, the wind, the open space – it was the closest he could come to re-creating his dream. He closed his eyes and focused, forcing himself back into the vision of driving rain and death. Rivulets of water poured across the worn rectangles of granite beneath his feet. To either side, castle towers offered momentary respite from the weather. They were also dead ends. He was trapped on this forsaken stretch of stone. There was no need to look over the castle wall. *What am I missing? What else is there?* The ground began to shake. Ry pressed his palms into his eyes to steady himself. A low roar followed, filling the air. He realized it was coming from behind him. He turned slowly, buffeted by walls of wind that pushed him steadily backwards. His mouth fell open. A gigantic black-and-gold dragon slowly rose above the far wall of the castle. Stream trailed from its nostrils. Flames crackled in its mouth. Each beat of its enormous wings swept it higher into the sky. *What are you? What are you trying to tell me?* Ry swore the dragon locked eyes with him. It let out a deafening screech and beat its wings in place, holding itself up in the sky, daring him to answer. Another screech followed, and then it plunged out of the sky toward him. He fell backward, his feet scrabbling for purchase. Its gaping maw came within inches of him. A pale underbelly, talons and hind legs blurred by. Its tail came through last, whipping from side to side. A sudden snap and its tail spear slammed into one of the towers, breaking it apart like so many toy blocks. Then the dragon was gone, headed for the horizon. Burnt earth and sulfur were the only traces it left behind.

Ry opened his eyes, stunned. Staring wide-eyed across the peaceful valley, a lost memory fell into his consciousness. They were on the hillside after the drone strike. The valley below had exploded in fire. The blast had knocked them all senseless. He coughed and struggled to stand. His ears were ringing and he could barely breathe. As the dust cleared, he saw Anna crawl over to Derek. She passed him a ragged piece of paper, whispered something in his ear. Later, as they made it down the hillside, he saw the paper fall from his friend's pocket. It came to rest near his foot, fluttering in the wind. He picked it up. Before he could do anything else, the paper folded open in his hand. There was a scrawled phone number. Nothing else. "You dropped something," he said to Derek later, and handed it to him.

Long forgotten, the details were razor sharp now. He had never asked. Derek and Anna had never said anything. But that piece of paper – *that number* – had been the most important thing in the world to Anna at that moment. The number blazed in front of his eyes, as if burned into a canyon wall. If she wasn't getting out of there alive, calling that number was her final request. Derek would have known how to reach out to her mother, or Luis, or Paul. This was something else. *Someone else.* He reached for his phone. For several minutes, he just stood there, daring himself to punch the numbers. His hands were shaking. He knew it could be a bridge too far. He had no way of knowing what might happen. But he could guess. His vision made no bones about it. That number summons a monster, he reflected. *But maybe we need one.* He thought about the call accelerating across the globe, leaping mountain ranges, plunging under oceans, pinging satellites, traveling hundreds of thousands of meters per second. And then arriving, slamming into a receiver, lighting up a screen, signaling…what? It was either put up or shut up. If he asked Anna, everything would unravel. If he did nothing, weeks, months, even years of frustration might lie ahead. Plenty of time for Wellsey to choose his moment. For him to end them. Ry saw it clearly then.

Making the call risked his marriage, risked their friendships, risked their lives. *But it gives us a chance. We have to take it.* He took a deep breath and dialed. It rang a dozen times. He hung up, puzzled.

A second later, his phone rang. The number was unlisted. He picked up. It was a poor connection – the line crackled and hissed. Whoever was on the line said nothing. "Anyone there?" he asked, trying to control the tremor in his voice. There was no response. He could hear someone breathing shallowly on the other end. He tried again. "We need help."

"You don't know what you need," a voice rasped, ignoring him. "Wrong number."

Ry flashed back to the mountainside. *Anna.* "She doesn't know I'm calling," he blurted out. "She's in danger."

Another long silence. A hacking cough ripped through the earpiece, startling him. He made out what sounded like a distant string of cuss words. Someone shouted what sounded like commands. A dog howled. Then the breathing returned.

"Dígame."

Jackie rolled her eyes. Derek had warned them. They were two hours in and council was still droning on about subdivision regulations. She looked down the row and had to smile. If the guys were trying to look casual, they were doing a lousy job of it. Ry, Sam, Paul, and Derek were all perched on the edge of their seats, tense and ready to go. They looked as if the meeting had just started. Fair enough, she thought. The day had finally arrived. She looked down at the meeting agenda for what felt like the millionth time. It said right there – Liz Conway was the night's first agenda item. Council had not made it out of their review of the previous meeting's minutes. Down in the front row, Liz's body language said it all. She was staring up at the ceiling. Her fingers rapped rhythmically on her presentation binder. *Let's get this show on the road.*

The men had all been jumpy as jackrabbits since the delegation got back. When Liz went into the hospital, she mentioned to Sam that she had managed to take photos of everything. "Even the Aponix facility?" he had blurted out before he could stop himself. "Yeah, I got a bunch in there. They were very nice. Quite a palace," was her response. While Liz had no idea, the news had electrified the men. Ry seemed to have written off the delegation's trip entirely. It didn't look like he was eating or sleeping much either, and the scraggly beard didn't help. But now he was wide-eyed and bushy tailed. Derek had rolled his agenda into a baton and was steadily drumming away on the seat in front of him. Paul and Sam were debating the finer points of new trails versus their all-time favorites. The ladies, she thought, not so much. At the far end of the row, Anna was staring off into space. It was fast becoming the new usual. They had not heard more than a few words from her in weeks. Jackie knew her firm was gearing up for a huge immigration case, it was all hands on deck across town. But things didn't add up. The investigation into her brother's death had hit yet another wall. That by itself should have been enough to light a fire. And Anna was usually way out in front of anything that hinted at conspiracy, running down leads and browbeating people into action. Now, she was just a warm body. Head nods, quiet murmurs, vacant looks had replaced the sharp questions, stinging sarcasm, and sly puns. *Chalk one up to…something else going on.*

At the other end of the spectrum, she knew Katherine was worried sick. Her husband was living full time in conspiracy land and she had her kids to think about. They both had a lot of time on their hands for the time being, until the valley sorted itself out, and it wasn't doing Katherine any good. She was pretty sure that if her friend had a place to go, she would have left town for a while. But her dad was here. Her mom was an unholy wreck living in Florida after her meltdown in the Antarctic. And at the end of the day, *we're each other's family now,* she thought. *Like it or not, we're stuck with each other. No one else can relate.*

The thought jolted her upright. *Where does that leave me,* she wondered. The possibility of ending up a spinster in a group of old friends had not crossed her radar. *I don't care how great they are,* she thought, *that isn't going to cut it.* She had been plowing through men at an impressive pace, even by her standards. Andy was a distant memory, and the muscleheads from the gym were not cutting it. Sam and Paul were sweet, but she was not looking for a boy toy. Whether Wellsey's alter ego showed up tomorrow or she lived to a ripe old age, something needed to change.

When Liz Conway finally stood and made her way over to the podium, she had another realization. *Maybe I've been looking in the wrong places.* Maybe I need a strong...*woman* in my life, she thought. One thing was certain. The woman cut quite a figure. Everything about her – her blonde hair, swept back in a bob, her simple black-and-silver A-line dress, the absence of makeup – suggested elegance and a minimum of fuss. Jackie saw she had small hands, just like her. Her gestures were small as well, measured, and precise. Her lips carried a slight hint of a smile. Piercing blue eyes sought out her audience. Her voice was soft but firm, commanding respect. For the first time all night, the councilors and the Mayor were quiet. Jackie was leaning so far forward she almost fell out of her chair. She looked around, embarrassed. Luckily, no one caught her daydreaming. All eyes were on the tall, willowy woman in the front of the room. *Sam never said the hospital hired a bombshell.*

Jackie took a deep breath and tried to tune in. "We worked hard...and we played hard," Liz was saying. "Sometimes, it was both at the same time." Her audience laughed as a shot of smiling people on a boat, beers in hand, flashed on the screen. Images of dense jungle and a sky filled with birds followed. "The Amazon Basin is obviously a huge tourism draw," she continued. "But the rainforest is also a global hub for sustainable forestry and agriculture, and for science of all kinds. Of particular interest to me, it is a research center for traditional medicines and pharmaceutical breakthroughs." Liz rattled off a string of brand-name drugs. "All of them," she followed up, "are the result of work in Amazonia." She barely had time to catch her breath before another, very different expanse of green popped up. She laughed. "I had to include this because I'm a huge soccer fan," she said. "This is me with some players from Nacional, one the city's soccer teams, and the two mayors. Arena Amazônia, you may remember, was recently the site of one of the greatest upsets in World Cup history."

Jackie watched the councilors and mayor smiling and following happily. Most of them think the World Cup is a sailing competition, she thought, or a medieval chalice.

"Anyway…enough of the fun and games," Liz continued, pressing on. A much-less compelling image appeared on screen. "Most of the trip was spent doing this, meeting in small working groups with local business leaders, touring facilities, brainstorming how Denver, Manaus, and us can bring our economies closer together." Jackie felt the hair on the back of her neck stand up. *Almost there. Any minute now.*

"Manaus does have quite a thriving, varied economy," Liz was saying. "Chemical and soap manufacturing, forestry, petroleum refining, tourism. Other major exports include beer, motorcycles, brazil nuts, computers…the list goes on. Most of our time was spent out near the airport, where many of these industries are based. Land is cheap, infrastructure is good. But we did also visit one huge multi-national based in the heart of the city." In an instant, they were looking at the gleaming interior of a massive, well-lit warehouse. A huge steel honeycomb rose to the ceiling and stretched away in both directions. Jackie could make out bundles of rebar, pallets of concrete, massive sections of pipeline in the storage cells. A forklift in the foreground was carrying a pallet laden with portable generators. Another was stacking huge coils of silver cable off to one side.

"Aponix is an energy company, as you can see," Liz said. "They're a household name in Brazil, and getting that way here. They got their start maintaining utilities and the grid, and now are promising to revolutionize how we get our power. For example, they claim their facility is powered entirely by sunlight. They say they have figured out how to store solar energy. But they're not sharing any of the details...not yet, anyway."

More pictures followed. There were more stacks of equipment, more vast expanses of gleaming concrete floors. Something nagged at Jackie. *It's too perfect.* It looked like a big stage set. We provided the actors, she thought. They provided the stage. *How thoughtful.* She realized something else. Everything in the photographs could be easily moved in or out in a matter of days. Not so much with the final image that flashed on the screen. *Wait a second.* It took Jackie's breath away. An industrial tanker ship the size of a football field filled the screen. Liz's take was that "Aponix isn't thinking small. Everything they do is big. I'm hopeful that their energy work may have medical implications down the line..." Jackie tuned out. She stared at the huge docking bay. Yellow cranes towered over the boat's hull, delivering cargo. She had a different perspective on what they were looking at. It was too big to hide, she thought. And what better place to stash stuff away from prying eyes. *Well played.*

The slide presentation went dark. Jackie tuned back in for Liz's concluding remarks. "I think Manaus has a lot to teach us in terms of resiliency," she was saying. "Rubber was at the heart of the region's economy for more than a century. The industry decimated the environment – it literally put itself out of business. Local leaders swore it would never happen again. Today, every business chartered in Manaus must develop and follow approved sustainability guidelines. Waste products from one industry are the raw materials for another. Industrial ecology, they call it. Everyone looks to natural systems to figure out how to design sustainable business models and factories. It was a privilege to visit such a forward-thinking place."

After applause and perfunctory questions, council adjourned for the night. Jackie shook her head in disgust at their incompetence. Add Liz's thoughts to the pile, she thought. That little cabal has several thousand recommendations under consideration. They were sitting on top of a mountain of good ideas, and acting on none of them. At least Derek's plans for the BMX park were finally moving forward. Still, she would not believe it was really happening until she saw the fences come down and people working on site.

She and the others made their way down to the front, pushing their way through the crowd of people headed for the exits. Ry got there first. Jackie could hear him lobbing questions at the poor woman. "Can we…I mean, could *I* get a copy of everything? I mean everything, like all of your photos. Even ones you don't like, plus any materials Aponix handed out…" he was saying as the rest of them caught up. Liz's head was bobbing up and down, and her eyes were wide – like a deer caught in the headlights. A tall, beautiful deer, Jackie thought, correcting herself. A beautiful animal currently in need of rescue. She reintroduced herself and offered to walk Liz to her car. She looked around the group, hoping they understood. We're much more likely to get somewhere with her one on one, she wanted to say. *A personal touch will go a long way.*

"That would be great," Liz gasped, seizing on the escape route. She grabbed her binder and coat. "It's good seeing you all again. Sam, see you tomorrow?"

The women made small talk on their way out. Liz admitted how nervous she'd been, and how waiting to speak had gone on forever. Jackie reassured her that there had not been a hint of nerves in her presentation. "You looked great up there. Really great," she said, and promptly blushed a deep red as the words tumbled out. If Liz noticed, she gave no sign. As they stood quietly, waiting for the elevator, Jackie suddenly thought of a possible way in. "It sounds like it was a really great trip, seriously well planned," she said, doing her best to bait the line. "Everything went like clockwork."

"Yeah," Liz laughed. "We didn't have much free time. I got the sense they didn't want to leave us to our own devices…"

"Did anything crazy come up?" Jackie asked hurriedly, setting the hook. "Anything completely unexpected?"

Liz's brow wrinkled. The elevator doors opened and they stepped inside. "Hmm, well, I don't know about crazy," she said finally. She reached for the buttons. "But there was something strange, and really sad in Manaus." After a short, jolting journey, the elevator shuddered to a halt, then made a half-hearted dinging noise. Its doors grudgingly opened. The city's ancient underground parking garage lay before them. Usually, the dim lighting and scurrying rodents freaked Jackie out. Not tonight. Every nerve in her body was on fire. Her mind was racing. I want to hear more about Manaus…but we have just these few moments. *Do I just go for it, out of the blue?* The moment hung in the balance. *I haven't had a crush on someone like this in an eon or two.*

Liz's hand brushed against Jackie's arm. They made their way over to a violet sports car, one of the few vehicles still in the lot. It matches her eyes, Jackie thought, struggling to think straight. The touch had been electrifying.

"Have you heard of the vanishings?" Liz asked.

Jackie shook her head.

"Neither had I. There's an epidemic down there."

"What epidemic?" Jackie asked, confused.

"Manaus is home to one of the greatest unsolved crimes in the world," Liz replied. Her voice was a whisper. "Every year, people disappear. Mostly young men. Always from the city's slums. Never a trace left behind. No one – not parents, the city, the military – has been able to stop it. It's been going on for years."

"How did you find out about it?" Jackie asked casually. *Could there be a connection?*

"We were there around the time of the annual memorial service," Liz replied. "It was in the news. Apparently, Aponix donates millions of dollars to charities helping the favelas. It's one of the largest corporate charity efforts in the world. They were drawn in by the crimes, and have been trying to be a good corporate citizen, I guess..." Liz stopped talking and looked at Jackie, concerned. "Are you all right?" she asked. "You've gone pale. It's a horrible story. I'm sorry if I've upset you."

"No, I'm sorry...I'm fine," Jackie mumbled. "Really, I just felt a little faint there for a moment."

"I feel awful," Liz said softly. "Tell you what, let me drive you home...please, get in." She opened the front passenger door and helped her get in. Her vision slowly settled. The queasiness in her stomach went away. She heard the sound of a door opening, but it sounded very far away. When she looked over, she was met by a warm smile. And there was something else...was that a twinkle in Liz's eye? Was that the slightest hint of a smile on her lips? Is it possible, Jackie wondered. *Could it be?* A moment later, the world went black.

Déjà Vu, All Over Again

The roads were still quiet. Anna hit the gas. She headed west, blowing through Fruita. She made it to the state road before dawn dared tug at the sky behind her. She pointed the car north and drove. As the miles passed, more and more headlights poured south. A semi hauling a huge silver oil tank thundered past. Anna watched it recede in her rearview mirror. It had to have come from where she was going. *There's no other industry out here.* She checked her rearview mirror. To her dismay, she saw it pass another gleaming cylinder in the distance before disappearing behind a ridge. What is it about this place, she wondered. I cannot believe I am on this road. *Again.* Labor strife, oil wars, crime syndicates. The world refuses to let the valley alone. Maybe there is something to the Utes curse, she thought. The tribe had been forced out of the valley more than a century earlier. Count on the tourism board to cheerfully turn it around into tacky boosterism and sloganeering. You Can Never Leave! If You Try, You'll Be Back! It runs deeper and darker, she thought. A stain on the land. *Maybe the valley is forsaken.* We are all condemned to cycle through tragedy after tragedy, reliving our ancestors' pain and loss. She grimaced. I'm not throwing in the towel, she thought. Look at it a different way. We have to prove we're worthy of living in this place every day. We have to fight to protect what others would take away.

Bill and Josie's report lay open on the seat next to her. "You're not going to like it," they told her when they handed it over. An off-hand remark from Katherine's dad had lit the fuse. On his way to a mustang roundup, he passed a freshly poured concrete pad and a cluster of trucks and tanks out in the middle of nowhere. Anna shook her head. It was a long way from there to here. Initial research uncovered the tip of the iceberg – long-dormant mineral leases were springing back to life. But not for oil, as she had always feared. They were starting on federal lands, which made sense. Keep a low profile, get established, build a track record before raising a ruckus. Running a fracking rig on private property was going to get a lot of attention. Particularly if the property owner did not want it there. Talking it through with Katherine and Jackie led them straight to Deep Jungle. No direct ties yet, but it was all there in their legal motions against the co-op. Lucille was still sorting through the tangle of company names they had uncovered. It's just a matter of time. All this for some leverage, she thought. They're keeping the pressure on them even after arbitration, to send a message. She saw the newspaper headline in her mind's eye. Don't Fuck With Us, Says Corporate Behemoth. I'd like to see them handle the publicity when the truth comes out, she thought. *Expose them, and this all goes away.* She saw the truck behind her gaining steadily; it had a serious head of steam. She pulled over to let it roll by. She gritted her teeth as the car shook, inches from the gleaming steel. She checked the rearview again before pulling out and did a double take. Another silver semi was hauling ass in the distance. *So much for the low profile.*

At least they were up and running. The associates were neglecting their other cases, sifting through the leases. Pieces of the puzzle were coming together. It hadn't taken long to come up to speed with the state and federal rules and regulations – the companies could do pretty much whatever they wanted. Other pieces did not fit...yet. The numbers were what kept her up at night, and haunted her thoughts each day. They did not add up, no matter how many times she went over the report's tables and graphs. There is no energy crisis, she thought, no spike in prices. And they're here for natural gas, not oil. Fracturing the shale to get at the natural gas took millions of gallons of water and chemicals. The water table simply could not sustain it. That's a lot of trucks, she thought. More evidence that Deep Jungle was simply pulling on levers. *How much is this deal worth to them?* One thing is certain, she thought. I know what this mess is costing me. Justice for my family. She gripped the wheel tightly with both hands. She had no time to even think about where to go next. *Damn you, Luis.* A clock is out there somewhere, ticking, ticking, ticking. Sooner or later, the man who came for you will come for us. The reminder was never far from her thoughts. *But in the meantime, we all have to keep living our lives.* I can't think of any way to stop them. I can't come up with a way to link that grainy footage to Aponix's doorstep. I need witnesses. I need evidence. And they're nowhere to be found. Some kind of leverage to stop those bastards moving on us is the best idea we've come up, she thought. *If the debrief from Liz's trip turns up nothing, we won't even have that.*

And everything takes a back seat to this mess, she marveled. Forty miles to go. I don't know if I ever want to get there. She glanced over again at the report. She flipped through its pages, as if new answers might jump out. The video camera taped to the dashboard might have better luck, she thought. She needed to see it with her own eyes. But they also needed something other than maps and the report when they met with the feds the next day. *We can only hope that a picture is still worth a thousand words.*

A huge plume of dust off to the left caught her eye. No need for GPS, she thought. Just follow the traffic. She turned off the highway and headed west. The Bookcliffs were close now, looming a few miles away off to the north. To the unfamiliar eye, it looked like a whole lot of nothing – grazing land, crazy desert rock formations, and endless blue sky. But we're looking at the watershed of the Colorado River, she thought. Summer storms turn these trickling streams and dry riverbeds into raging waterways. The car bounced and skittered over miles of crushed stone. Eventually, she caught up to the truck that had passed her earlier. Clouds of stone dust replaced the views. The pace slowed to a crawl. It's as good a place as any to start filming, she thought. She turned on the video camera. "My name is Anna Garcia," she said. "I am an attorney in Grand Junction, Colorado. I am making an unannounced visit to Kriegler Enterprises' hydraulic fracturing facility, in the northwest corner of Grand Valley. I'm driving west on Mitchell Road. Or, what used to be Mitchell Road. Tons of rock has been laid down on top of what used to be a dirt road. The road is wider now, able to support two-way truck traffic. The rock is everywhere. Spilling into gullies. Crushed up against gates and fence posts. I am in a convoy of tanker trucks headed to the facility. Visibility is poor."

Miles crawled past. Eventually, more than an hour later, the convoy stopped. As the dust settled, Anna began to make out shapes ahead – barbed wire fencing, trailers, enormous storage tanks. They pulled slowly forward, then stopped again. A few more minutes, a few more feet. Above the back of the truck, she could see the top of a well rig, the telltale methane flame burning orange against the sky. The truck in front slowly pulled away. She realized she was only a few yards from the entrance. A guard station lay ahead, off to the left. The barrier arm was just settling back into place. As she drove forward, a guard stepped out and stared at her license plate. He motioned for her to stop and walked over, checking something on a clipboard.

She put her window down and almost gagged. A thick, heavy soup of chemical smells poured into her car. "What died out here?" she asked, coughing.

"Ma'am?" The man's face was blank, his eyes hidden behind

metallic sunglasses. He was dressed in military fatigues. A black cap with the company's lion logo was pulled low over his face. Serious business, she thought. "Nothing," she replied. "I'm a concerned citizen. I'd like to see what's going on out here."

"I need to see some identification."

Anna dug out her driver's license and handed it over. The guard studied his clipboard even more intently. "Your plate isn't on our list," he said finally. "Are we expecting you?"

She tried to smile despite the smell. *Keep it casual.* "That shouldn't matter," she replied. "These are public lands."

The guard ignored her. He looked past her, checking out the inside of the car. He cocked his head and froze when he caught sight of the dashboard camera. "Ma'am, this is a private facility." His tone rose and his jaw set firmly. "For media requests or interviews, I suggest you contact the main office."

Good to see a reaction, she thought. You're not a robot after all. "The main office?" she asked, trying to draw out the conversation. The dust inside the facility was settling. "Isn't there someone here I can speak with?"

"No ma'am. Just showing up like this, we can't help you." The guard glanced behind her car. The next rig was pulling up. Time was short. She stared straight ahead as the guard made several increasingly urgent requests. The size of the operation was clearer now. There were several well rigs, several dancing methane flames. At least a couple dozen trailers. Something huge and dark covered the ground in the distance. *A tarp?* She scanned the ground inside the fence. Something she had expected to find was missing. No network of pipes. No distribution network. They had to be trucking everything on and off the site. That makes no sense, she thought. There is no way that's feasible.

"What is *that?*" The words flew out of her mouth. She was looking back over at the huge dark shape. It was moving. *Oh my God.* It was a wastewater pond. An ocean, more like. It was the size of a dozen football fields. At least.

The guard leaned in. His hand clamped down on her arm. "Ma'am! You need to turn your vehicle around. *Now!*"

Startled, Anna turned to look at him. The man's mask was gone. She was staring into a red, snarling maw. She shook his arm off and slammed the car in reverse, narrowly missing the truck behind her as she spun around. She was shaking with anger. *What is going on here?* It was a thousand times worse than she had feared. Nothing more than an earth berm was holding back that ocean of toxins. *Multiply this facility by all of the lease renewals and the far end of the valley is turning into a mini-Alaska.* She shifted gears and gunned the engine. The miles flew past. Tomorrow's meeting just turned into pre-trial discovery, she thought. And I'll have an injunction filed hours after that.

They were ushered into a small, square room. Anna squinted. Everything – the walls, a desk, end tables – was made of dark, burnished wood. A small window behind the desk let in a few weak rays of light. The air was dense, hot, and close. It felt like they had stepped into a coffin. "The director will join you shortly," the secretary said, standing in the doorway behind them. "Please, have a seat."

If we could find them, we would, Anna thought. The secretary pulled the door closed and she fought an urge to claw it back open. "Quite a place," she said drily to Josie and Bill. "I'd hate to see what the assistant director's office looks like." They stumbled around in the murky light, finally discovering several dark leather armchairs near the large slab of oak in the middle of the room. Anna could make out a couple of framed family photos and several pens scattered across the massive expanse. Please tell me he carries a laptop with him, she thought. Please tell me this meeting is not going to be something out of Mad Men.

A wall panel on the right side of the room opened silently, revealing a rectangle of pure blackness. A few moments later, a figure strode in. "Good morning, Ms. Garcia," a voice boomed. "Sorry to leave you in the dark like this." There was the sound of a lamp chain being pulled. The room was suddenly bathed in a tired, pale yellow light. The man standing by the lamp straightened up, half brightly lit, half hidden in shadow. He walked over and shook each of their hands. "Director Allen Williams. Good to meet you." Each word was warm, perfectly enunciated and much too loud. They were watching a politician in action. He doesn't have a non-campaign gear, she thought. Everything is a photo opportunity.

She introduced Josie and Bill, then watched Williams closely as he made his way back behind his desk. He was tall, reed thin, and impeccably dressed in a tailored three-piece suit. Thick brown hair and a perfectly trimmed moustache finished off the ensemble. "How can the BLM help you?" he asked, slipping a mild, tepid smile in place. He sat down and stared at Anna.

"We're here to discuss an urgent environmental issue," she replied. "Hydraulic fracturing in the valley. There are only a few active operations now, but that is going to change rapidly." She slid a copy of their research findings on the director's desk. "There are dozens more in the pipeline."

"What does this have to do with the BLM?" Williams asked, ignoring the report. He kicked a pair of hand-tooled cowboy boots up on his desk and rocked backward in his chair, resting both arms behind his head.

Don't play dumb, Anna thought. It was not a promising start. "Many of the leases are on BLM lands," she replied. "Public lands. I tried to visit one of the facilities yesterday and was improperly denied access."

Williams' eyes narrowed. "That would depend on the terms of the lease," he said coldly. "Could be you were trespassing." Next to her, Bill and Josie shifted uncomfortably in their chairs. The tension in the room was steadily building. "There have been no public hearings, no environmental impact statements," Anna continued.

"Our research could not find any sign of BLM oversight or management."

An uncomfortable silence settled in the room. Williams was staring at a point somewhere above her head. "I appreciate your interest in our operating procedures," he said finally. "These facilities are providing jobs and paying taxes. Which as you probably know, are two of the governor's top priorities. You may not have noticed, but we are in the midst of an unprecedented energy boom. Natural gas is lowering electricity costs and home heating bills. *For everyone,*" he emphasized, jabbing a finger in the air. "Colorado had been on the outside looking in until Governor Johnson's administration. Bureaucratic red tape held us back. Now, we're a player in this incredibly important market."

What does he think this is, Anna wondered. A public service announcement? "I'm glad you brought up economics," she replied calmly. "We took a detailed look at the financial bottom line. Our understanding is that these operations require water. A lot of it."

"Sure, makes sense to me," Williams huffed impatiently. "What of it?"

"Well, they're trucking it in," Anna replied. "The water table out there cannot sustain even basic operations. Trucking in water is expensive. And if you look at the company's own estimates in the lease agreement, the amount of natural gas they're getting doesn't even begin to cover their bills. The economics make no sense."

Williams took his boots off the desk and leaned forward. "No offense, Ms. Garcia, but if there's one thing I know, it's that the market doesn't lie," he said in a low voice. "Kriegler Enterprises is out there because they're making money."

Anna cringed. It killed her that they didn't have anything yet to throw back in his face. "Has the BLM considered potential environmental costs?" she asked instead. "Kriegler has been cited for poor facility management and water quality violations in eight states. There is an ocean of toxic wastewater out there already. Held back by nothing more than an earth berm. A breach and a good afternoon storm and those chemicals would wash into the Colorado River before the sun went down."

Williams did not respond. Instead, she watched his eyes glaze over and his body language stiffen. His smile was long gone. To hell with this, she thought. The gloves have to come off sometime. "We believe these operations have nothing to do with energy production. In the meantime, how long until people taste diesel fuel in their well water?" she asked sharply. "How long before livestock start dying? How long before our food supplies are contaminated?"

Silence descended once again. Anna glared at the director, daring him to respond. "Sir, have you visited any of these operations?" Josie asked. "Perhaps you could –"

"Ms. Garcia, I would hate to see us on opposite sides regarding this…beneficial matter," Williams said curtly, cutting the paralegal short. "If you have evidence, I suggest you produce it. Though I caution you, there are a lot of conspiracy theories out there. While I appreciate your concerns, the permitting process for these facilities has been by the book. It may interest you to know that this has not always been the case. For example, permitting for the Bookcliffs Challenge was, shall we say, highly irregular. But, I have continued to honor my predecessors' wishes. And it is my understanding that your husband's race continues to be a great success." He paused to let the words sink in. He tapped his fingers together, savoring the anger blossoming across the table. "If you think about it, we share a surprising amount in common," he continued. "I hope –"

"Thank you for your time," Anna croaked, cutting him off. Deep Jungle had tentacles everywhere. She wanted to reach across the desk and throttle the smug smile off the man's face. Instead, she stood and turned to leave. Her body was shaking. "Josie…Bill, let's go. Director Williams, we'll be in touch." Please let there have been a breakthrough in Chicago, she thought. Because this is going to get ugly.

Fortinbras poured himself a whiskey. He walked into his bedroom, turned on the television and sat back. The commercials ended and the screen went black. "Everyone remembers the Trans-Alaskan Pipeline tragedy…" the devastatingly handsome host intoned. Iconic images from the disaster flashed on the screen. "Oil companies say it will never happen again. A recent review by the federal government gave the nation's energy grid a passing grade. But, a CNN special investigation has uncovered a different story, one that suggests America is facing an energy crisis. Tonight, we take a closer look..."

Fortinbras closed his eyes and silently mouthed the narrative. They had seen copies of the script along the way, and provided occasional comments through a cheaply bought producer. Getting them started had been easy enough as well. People had lots to hide, if you knew where to look. "We start this evening's broadcast in Hadensville, Pennsylvania," the host said solemnly. "Carol Forster is a homemaker who lives with her husband and two young sons in this former coal town." A short, plump woman with scraggly blond hair appeared on screen, standing in front of a small brick ranch with a mildew-stained roof. "It's turned neighbor against neighbor. If we don't sell out, we know someone else will," she said, struggling to hold back tears. "People are making money while our children are getting sick. Both of our dogs had to be put down. We can't get a straight answer from anyone. The state says more testing is needed. It's too late for that now. We can't sell our house, and it's not safe to stay here."

The broadcast returned to the studio. "Environmental groups claim fracking spills and ground water contamination happen every day," the host said, looking straight at the camera. "Energy companies argue that small, wildcat operations are to blame. Hydraulic fracturing done right, they argue, is safe and vital to our nation's security. Energy expert Steven Bracken notes that, with the U.S. awash in inexpensive natural gas, oil imports are at their lowest levels in decades. According to him, fracking could one day help the U.S. end its reliance on foreign oil."

Fortinbras laughed. Edward R. Murrow must be turning over in his grave, he thought. Journalism has been reduced to this. Talking heads parroting talking points. He had expected more headaches getting a propaganda piece lined up. In the end, they had the choice of any of the networks to run with. He headed for the bathroom during the commercials. The next section was his favorite part. *To really scare people, they have to see the big picture.* He came back to find the tape already rolling. The ken-doll host had been replaced with a brunette cyborg. Every wrinkle had been botoxed away. Long lashes fluttered over huge doe eyes atop a highly sculpted nose. That lady is way too well-packaged for this, he thought. The distance between her digital perfection and the story on screen was jarring. An occasional muscle twitch in her cheek suggested she knew her talents were needed elsewhere. Who needs substance anymore, he reflected. Image is all that matters.

"Hydraulic fracturing represents some of our nation's newest energy infrastructure. What about the utilities, coal plants, and dams we all take for granted?" the woman said, peering out from behind a shimmering desk in the network's neon-backlit studio. "We hear a lot about America's aging transportation infrastructure – our bridges and highways failing after years of neglect. How is our nation's power grid operating? What about the utility lines outside your home? How safe is your community's power plant? What we have learned may surprise you."

Fortinbras gritted his teeth. Maybe they should have dialed that part back, at least a little. The story was powerful enough, without having to run over puppies or send every mother in America into a panic. He pictured anxious parents standing at bedroom windows, staring out into the darkness at perfectly functional power lines and transformers. Maybe that isn't such a bad thing, he thought. It was the most powerful motivator in the world. He had smelled it in the halls of Congress. It haunted every election. It came wrapped in many guises – uncertainty, anxiety, anger, ignorance, exhaustion, confusion. Fear made anything – and everything – possible.

"Here, in this rural part of Kentucky, coal is king," the lady intoned. Fortinbras was surprised to see the fembot on the ground. She was standing on the side of a road next to a high chain-link fence. A massive smokestack towered in the background. Impressive that her life support systems can function outside of the studio, he thought, snickering. That much fresh air could be fatal. "But for how much longer?" she continued. "The Tennessee Valley Authority recently announced plans to shutter three nearby plants, including this one. Each is more than fifty years old. Safety records document mounting workplace injuries and three fatalities in recent years. Annual maintenance and repair costs at TVA facilities in the southeast alone run into the billions. Nationwide, there are hundreds of plants in similar shape."

The woman paused. The camera panned as she walked across

the road, revealing a row of houses with peeling paint and sagging porches. Battered pickups sat in the driveways. "Surprised?" she asked. "These families live just feet from the plant entrance. These moms and dads have worked there for years. All of that is about to come to an end." The camera lurched into motion, following her across a crabgrass lawn, up cinderblock steps and past a rusted-out screen door into a dark cave. The woman reached up her arm, and the room flooded with light – stained shades, torn carpet, an empty parrot cage flashed into view. "Flip a switch, and we have power, right?" she said, turning to face the camera. She stepped out of the house, back onto the porch. "We all take energy for granted. This is what we see, and count on. What we don't see will take your breath away." A series of charts flew on screen. "Generating power can leave behind more than sixty percent of the energy available in the raw materials – water, coal, uranium," she narrated in the background. "Energy losses from transmission and distribution of that power are usually assumed to be another six to eight percent. Our research indicates this number may be as high as twenty-five percent, as our electrical grid ages. Less than fifteen percent of our energy resources actually reach where we work and live." The screen faded to black for a long moment, before the inevitable onslaught of shiny cars, insurance gimmicks and cereal boxes.

Fortinbras nodded, pleased. They handled that moment well. No need to rub the audience's faces in it. A whiff of poverty was all that was needed. He was also increasingly preoccupied; there was something incredibly sexy about the fembot's voice. Slightly husky, with a hint of longing, as if she might start moaning softly if a man with the right touch came along. He muted the commercials and reached for his phone. Two girls tonight, to celebrate. He asked if any brunettes were available. Tall, preferably with big brown eyes. In an hour would be fine. *First things first.* They were just getting to the good part. When the broadcast returned, he felt a flash of jealousy. The ken doll and the hot cyborg were now sharing the shimmering studio desk. Ken spoke first. "We interviewed U.S. Energy Secretary Daniel Tyrell for tonight's report," he said solemnly. "He did not mince words regarding our energy future."

A small, weasel-faced man in a navy blazer and open-necked dress shirt appeared on screen, hemmed in by shelves of fake books and a limp fern in the background. "Overhauling the nation's grid is a massive project, there is no doubt," he said. He squirmed in his seat, looking distinctly ill at ease.

"Trillions of dollars? Millions of miles of cable and pipeline...thousands of power facilities..." the male host's voice prodded off screen.

The secretary frowned. "I can't comment on total costs, we are looking into that...But I can say, it will require one of the great collective efforts in our nation's history. We have risen to such challenges before, and I am confident we can do so again."

A great collective effort...*really?* Fortinbras marveled. The country can't come together around gun violence, failing schools, social inequity, pollution, deficit reduction, entitlement reform. *Anything.* Name an issue, and I'll show you the broken dreams, he thought. Calling for collective action was downright naïve. The awkward little man faded out, and the broadcast returned to the studio. "Everyone we interviewed stated there is no silver bullet, no way to avoid the hard choices we face," the fembot followed up. "But is that really the case?" He was pleased to see she would be bringing the story home. He started mentally unbuttoning her blue silk blouse while she spoke. "Energy company Aponix has been hinting for several years that a game-changing technology is in the pipeline," she said, slightly breathless and blissfully unaware of the word play. "While the company declined our repeated requests for an interview, it did release this statement."

The company's letterhead floated across the screen. The camera zoomed in on the second paragraph. "Aponix believes that new technologies and innovation are at the heart of any solution to meet and address our energy needs," the woman narrated. "We also believe that localized energy resources, tailored to local needs, are essential." She has a gift, he thought. It sounded nothing like that when I said it. Perhaps she might consider a career change. He turned off the television before the credits rolled. He waited for his phone or the door buzzer to make a sound. Either was fine. Although it would be nice to take the call after the girls had finished their work. His erection surged as he imagined lying there, tangled in all that female flesh, and giving the green light. They were so close…but it was time for a final demonstration first. He had insisted on it, in fact. He had denied himself so much. If revenge was a dish best served cold, his had been in the deep freezer for far too long. Lining up Grand Valley was like shooting ducks in a barrel. The spills would wipe out every inch of fertile land in the valley. Ground water would be poisoned for a thousand years. To hell with the Indians, he thought. *Now that's a curse.* And they could come in and quietly take care of business in the noisy, nationally televised aftermath.

He had enjoyed taking out the lawyer. That stinking rat had to pay. It had been his only indulgence. Maybe I would have stopped there, he thought, toying with the possibility for a moment. He sneered. *Probably not.* Once the others dared sniff around the business, dared bring about that laughable civic visit, there was no alternative. Now they were running around like Chicken Little, thinking a glorified warehouse had the cojones to make the sky fall in. Like they were that important. Fortinbras shook his head in disbelief. Burying those companies in an untraceable web of paperwork had not even been necessary. That paranoid crew projected a paper enemy out into the desert for us. We could have just stepped back and enjoyed the show. They will know the truth before I put a bullet in their heads, he promised himself, grimly satisfied. They should all have died that day in the desert. Now their children and their precious valley can pay the price as well.

The tall, hulking Russian stepped off the pitch, raising his hands to clap in appreciation and say good night. Hoots, catcalls, and more than a few cries of "Dolph" trailed behind him. He smiled. Almost a regular these days, he thought. *Almost.* The moment passed. There were lots of others looking for a game tonight. A barefoot kid with a flashy mohawk took his place before he could tug off his shirt. With a deft first touch, the kid danced past a defender, then sent a shot high into the trees. Friendly jeers rained down. Harper sat on a ragged stump and reached for his bag. There were some nods of appreciation from nearby spectators. That would be it. Everyone there had other lives and he liked it that way. He was barely able to keep up with the patois of Portuguese, English, Amerindian, and Spanish anyway; the words flowed around him faster than the passes and shifting runs. He could guess at the other men's occupations – dockworkers, busboys, delivery drivers, carpenters, waiters – but it made no difference. Men walked into the clearing day and night, tired from their shifts. A touch on the ball brought them back to life.

He watched the action for a few minutes, then got ready to leave. It was a perfect night for pelada – a light breeze was keeping things cool. On a map, the field was nothing special, an old sand pit on the eastern edge of the city. On the ground, at night, it was a magical place, an oasis hidden away in a tangle of forest. Macaws fluttered overhead, adding their chatter and screeches to the conversation. Good-size lizards sometimes skittered onto the pitch, disrupting play. Harper swore he had seen a panther one evening, its ink-black pelt moving soundlessly through the dense vegetation.

Pelada had been a poorly kept secret at the warehouse. The word mystified him for months. At first, he thought the men were spending all of their paychecks at the city's strip clubs and whorehouses. Only later did he understand it was about the game, stripped down to its essence. He had never played barefoot before; now the soles of his feet were rough and calloused. Here, yesterday and tomorrow meant nothing. Only now mattered.

Well, almost, he thought. Everyone has to get back. He checked his watch. As long as the bus was on time, he would have a few minutes to spare. He walked gingerly away from the pitch, making sure there were no new twinges or aches. Finding none, he jogged through the woods and headed for the bus shelter. He flagged down a number fifty-three just after reaching it, and was pleased to find the bus almost empty. He collapsed into a seat, leaned back and breathed in deeply. Blocks jolted past in the stop-and-go traffic, a blur of nighttime neon, dirty sidewalks and crowded street corners. Before pelada, it had all felt completely alien to him, a place to leave whenever possible. The days were too hot and his Portuguese too poor to make it far. He ate, lived, and slept on base. He figured that was what Fortinbras intended. The Alaska trips had been a welcome change from the monotony, despite the distance. Now the North Slope was a distant memory. The D.C. trips had dried up as well. Not that he liked all the bluster and bullshit up there. But Georgetown was his speed. He could get used to a row house there, with good bars nearby, no shortage of fine-looking women with a taste for the finer things, a sports car in the drive…he was pretty sure Fortinbras knew all that too. *I don't get the sense I'm leaving Manaus any time soon.*

Pelada had at least made life tolerable. He was out there most nights. The base pretty much ran itself. Production for the first run had long since finished. He often stared at the stacks of crates, willing the orders to come through. *Not until the man in charge deigns to release them.* He had stopped trying to guess if that was days or weeks or months in the future. He sighed. Tonight, another thrilling late-night security shift awaited. Nursemaid to a thousand energy orbs, he thought. I didn't sign up for this.

He saw they were within a couple blocks now, and made his way down to the front of the bus. He stepped out into the throngs of people crowding the riverside docks. Do these people ever sleep, or go to work, or school, he wondered for the umpteenth time. He stepped out to cross the street, pushing his way through the crowd. He made it to the far side…and his eyes went wide. There were no guards on duty. He ran to the massive gates; one of them was slightly ajar. He looked back at the crowd. No one paid him any attention. He scanned the ground, glanced in the guardhouse. There were no signs of a struggle. *Shit.* He reached for his phone, then staggered forward as a bolt of excruciating pain tore through his lower back.

"No need, my friend," said a low voice. "Let's take a walk. Trust me, you don't want me to really use this thing." The sharp edge of the Taser dug into his skin.

"Understood," Harper whispered. In a heartbeat, his military training took over, tamping down the adrenalin rush. His breathing slowed. *Buy time, identify weaknesses, exploit them.* Whoever they are, they want something badly, he reflected. And they need me alive.

"We're going through the gate. Now!" the voice barked. Harper stared straight ahead and started walking. He went slowly, trying to take the measure of the man behind him. Making a move was tempting – he had at least a couple of inches on him. Plus, people were nearby. Always a good thing. Once inside the gate, all bets were off. *But what if no one else was left, damn it.* Images of crowds looting the base flashed through his mind. The man's other hand suddenly slid close to his neck. The sharp prick of a knife blade ended the debate. "Open the gate with your boot," he hissed. "Try any of your pretty *pelada* moves and I'll end you."

Harper ignored the jibe. Surveillance was not good news. He pushed the gate open, trying to remember anything out of place at recent matches. I let my guard down, he thought, cursing his shortsightedness. *I bought in.* He barely made it inside when several swift, expertly placed kidney punches knocked him to his knees, scattering his thoughts. Before he could respond in any way, the man had pinned his arms behind his back and whipped a plastic zip-tie around his wrists.

"Llevarlo a él," the man said to shapes in the shadows. He hauled Harper to his feet. "If he tries anything, shoot him." Several men emerged from the darkness, dressed in camo fatigues and ski masks. They frogmarched him the length of the entrance road, straight up to the main facility.

Every light in the building was blazing. More masked men stood at attention at each door. They're not shy, he thought. *Where the hell is our cavalry?* He risked a quick sideways glance at his captors. What he saw made his blood run cold. Their masks had a small red diamond sewed in just above the eyes. He struggled to maintain his composure. Everyone in the business knew the stories, the rumors. But that was years ago.

"Keep walking." One of them pushed him forward with the butt of a rifle. "Speed it up, gringo." In another time and place, the inaccuracy of the insult would have been hilarious. Now, it was all he could do to put one foot in front of another. He was hustled up a set of stairs, through a service door into the main warehouse hangar. He looked around quickly, looking for anything he could turn to his advantage. Nothing was out of place. The floors were gleaming. Storage areas were full. The rows of stacked crates remained intact. People were the only thing missing. They marched him across the warehouse, over to the crates. "Wait here," growled one of the men. "You know the deal." Another kicked his legs out, sending him sprawling across the floor. He rested his head on the cool concrete, watched as the six men walked away. They opened the service door and left without looking back. Then...nothing. He was alone with the whir of the ceiling fans. He thought back, trying to dredge up anything he could remember about the brigade. The men were phantoms, figments of fevered imaginations, unicorns cursed by every government in Latin America at one time or another. Nicaragua. El Salvador. Honduras. Guatemala. Chile. It had to be a cover, he thought, and a damn good one. If it still existed, or ever had, the brigade would never hit us. There was only one thread linking their work – disappearing those responsible for the continent's dirty wars, avenging the deaths of innocents. Back in the day, there had been no shortage of work.

Another possibility suddenly lit up Harper's mind. He gasped as memories flooded in. He was at the controls. They were on the belt. The loose ends. The accidents. Employees with second thoughts. Or, whoever the city's crime syndicate brought in. They needed the raw material – it wasn't like they could bring in stacks of animal carcasses from the Amazon without someone noticing. It had been the price of doing business in Manaus. For years. Fortinbras' bright idea, branching out to make things happen. But he's not here now, he thought. I am. *They think we're no different from Pinochet.* As recognition sunk in, his veins turned to ice. This was no imitation army. Either the band was back together...or they had never broken up. *How could they know? How much do they know?*

He did not have time to ponder the possibilities. He heard a scraping sound; the service door had opened. An elderly man hobbled into the warehouse. He leaned heavily on a cane for support as made his way across the floor. Harper sat up to get a better look. Correction, he thought, as the man came closer. He is not old. He's ancient. The man looked like an Andean mummy brought back from the grave. He was wearing a pair of leather slippers, hemp pants, and some kind of traditional, hand-woven shirt that fell to his knees. He stopped several feet away. Harper stared at his face, trying to find a way in. The man's hair was a wild, gray, matted mess, but his dark eyes were sharp and focused. They gave nothing away.

"You're making a big mistake," Harper offered. "As pessoas vão ser aqui a qualquer minuto."

"Stick with what you know, Mr. Harper," the man replied, waving his words away with his hand. While the old man's tone had a Latin American lilt to it, his English was perfect. "I would not be here if we could not take care of such things."

"Who are you?"

If the old man heard his question, he gave no sign. "Your boss, he understands force, yes?" he asked. Harper said nothing. He knew nothing about the brigade. Its history, size, membership – all were mysteries. He could not begin to guess at who he was talking to. No one could, he realized. *I'm talking to a ghost.*

The old man shrugged. "No matter. I will speak your boss's language. We are going to burn this place. Chances are, whatever is so important to you, some of it will survive. Most of your people are safe. We will let them go. If we have to come back, we will kill all of them. Then we will come to Washington. Understand?"

Harper nodded slowly, increasingly worried about where this was heading. The old man had spent most of his speech talking to the small black security camera overhead. *If I'm not the messenger...* The man dissolved into a hacking coughing fit, disrupting his thoughts. A nugget of blood-red phlegm splashed on the floor. He's not long for this world, he thought. Maybe I can bull rush him and help him on his journey. "Why are you doing this? What do you want?" he asked, doing his best to slow things down. He slowly shifted his weight as he spoke, trying to get in a decent position to burst forward. His knees betrayed him, slipping on the slick, smooth concrete. He struggled awkwardly to maintain his balance.

The old man looked down for a moment. "Mr. Harper, your questions...your actions," he said, gesturing at the floor, "they are beneath you. We pay our debts, we seek forgiveness, no?"

What does that mean, Harper wondered. "I'm sure we can work something out," he offered. "Aponix –"

"There's no time for the five stages of loss," the old man snapped, cutting him off. "We need acceptance." He hobbled over next to Harper while pulling at a rope around his neck. A small, dark leather pouch was attached. "Thank you for this moment of indulgence," he said. He placed the loop of rope over Harper's head. "I'm a traditionalist, and this is my last rodeo."

Harper's mind raced. Acceptance of...

"Death," the old man said quietly, reading his mind. "You are our message to your boss. This, he will understand." He moved like lightning as he spoke. He stepped back, reaching under his tunic for a hidden holster. The cane clattered to the ground. He fired three times. Harper did not make it off his knees. The old man holstered the weapon, reached for his cane, and hobbled away.

Best Laid Plans

They sat around Katherine and Ry's living room, eating pizza, washing it down with beer, watching the footage. A shaky cellphone video captured flames leaping high into the air. A section of the warehouse roof collapsed in a fountain of sparks and smoke. Aerial footage from the following morning showed a skeleton of tangled steel and piles of blackened debris. The tanker ship was clearly visible in its docking bay, scorched but otherwise intact. The footage looped while the local newscaster chattered away excitedly. Anna did her best to translate. "She's talking about Aponix, saying it's an energy company with contracts in many countries," she noted. "She talks about the bravery of the firefighters. It took several hours to get the blaze under control. It's too early for investigators to know the cause of the fire. There were several casualties. Most people escaped."

"As far as we can tell, news of the fire hasn't been picked up outside Brazil?" Derek asked.

"So far," Anna replied. "There's nothing on the AP wire, not even a headline. The only reason we know is because of an online news alert I set up a year ago."

"Well, let's start with the basics," Derek offered. "It's for real, right?" His words were met with nods and shrugs from the group. "Beyond that, the mind games begin," he continued. "When was the last time we could take anything to do with these people at face value?"

"Everyone screws up sometime," Katherine said. She was clenching a napkin tightly in her hands. "I take this at face value. Someone didn't do their job or a system broke down. This has to be good news. That fire is a beautiful thing. A beautiful accident."

Ry had his doubts. He shoved his hands in his pockets. *I make a phone call and days later, this happens.* He looked over at Anna, searching her face for any sign of recognition. She looked as confused as everyone else. Who does she know with this kind of power, he wondered. Couldn't we have ended all of this long ago? Haven't we been saying for years that we wished we had some firepower on our side? Mostly, he was furious. *It sure looks like one of us has been holding out.* He had tried the number again, right after Anna called with the news. It was disconnected. I have nowhere to go, he thought, except for asking her point blank. *Now is not the time or place.* Instead, he spent the evening dredging up every memory he could think of, all the way back to when he and the other guys had come back from a biking trip to meet Katherine and Jackie's new hire. From that first meeting at their offices, it was clear Anna was a straight shooter. She was brutally honest, held nothing back. She shouldered a heavy load for years, gutting out life as a working single mother while putting herself through school. She loved the valley more than life itself. He could not think of a single instance where she had lied or even put herself first. Her brother's murder investigation was still a hot mess – no special access or behind-the-scenes magic there. And yet...and yet...his thoughts kept circling back...and yet, when push came to shove out in the desert, she had slipped Derek that piece of paper. A scribbled bunch of numbers that led to a voice that led to...*this*. Something did not add up.

The night wore on. They ate, stared at the footage, checked for nonexistent news updates, and tossed out half-baked ideas. A rough consensus seemed to be emerging – Derek, Katherine, Paul, and Sam were in favor of chalking the flames up to some vague combination of chance, justice, and fate. Anna had barely spoken. Ry just sat there, worried about what he might say if he opened his mouth. "How about you, Anna?" he asked eventually, a little too loudly. "You have any thoughts to share?"

"I don't know...yet," she replied testily, glancing in his direction. "If I had something to say, you'd know about it."

Ry stared off into space, cracking his knuckles in frustration. His thoughts turned to the evening's no-show. Where the heck is she, he wondered. No one had seen or heard from Jackie since Liz's presentation at city hall. Nothing unusual there, Katherine had reminded them. "This is the woman who drove a thousand miles to see a butterfly migration, on a whim," she pointed out. "Who flew to the Toronto film festival the same day she read a movie review." But Ry was still uneasy. I can't help it, he thought. I am officially turning into our resident conspiracy nut. Phone calls lead to fiery explosions. Friends drop off the radar around the same time. *With our past, nothing is imp–*. A new possibility smashed into his thoughts, sent a cold bolt of fear up his spine. What if Wellsey traces this to us, or even suspects we're involved, he wondered. Aponix could be coming after us as we speak. *I made that call to ask for help, not to start a war.*

His mind was still churning later that night. People were heading home, and he walked around in a fog, murmuring goodbyes. A short time later, he found himself alone in the hallway with Anna. She had opened the closet and was reaching for her jacket. Maybe now *is* the time, he thought. This could be a matter of life and death. "Have you thought of anything?" he asked, trying to keep it casual. "Is there anything else you'd like to tell me...I mean, tell us, about the fire?"

Anna laughed. "What's with the third degree tonight, Ry?" she asked, stepping back. "Why am I the resident expert?" She turned to look at him as she spoke. She saw the truth in his eyes. In an instant, her face changed completely. Her jaw clenched and thunderclouds exploded across her brow. Her eyes narrowed and she stared daggers at him. "What did you do?" she asked, her voice rising. She was looking at him as if he had lost his mind. "WHAT DID YOU DO?"

Ry no longer recognized the woman in front of him. The cords in her neck stood out like ridges of sculpted stone. An angry red vein throbbed across her forehead. He tried to speak but no words came out. Anna had no such difficulties. She was yelling and the words were crackling and snapping around him like a brushfire. Concerned faces appeared down the hall. Eventually, a few simple words escaped. "I made a phone call," he whispered.

Anna's eyes went wide and her skin flushed purple. She lunged forward. Ry stumbled, almost fell, then slammed into the front door. "Open it," Anna snarled. He reached behind him and tugged at the doorknob, then reached to open the screen door. Anna pushed him outside and slammed the doors behind them. Ry crouched and raised his arms to defend himself, expecting blows to start raining down. None followed. He looked up to see that Anna was not even looking at him. She was pacing on the bricks, talking quietly, hugging herself with both arms. Tears were streaming down her cheeks. *Oh shit.* What did she go through, he wondered. What did she see? "Anna, I thought I was doing the right thing," he offered, trying to find a way to comfort her. "I can see I have no idea what I've done."

The words fell miles short. Anna stopped pacing and glared at him. "That's right. You have no idea," she growled. "You had no right. That piece of paper…that was in case *I died.* To tell him I was gone…Jesus, what did you think would happen?"

"I thought I could talk to someone…someone who could help us…who was that on the other end of the line?"

If Anna heard his question, she gave no sign. "He gave that number to me years ago…I thought he might even be dead," she murmured. "I hoped…"

Ry said nothing, respecting the silence. When Katherine appeared in the living room window, concern and worry written across her face, he waved her away.

"I hoped he was dead," Anna said quietly. "Pepi, we called him. Around here, he and my mother were folk heroes. They crossed the border looking for a better life, and found a nightmare. Thousands of immigrants picking the fruit trees, gathering in the crops, paid with pennies, beatings, and threats. If you spoke up, you vanished. We lived in fear for our lives. Pepi and some men, they fought back. The growers did unspeakable things in response. It became a war. In the end, they escaped back across the Rio Grande with their lives. They left everything behind…"

Ry took a step back, stunned by what she was saying. "I'm sorry, Anna," he said simply. "This man, Pepi…he's your father?"

Anna bit her lip. "He was my father," she replied. "That was a long time ago. Dammit, Ry, you don't need to hear any of this. My father went on to raise a private army. He killed and killed and kept on killing. He worked in the shadows. Justice, he called it. But the truth is, he found his calling. He liked it and could not stop. And no one could stop him. Not even his family."

"I think he answered the phone," Ry said quietly. "It sounded like an old man. He didn't say much. I said you were in danger. I talked for maybe a minute and then the line went dead."

Anna nodded but did not say anything. She had stopped pacing and wiped away her tears. Now, she was staring off into the distance. Minutes passed. "What now?" Ry asked finally, unable to take the silence any longer. His heart began to race again. "What have I started?" *And where does it end?* We're caught between a madman and a vigilante, he thought. I don't know which is worse.

Ry's words reached her as a quiet murmur, as if they had traveled a great distance. She vaguely noticed when he touched her shoulder. At some point, she realized he had gone inside. She was aware of her own breathing, shallow but steady. She heard a breeze rustling leaves and branches. Otherwise, she simply stared – at the railings, bushes, a tree, parked cars, the street. It took looking overhead to bring the first thought back into her mind. The future is as unknowable as that night sky, she thought. The present slips easily through our hands like so much water. All of these things in the world – so tangible, so concrete – are nothing but a backdrop…for what? A past that leans and lurches and preys on every moment…that rides shotgun on every trip, haunts every conversation, then rips apart your life like it was made of paper. *Once upon a time, I thought things could be different.* Paul was tiny. She and Tariq were getting by, living in that lousy maintenance apartment. Money was tight. Time was tighter. But for a short while, before the fights, before he left, there was enough love to go round. Mami rode the bus north to help out, and mostly to hold that beaming baby on her lap. Pepi came only once. She could see the marked-up pantry boards in her mind's eye, and wanted to reach for them. She could see him there still as if it was yesterday, the red heels of his worn cowboy boots wavering as he squatted to scrawl a quote from his hero.

> "No one owns the truth. Everyone has the right to be heard and understood…el poderoso siempre creerá que tiene la razón y el que se opone a él es un traidor o, por lo menos, alguien dispensable."
>
> – Carlos Fuentes

She and Derek had started anew, but the old pathways stayed with her – the haikus and lists, the bad jokes, the pencil lines marking the passage of Paul's childhood. The black ink surged up one side of the alcove like a swollen river, then poured across the top of the entranceway. The Garcia family annals had made it partway down the other side before they left. Until Derek, the alcove was what kept them there. Even now, when she and Paul went back to visit Francine, she was still drawn to those tired front windows, seeking a glimpse of the words. Part of her knew they had long since been whitewashed. But like everything past, those words were still there, hidden away, waiting, reaching out to her. She was sure of it.

She asked him to choose a different path, barely understanding then what he had become. And in his way, he answered. His dense, narrow handwriting told the story. He could be nothing other than what he was. The world had made him, and that could not be undone. That same night, his mustache brushed her forehead while she slept. She realized what it meant when the front door opened; by the time she flew down the hall, he was gone. Mami stayed. They never heard from Pepi again. Now, there was a fire burning in Brazil.

Anna pressed her palms against her eyes, trying to focus. The initial shock was wearing off. If Ry's call had led to this, there would be proof in the ashes, somewhere. She knew that much. If it was mere coincidence, two possibilities are in play, she thought. One, Pepi is dead and there really was a gas leak in the warehouse. Or two, he's biding his time, waiting to make his move. It would be good to have a PI tail Wellsey for a couple of weeks. Striking at Wellsey in the U.S. seemed like a stretch, but in Brazil, all bets would be off. Hot tears cascaded down her cheeks again. Thinking it through like my father the assassin would, she thought. *But what about my father, the farm worker…my father, the husband…my father, the father?* One had blotted out the others, and she had buried all of them long ago. Now, the graves were shifting and the coffins were splintering. Long-forgotten questions, possibilities, realities were surfacing. *Pepi could be alive.* Does he know that Mami and Luis were gone? Does he know anything about his grandson? About Derek and I? About the lives and love he left behind?

They had only one family photograph. In most of her early memories, Pepi was a blur of motion, coming into camp, leaving moments later. He could pick a row of soybeans or clear a fruit tree before others had stopped yacking and put down their sacks. Mami was never far behind. She and Luis could always find her, even on the largest truck farm, amid the tomatoes, melons, onions, and strawberries. Her father dressed like the other men, indistinguishable in a sea of gray-and-brown cotton and hemp. But they could spot her colorful patchwork skirts, the long, braided black hair wrapped in a sky-blue bandana a mile away. And even at a distance, you could tell they were flying. But in the picture, for that brief moment, the family stood still. It was no perfect Kodak moment. She and Luis were squinting in the bright sunlight. Her hair was a tousled, dusty mess. Mami's bright colors were washed out by overexposure. Pepi had a slightly stunned look on his face, as if to say, "really, we're paying this man a dollar?" But it was their eyes Anna loved. Her parents' eyes sparkled. It was before everything happened, when their lives moved with the seasons and there was always a little something left over for the people who worked the fields. When they had time to sit around the fire in the evenings, had time to wash up and help their children learn to cook and read. She could remember sitting in Pepi's lap, burrowing in against his chest, seeking warmth on cold nights. He knew the constellations by heart, and would take her and Luis on journeys across the ancient sky. Luis begged for tales of heroes and monsters, of Hercules' labors and Perseus' bravery. She dreamt of Cassiopeia and Andromeda, trying to imagine the stories the women would tell if they could escape from the well-worn legends. Pepi patiently told and retold the stories without complaint, his low, calm voice lulling them to sleep.

She sighed. Nothing good can come from living in the past, she reminded herself. That was then. A million miles away. *Focus.* Bottom line, whether he's alive or not, some time just went back on the ticking clock, she reflected. The grainy video from Sandoval Hills slid into her thoughts, pushing out the Kodachrome print. Sudden moves and all-out war were not Wellsey's style. He liked things in the shadows, cloak-and-dagger style. *Like someone else I know.* And accidental or not, that fire is going to consume a lot of his energy. She drummed her fingers on the railings, thinking things through. The fracking case was going to take a lot. *But every other waking moment needs to be on this.* It was time for their plans to get some teeth. The twinning tour had not turned up jack. We need leverage, we need evidence, we need motive, she thought. Something, anything, to push back at Wellsey with. Something we can take public, something we can take to the cops, or the feds, if need be. It was time to rope in Lucille full time and put a tail on Wellsey. And…Ry and I need to convince the others. She figured Derek would be on board. The others might take some persuading. They would need to know about Ry's phone call. "And Pepi," she said under her breath. She shuddered. She had never talked about him with anyone other than Mami, Luis, and Paul. *That's about to change.*

Lost in her thoughts, she did not hear the front door open. She jumped slightly, startled, as two strong arms wrapped around her from behind. Derek nuzzled her neck with his face. "Hey there," he said simply. Anna reached her hands back to tousle his hair, then turned into his chest for a long hug. "I'm good," she said quietly. "We need to talk, but I'm good. Or better, anyway…You up for a walk? We can come back for the car…" Derek nodded. "Of course, lead on," he replied. "I've seen enough burning buildings to last me awhile."

Anna tried to smile, but ended up wincing instead. We can only hope, she thought. They say the darkest hour comes before the light, right? She looked around at Katherine and Ry's neighborhood. Windows were dark. Roads were empty. No one was out walking dogs. The breeze had dropped; the low, distant thrum of the interstate was now the only sound. Her thoughts circled back to earlier. Everything seems so damn normal…until one day, invisible men in ski masks slip inside your home and end the world as you know it. The past is just as real, just as present, as those curbs and that fire hydrant, she thought, scanning the street. She thought back to the slums, markets, and port crowds on that searingly hot day in Manaus. Time passed, and people forgot about the fence. They went about their business…until one day the world on the other side of the chain links erupted in fire. *Time and routine lulls us to sleep, just in time for the nightmares to roll in.*

Enough, she thought. No more pushing this sweet man away. She led him down the porch steps and headed for the street. She took his hand as they walked and started at the only place she could –

the beginning. "I've never told you about my father," she began.

"Is that what this is about?" Derek asked, surprised. "I was worried the sky was falling."

Anna stopped in mid-stride. "It kind of is," she said with a sad smile. "I wish I could say you could walk away, but..."

Derek's eyes darkened. "Is this to do with whatever Ry did? I swear, I'll –"

"No, sweetheart," Anna replied, cutting him off as gently as she could. "There was a misunderstanding back there. He meant well...he called my dad." She paused for a moment, startled by the simplicity of the statement. From here on out, everything else is complicated, she thought. A mix of guesswork, detective work, and blind luck.

She saw confusion replace the anger in Derek's eyes. "Let's keep walking," she said quickly, "I'll tell you everything." The two of them crossed the street, headed for downtown.

They walked and walked. Anna talked and Derek listened. At times, there were tears in his eyes. At others, his fists were clenched and his jaw set. For her part, Anna felt only one thing – a need for speed. She wanted to speak faster and faster, and to run rather than walk, to pour her family's hidden history out in a torrent of words. "Tonight...earlier...I felt trapped, like we were in a dead end," she said. They were close to home now, about a block away. "I felt betrayed, like Ry had opened a door and the past was going to come roaring through it any moment. And don't get me wrong...it is coming. But we don't have to just sit here and take it. We're a part of Wellsey's life, no matter how much he may want us to be nothing more than bugs splattered on his windshield. We don't have to sit here and take anything. We don't have to go quietly. We don't have to go anywhere at all. We can come roaring right into his life as well. We can —"

Anna stumbled over something as they walked up the path to their front door. She looked down and saw a small package. "Hold that thought," she said, headed for the steps. Derek reached for the door and followed her inside. She flipped on a light and together they examined the delivery. It was a padded mailing pouch, just larger than a sheet of paper. There were dozens of small tears and rips all over it, exposing the bubble wrap stuffing inside. The postmark had been inked out with a black marker. Scuffed, mottled squares remained where the stamps had been. There was no address. She flipped it over. No words there, either.

"Shake it?" Derek offered. When she did, something slid around inside. The package bent easily. It was fairly light. When Anna turned it back over, however, she noticed something for the first time. Someone had glued a small rectangle of paper over where the mailing address should have been. It had been done carefully, something to be noticed only upon close inspection.

Anna went white. Her fingers began to tremble; she almost dropped the package. She took a deep breath and plucked carefully at the almost imperceptible seam. Slivers of paper fell to the floor. She stood there for what seemed an eternity, staring at the fragments of meticulous handwriting underneath, unsure whether to shout in happiness or dread. If Derek said something, she did not hear him. If he touched her, she did not notice. Her bold, confident pronouncements only moments earlier now sounded like strings of unfamiliar syllables in her ears, like wisps of mist that could blow away before her in an instant. She tore at the seal and shook out the contents. A safe deposit box key and a small silver medallion fell out. The silhouette of a baying wolf lay across her open palm. She turned over the key and the medallion. No more surprises, she thought, relieved. Her mind stopped racing and she looked up to meet Derek's concerned gaze.

"Luis sent this package to Pepi before he died," she said quietly. "My father opened it. And now, it's here." More doors are opening, she thought. It's time to step through them.

Gazinsky threw a small metal disc on the desk. Blackened, scratched up and partly melted, the face of the animal was still visible. Fortinbras did not say anything for a long time. "Did anyone else see this?" he asked finally.

"I don't think so, sir! I talked to the coroner before the autopsy. It was fused to the body, sir!" Gazinsky barked the words as if he were on a parade ground, answering his drill sergeant.

Fortinbras sighed. The two men each had their strengths, but if he had to choose…"Inside his shirt?" he asked. He leaned forward, his fingers rubbing circles in his temples.

Gazinsky nodded. "What remained of it, sir! There were a few rope strands. Everything else was ash. It was like you said."

"And our inventory?"

"Spare parts and supplies took the biggest hits, sir! There were two hundred orbs on the warehouse floor. The electronics are fried, but the cauldrons just need some refinishing. The boat is in rough shape. The hull is all scorched up, the windows blew out, but everything on board appears to be in good condition."

Fortinbras was impressed. It qualified as a major speech for his second in command. He tapped his fingers together, savoring the small wave of relief. *That boat is something.* He smiled grimly at the irony. Their stupid visit actually helped us, he marveled. Without that jolt, everything would have been burned to a crisp. I have those irritating gnats to thank for saving our butts. He snorted. No need to get sentimental. They've already received a bigger thank you than they ever deserved, he mused. Holding off had been a bitter pill to swallow. But a demonstration wasn't worth much when there was no product to back it up. *In the meantime, I'm sure there are small things we can do to make their lives…unpleasant. Ruining that oh-so-precious ranch seems like a good place to start.*

The moment still made him shudder. The phone rang first. He dropped it an instant later – a sharp, piercing whine exploded next to his ear. "What the hell?" he shouted, reaching for the shattered screen. He could hear other noises…popping sounds, shouts, screams. And one calm voice, speaking commands in Spanish in the mayhem. The techs said the call lasted forty-eight seconds. It had been bounced around networks in dozens of countries. The taunting ended in squeals of feedback. He took out his frustration on the whores when they showed up.

Fuck. He had been holding out hope…but that damn wolf pin made his stomach turn. Few people would have any idea what it meant. Anyone Gazinsky's age would have no idea. Those guys hung up their spikes years ago. Whoever they had been, they remained a bunch of ghosts and shadows. *Why would they come out of retirement for us? They dealt with monsters, dictators, enemies of the people.* His lip curled in disgust. The only possible answer seemed way beneath them. So what if we were cleaning up the streets? The neighborhoods invited us in. He wanted to believe this was some new crew ripping off the past, but his gut told him differently. The operation was too big, too seamless, perfectly handled, no loose ends.

Gazinsky was still standing there, awaiting orders. Maybe it had worked out for the best, he reflected. He preferred brains, but whatever came next was going to require a lot of muscle. He could take care of the thinking. "What about the hard drives?" he asked.

Gazinsky slipped off his backpack and pulled out a small black bag. "They're all here, sir!" he replied. Fortinbras shook the drives out onto his desk and stacked them.

"So you went down there…"

"Sir yes sir!"

Fortinbras rolled his eyes. "I need you on the next plane back to Brazil," he growled. "Collins and Stewart will take over the reins in Alaska. I need you to be our ears and eyes on the ground. I need you to take charge of the rebuild."

"Sir –"

"Enough!" Fortinbras held up his hands. It was his turn to bark. "Three months. You have three months. Understood?" Gazinsky nodded. The meathead had better work out, he thought. He knew boots on the ground were stretched thin. A review of security staff in the field should take care of it, he thought. Cream always rises to the top. "And Dmitri, there's one other thing," he followed up. "Forget this conversation. Forget what you found. Get the warehouse up and running. That is all that matters. I'll take care of everything else."

"Sir?" Gazinsky's face creased in confusion.

Fortinbras slammed his hands down on his desk. "Stop saying that! Nod and agree! Then go do your job. I'm not paying you to think. Get out of here!" He swiveled around in his chair and waited for the footsteps to recede. Eventually they did. He heard the door close. *I need a drink.* He walked over to the bar, dumped some ice in a glass and poured himself a double. He strode over to the window and stared out at the city. Traffic was backed up. People were everywhere – stuffing themselves into buses, yakking away on park benches in McPherson Square, marching to get out of the heat and humidity. *We all make choices,* he reflected. *Most of you don't think past the next* moment, the next paycheck, the next ballgame. You respond, you react, like some primitive organism fumbling through the universe. Like humankind can't do better. *Screw that.* He knocked back the rest of his drink, nodding with approval as he looked down at the floors below. We've gone from being invisible to holding down a chunk of prime real estate, he thought. The suits in the other buildings think they are better than everyone else. But they're a bunch of leeches, living in the moment just like those lemmings outside. Think tanks, lobbyists, advocacy groups, they've owned K Street for decades and for what? They line their own pockets, they ensure their own survival. It makes me sick.

He realized the drink was not helping. His hands were shaking. Aponix is not about to be derailed by a bunch of Latin American vigilantes looking to play hero, he seethed. *We're the ones changing the world.* He had made the necessary moves quickly. Additional security for all other company facilities was in place overnight. The Brazilian army had the warehouse under military lockdown. Too little too late, but whatever…they were treating it as an act of economic terrorism, which suited him fine. The ambassador's sweaty handshake and vague promises had been disappointing. "We will find whoever did this, we will track them down. We will do whatever is needed," the man said, ushering him into a massive office hung with huge landscape paintings. He spoke too quickly. His eyes darted from side to side. With his thin pointy face and uneven buck teeth, Fortinbras thought the man looked like a rodent. He had an appropriate response – "your assurances are not worth a warm bucket of spit" – lined up but held his tongue. Maybe some bureaucrat down there would be useful, somewhere down the line. They did not have a clue, and he intended to keep it that way. The official finding would be arson, so at least insurance would pay out.

Message received, he wanted to shout. Thinking about it drove him crazy. Testing for the orbs had wrapped up earlier in the year – all remaining issues with organic and inorganic materials had been resolved. The brigade's Robin Hood crusade was completely unnecessary. He walked over to his desk and sat down to do what he had been dreading. He plugged the first hard drive into his laptop. He zipped through footage from four cameras before finding it. A crew of masked armed men. Harper left alone, sprawled on the floor. Minutes passed. He fast-forwarded again. He was startled by what came next. A figure shuffled across the floor. It looked like someone who spent their days living under a bridge. Crazy wild hair. Filthy clothes. Completely harmless, he thought. Until he started talking. The man lifted his head and spoke directly at the camera. A chill went down Fortinbras' spine. It was the brigade. *And the chameleon, the man of a thousand faces, is now…an old man.* I would be surprised if there is another picture or video on Earth that shows his face, he thought.

This is his final act.

Fortinbras flinched at the muzzle flashes, watched the old man pick up his cane and shuffle away. There had been no hesitation, no request for information. The whole thing was choreographed for his benefit. He hit rewind several times to read the old man's lips. Everything went down just as he said. The threat was convincing as well. *I understand.* No need to lead your militia into the nation's capital, old man. He sat back in his chair, grinding his teeth. He didn't like the situation, but it could be worse. Much worse. Anyone else, they would hit back and hit back hard. This situation called for...restraint. *For now.* He thought fondly of the first mercenaries he had hired. Nothing more than a minor skirmish for their first outing. He had walked through the smoking remains of the shelter, poking at the bloody corpses with his foot. He was vaguely disappointed that it was so easy, was over so quickly. The natives had been too wasted to put up much of a fight. The men led him to the shaman, lashed to a pole, wounded but alive, as requested. The shaman's eyes went wide in terror when he squatted by his side. The shaman started babbling. Spittle frothed at the corners of his mouth. "Glad you remember me," Fortinbras hissed. "Incantations and spirits can't help you now." He turned to his lieutenants. "Mark him, then let him go." They sent dogs after the few who ran.

Now he could take on a small country if he had to. *I have an army on call.* But this clearly called for a different approach. *Patience.* That old man is going to need medical care sometime soon, he thought, staring at the dark splotch on the warehouse floor. And when he does, we'll be there. The queen of chemistry could take care of the end game. He smiled. She was safely tucked away. And earning her keep to boot. *There will be no trace left behind.* He sighed. Time to get back to the endless conference calls and glad-handing. He still had nervous investors and politicians to talk down. He repeated the magic number like a mantra under his breath. Three months. Three months. Three months. *Three months and we will finally change the world.*

Liz slid back into the booth. "Hey! Glad the food finally arrived," she said cheerfully. She was still working on the tone. The goal – not too bubbly, but not too reserved, either. Cheeks a little flushed. Shy, warm smiles. Like we're really getting to know each other, and I like what I see. She was hoping the usual playbook still applied. *We're all looking for warm affection and a safe harbor, right?* "You know, there's a great place nearby for dessert," she followed up, "if you don't mind a late night…"

Her date caught the hint and smiled. A late, uncomplicated night, Liz reflected. The trip to the ladies' room had been uneventful. No new instructions. It looked like the last-minute course correction was going to take. *I deserve a medal if I pull this off.* "So you grew up near Baltimore?" she asked, making sure the spotlight stayed firmly on the other side of the table. "Siblings? Parents still together?"

Her date took the questions and ran with them. The mark was making it pretty easy, she thought. Talkative was good. She could sit back and relax. *The last few days have been surreal.* She was guessing only child, doting parents, suburban upbringing, Catholic school, with massive rebellion in there somewhere for good measure. She listened for gaps and inconsistencies. They made it through college without a hitch. But then they finished dinner and hit a brick wall. Life after college was off limits. For now anyway. Just when things were getting interesting, she thought, masking her frustration with a tight-lipped smile. *So close. That's why I'm here. I want to know what happened.* Once they're gone, there will be no one left but him, she thought. And not that I don't trust him…but come on, we've all got agendas. And his have a funny habit of getting people killed.

The waiter brought the bill. Now the questions started coming back her way. Deflecting them went nowhere. *Take evasive action.* "Let's get out of here," she said finally. *Time for a reset.* They split the check, grabbed their coats and walked out into a delightful summer evening. Her date took her hand as they walked. A promising sign, Liz thought. She tried a different angle. "Did you like living in D.C.?" she asked casually.

"Enough about me!" her date replied, laughing. "Geez, I hardly know anything about you. I swear, not one more detail about me tonight. Spill the beans."

Liz thought it over. Giving a cover a full workout was a rare opportunity. It would be good practice. And no duress, no sweating the details. A nice change. "Okay," she said finally. "There's not much to tell. I grew up in Santa Barbara. No brothers or sisters. Parents are divorced. My dad's in the wine business. My mother is a home care nurse. I lived on the beach."

Her date didn't bat an eyelid. "Doing what?" she asked.

Liz blushed. "You sure you want to know?" she asked. "It's not my crowning achievement."

"Of course I do!"

"Surfing, sunbathing, selling weed. And dating rich men. I liked young, rich millionaires. And they liked me." Liz looked down at her feet while she spoke. "One guy, he was in biotech, he ran and sold several startups. He had more money than God. I went in the labs with him, and fell in love." She stopped walking and laughed. "Sorry, that came out all wrong. I fell in love with *the work*. It was the weirdest thing. It felt completely natural…and important. Like, life-changing important. I found what I was meant to do. I ditched the guy, somehow sweet-talked my way into school."

"I envy you," her date replied. "I've always been good with people, so that led me to marketing and public relations. But nothing has ever felt like that. I'm still looking…" Now it was her date's turn to stare at the ground.

"What's up?" Liz asked. "Something on your mind?" It was time to push the evening along. If this is as far as we can get tonight, she thought, I could really go for a hot bath and a glass of white wine.

Her companion looked up and met her gaze. "Nothing, sorry…I was just thinking about connections, fulfillment, fate…anyway, I'm a mess!" she replied. "I have an idea – I think I'll stop talking! What if we go back to my place for a drink?"

This is different. Nicely played, Liz thought. She appreciated subtlety. The vulnerability seemed genuine too. Most men either didn't have the cojones to lay it out there, or had the gentle verbal caress of a wrecking ball. You. Me. Sex. Now. The old saying boiled it down nicely. Say what you want, and mean what you say. You want me for dessert, she thought. I figured this was coming somewhere down the line. But now feels good. More than good, she realized. Hot. *This is going to be fun.* A few minutes' walk and they were standing outside a townhouse. "This is me," her date said, turning to walk up the front steps. Liz nodded and smiled. She hung back while her date fumbled with keys. "There's something you should know," she said tentatively. The door opened. "I've…I've never done this before." She followed her date inside.

Her date looked back at her and smiled shyly. "Me neither," she whispered. "Maybe we could start here." She pulled Liz close and kissed her gently. Liz slid her fingers down her shirt, tracing the swell of her soft, firm breast. Jackie smelt like a summer day – ripe peaches and a hint of honeysuckle. Liz nuzzled her neck, licked at the small, tight curls of hair. Her skin was incredibly soft. When she sought out Jackie's lips a second time, their warm, wet tongues came together. Liz closed her eyes, sighing with pleasure as Jackie's hands moved down her body. She dropped her bag, nearly tripping over it as Jackie led her toward the stairs. A second later, Jackie dropped her hand.

Liz opened her eyes to find her date looking behind her. She turned and saw the blindfold, handcuff and ties scattered across the floor. *Oh shit. Not this, not now.* She froze, desperate to keep her emotions hidden. Her cover was in tatters. "Sorry, tools of the trade, pretend you never saw them," wasn't going to cut it. Unless...

Jackie got there first. "First time, huh?" she asked, a wicked smile on her face. "You sure about that?" Liz's took one look at her smile and knew she was safe. "I didn't say I didn't know what I like," she said huskily. She reached for the gear and walked over to Jackie. "Close your eyes," she demanded. Jackie did so. "Turn around." Jackie spun on her heels. "I want you to think of your safest place," Liz said in a low voice, slipping the blindfold over Jackie's face. "I want you to go there..."

She counted silently to twenty. "Ready?"

Jackie nodded.

Liz dropped to the floor. She ran her mouth slowly up her leg, kissing Jackie's calf and thigh. When she reached her skirt, Liz tugged at it with her teeth and growled, then turned her attention to her other leg. Tremors of anticipation shook Jackie's body.

"I want you to stay there," Liz whispered, "and invite me in...pretty please." She hovered behind her, waiting. The job never failed to surprise, she thought, but going from Plan A to...*this* in a matter of hours set a new personal record. You do what you have to do. And I've done plenty, she thought.

She had nearly driven off the road when she saw the text. "Change of plan. Return package to service center. Immediately." What kind of sense did that make, she wondered. The mask could come off only once. "Screw that," she growled, and turned around at the next stoplight. The hospital was a lousy option. Only one place made any kind of sense. It wasn't great, but it was something. *Thank God they found me a place with a garage.* Traffic had been light and the drive uneventful. She pulled in and parked, looked over at sleeping beauty. She had checked Jackie's pulse. It was strong and regular. If the meds were as good as advertised, she thought, everything should be fine. When the garage door closed, Liz got out and headed inside. She took a quick glance around, picked up stray laundry and papers that had fallen under the kitchen table. She sighed. Hopefully, Jackie wouldn't be paying too much attention when she came around. The crappy rental furniture and bare walls didn't exactly paint a picture of domestic bliss. Playing off the drugs was the next step. Liz played it cool and casual when Jackie started to stir. "Hey there…" she called out, pretending to be busy in the kitchen. "Can I get you some tea? A glass of water?"

"Ohhhhhh, my head," came the muffled response. "What happened?"

"You passed out on me," Liz said brightly. She walked into the living room and found Jackie sitting on the edge of the couch, holding her head in her hands. "Have you had fainting spells before?"

Jackie winced. She moved her head gingerly from side to side. "I feel like I'm at the bottom of the ocean," she murmured. "The world is swimming and I weigh a million tons. I can barely keep my head up."

"Don't fight it," Liz said gently. "Lie back and rest." She did as she was told. Jackie's recovery was slow but steady. Cold sweats came and went. Ditto for a blazing fever. Liz made sure to be the warm, smiling face waiting each time Jackie woke up. In between, she tried to think through the possibilities. With the change in plans, it had to be all about buying time. Which meant making Jackie the center of her world. And doing a pretty good job of it too, if I say so myself, she thought, smiling. *Three days later and here we are...*

"Unnnhhhhhhh..." The moment Jackie opened her mouth, Liz slid her hand between her legs. "Please come in," she moaned, rocking gently against the pressure. Liz tore away her panties. She held back for a long moment, then began to trace slow, gentle circles. Jackie threw her head back in ecstasy. Liz smiled. I've always wanted to have a man do this to me, she thought, but it seems to translate just fine for others. She slowly stood up, and put her lips next to Jackie's ear. "We're just getting started," she whispered. "Here's where I make you scream." She reached for the handcuffs and marched her prisoner upstairs.

Connections

Katherine pulled into the carpool lane. She sighed. At least something was working out. On a school day, there would have been pleading and squabbling. Not with adventure camp. The excitement and anticipation pouring from the back seat was palpable. They were chattering away. Jonah was headed for archery lessons and a massive game of capture the flag. Nora was building some kind of robotic monster controlled by laptop commands. Childhood isn't dead, she reflected, but it sure is different.

Her phone buzzed again. She ignored it, again. *Leave a message.* She pulled over and one of the counselors opened the rear door. "Bye mom!" The kids were gone in a flash. She was about to pull away when fingers rapped the driver's side window. Jonah cocked his head and waved. "Love you!" he cried.

"See you tonight. Have fun!" she replied, trying to put on a bright smile. *Someone needs to.* Reluctantly, she put the car in gear. When she checked her rear view mirror, she noticed a dark green SUV behind her. It had been there each morning. Family schedules aligning, she decided, dismissing the possibility of anything more sinister. *I'm going to be seeing conspiracies in the grocery store at this rate.* Where to, she wondered. What next? A stranger was working in her old office. Until Jackie came back from wherever she was, their plans were on ice. Heading home meant seeing Ry. *I have nowhere to go.* Things had felt so different only a few days earlier. New possibilities, she thought. Yeah, right. That was before a fire thousands of miles away lit the night sky and Anna attacked my husband...

She could not believe it. Explanations were still forthcoming. The previous evening haunted her thoughts. Derek pacing the hallway. Standing with him at the window and Ry waving them away. The front door opening and closing, and then opening and closing again. Ry walking into the kitchen. "Everything's fine," he said quietly. "Everyone can go home." Paul and Sam nodded and headed out quickly, visibly relieved by an escape route opening up. She was foolish enough to expect answers when it was just the two of them. "I made a huge mistake...I didn't know..." he started out.

"What did you do to her, for God's sake?"

"I can't tell you," he said lamely. "It's Anna's to share. But trust me...it's all going to work out, I think..." he pleaded.

She stood there, speechless, hands on her hips, angry, confused, and hurt. "That's all you have to say?" she asked finally. "It's going to work out, *you think*? Wow, thanks for that."

"Sweetheart —"

"I'm going to bed."

Earlier that morning, things went from bad to worse. A brief email from Anna dropped the bomb that she and Derek were hopping a morning flight to Chicago. "I have no clue," Ry said, looking over her shoulder at the single line of text. "She's going to straighten everything out, I promise." Such reassuring, confidence-inspiring words, Katherine thought. *In the meantime, I'm living in the dark, bumping around running errands, shuttling the kids, filling my time with anything to avoid thinking about the elephants in the room. Is Wellsey coming to kill us? Or did that fire wipe him out?* Another call came in, rattling her further. She mashed the car's console with her fist in frustration. "Yes? Hello?" she said brusquely.

"Katherine, I'm sorry. We need your help." The voice on the other end was hoarse, frantic. "A drilling crew is outside. A contractor for an energy company. They want to put in test wells. They say they have the right to go anywhere on the property." Katherine struggled to make any sense of the woman's words, when it suddenly registered. She knew the caller. The calmest, most even-keeled lady she had ever met was in distress.

"Hang on a second." Jill's hand muffled the receiver, but her words were still clear enough. "Tell them to cut the engine," she said to someone. "It's scaring the horses." She was shouting. There were more muffled sounds and words, and then Jill came back on the line. "I'm staring at a piece of paper with seals that look official. What should I do?"

Katherine's mind raced. *Deep Jungle is tightening the screws...again.* Anna's discovery had been breathtaking. Now this. All of it months before their non-compete clauses expired. Holding the valley's producers hostage by threatening Armageddon seemed like bad business. Whatever, she thought. I'll never understand the logic of corporate behemoths. Considering options didn't take long; there weren't many. Anna was in Chicago. A judge had thrown out their complaints against Kriegler Industries. She thought back to Anna's tattered mineral rights map and shuddered. *The oil companies own everything under the ground.* Not today, she thought, her anger rising. Not these puppets. Not on my watch. I don't care if that drilling crew has forty-seven permits and the Supreme Court on their side. We're not going to roll over and take it. "Jill, put the foreman on the line," she said quietly. She heard footsteps. A screen door slammed. A man's voice grunted a hello.

"This is Ms. Gibson's attorney," she replied, taking a little creative license. "If you take any action, if you so much as unpack a toolbox, you will face civil and criminal proceedings. Leave the property immediately."

"Ma'am, we both know that's not how this works. All of the paperwork is in order." The foreman had a slow, patient drawl. He sounded well used to explaining to people how the world worked. Funnily enough, Katherine thought, it was always in his favor. *Not this time.*

"Suit yourself," she said coldly. "Law enforcement is on the way. Smile for the ranch's security cameras in the meantime." She hung up. She gripped the driving wheel tightly and hit the accelerator, headed for the valley. There were no cameras, but the other bluffs seemed reasonable; they would be replaced by actual, real-world muscle in short order. Anna's associates could handle the legal side. Andy was her next call. Things had not ended well with Jackie, but whatever. He would eat this up. He believed in individual rights, private property, and small government above all else. He wasn't quite a right-wing lunatic. No nut job. But he took protecting the Constitution seriously. It was part of his job, as he had reminded her on multiple occasions. She had never thought that nodding through those dull conversations might actually pay off.

When she pulled into the ranch, she was pleased to see he brought friends with him. There were four squad cars with lights flashing, surrounding a huge, gray-and-black beast of a vehicle – it had to be a drilling rig – and a couple of pickups. Another idea came to her as she pulled in to park. Let's get this on the evening news. She sent quick texts to the two stations in Grand Junction. That should be enough to slow them down.

After she got out of the car, she found Andy and the other deputies standing over by the drilling rig, talking to several men in wader boots and overalls. Ready for a day's work, she thought, surprised by their optimism. They had to know this was going nowhere fast. Andy made brief eye contact with her and turned back to the conversation. She ran over to the farmhouse and found Jill and her dad in the living room. Jill was staring off into space, her eyes wet with tears. Her dad was wearing a path in the carpet. "Hi hon," he said, his eyes wide and panicked. "Thanks for coming."

"I got here as fast as I could. Tell me everything," Katherine replied. "Start at the beginning."

Jill seemed startled by her voice. "There isn't much to tell," she said, looking nervously around the room. Her hands were shaking. "I was in the horse barn. I heard engines idling, then raised voices. We have the ranch hands to thank. The brutes nearly ran a couple of them over on the way in. I don't think those men had any intention of saying anything to anyone. One of the hands ran to find your dad and me. We took one look at that rig and grabbed anything we could find – jumping posts, empty buckets, baling wire – to block the way in. They shouted and cussed at us and shouted some more."

Katherine's dad stood beside Jill and rubbed her shoulders. "We stood our ground, though," he said quietly. "Pretty soon, everyone on the ranch was standing on the other side of that barricade."

"They're a bunch of vipers," Jill said under her breath. "Who do they think they are?"

"I have a pretty good idea," Katherine replied. "Can I see the permit?"

Jill reached for a paper on the couch and handed it to her. Katherine's breath caught in her throat as she looked it over. It was just as Anna had said. These pieces of paper really were filed away in a safe somewhere. The document listed a consortium of international energy companies as the owners of the mineral rights. Kriegler was an afterthought. She glanced at the boundaries listed and winced. The permit covered every inch of the property, as the foreman claimed. Way down at the bottom, a chronological parade of numbers caught her eye. The permit had been renewed annually more than thirty times. There were few other details. Nothing about notification requirements. Nothing about the rights of homeowners. The permit was a blunt instrument: drill, baby, drill.

Katherine sighed. She ran a hand through her hair. She had assumed the men were full of...hot air. They appeared to have everything nailed down tight. That left only the back story..."Have you had any contact with the co-op or Deep Jungle?" she asked Jill. "Phone calls, emails, anything?"

Jill snorted. "Of course!" she replied. "The new contract came in the mail last week. I checked the producer opt-out clause faster than you can say, 'new day dawns in the valley.' And I wrote a note on the bottom saying I would be urging all of my neighbors to opt out as well. Sent it back the next day."

Katherine's thoughts swirled. *Deep Jungle was sending out contract renewals already?* She was working so hard to put the whole debacle in the rear view mirror, to finally wash the bitter taste from her mouth. Starting again was somewhere down the road. When she and Jackie were reenergized and ready to go. When their non-compete clause was up. *Not today.* Cold fear washed over her. If people opted out now, there were no systems in place, no storage facilities, no staff, no customers...*nothing*. Which is exactly what Deep Jungle wants, she realized. Make us look incompetent before we ever get off the ground. Throw in a drilling rig and you've got a full-court press. *We never specified when the short-term contracts would start or finish.* "You didn't think to give us a heads up?" she asked in frustration. "You didn't think this was something to talk about?"

"Wait a second. You're angry...*with us?*" Jill asked, incredulous. She planted her hands on her hips. "An energy company just pulled up and asked to destroy the ranch, in case you'd forgotten. Nothing about co-ops or production contracts or opting out. Just good old-fashioned fracking. They're not connected. If they start drilling, they could wipe out our turkey and livestock production. A fat lot of good that would do them."

"That's exactly my point," Katherine said steadily. "Deep Jungle has found a way to keep everyone in the valley in line. There's no direct connection, no trace of meddling. The new co-op can replace a few producers here and there. But the farms and ranches lose everything. Clean water. Clean air. Clean soil. You signed up to be their test case."

Jill gasped as she absorbed the news. "We may have to find a new home for the horses," she whispered to Katherine's dad. "Start again." Fresh tears welled in her eyes.

"We're not there," Katherine said firmly. "Not yet. Not ever." We should have been treating the ranch as the front line of a war, she realized. Jill was unafraid, a lightning rod for controversy in the first place. Throw in her close ties to the co-op's former owners and you had a tempting target with a big red bulls-eye painted on the ranch's front gate. A nice high-profile example to use to scare everyone else to death. No one would need to connect the dots. That's our job, Katherine reminded herself. Shining a light on the darkness. Lucille had come up with nothing so far. That was going to have to change.

"How do we fight back?" her dad asked. "What can we do?"

"We fight for time," Katherine replied. "Time to get the answers we need. Hours, days, weeks...whatever we can get, while our legal team goes into overdrive. There has to be a loose end somewhere – a forgotten memo, a deleted email, a staff person looking to do the right thing."

"And if there's not?"

"Then we man the barricades. And win the battle of public opinion. We get 60 Minutes to come out here, and see how Deep Jungle likes the national spotlight. I'm guessing they may be trying this strong-arm stuff in the co-op's other states as well."

"Suits me. I like a good fight," Jill snarled, wiping away her tears. "Just ask the cop standing behind you. He had to keep me from taking a swing at them earlier."

Katherine turned around. She was surprised to see Andy standing in the doorway. "How long have you been there?" she asked.

"Long enough to say I never had you pegged as a conspiracy theorist," he replied. "You are out there!"

Katherine squinted, trying to decipher if he was giving her props. She remembered Jackie saying he was hard to read. His flat, even tone gave little away. "Not sure I appreciate being roped into your little fantasy world," he followed up. "But I'll say one thing. They are confident sons of bitches. They say we'll be back as their police escort. How do you like that?"

The three of them looked at each other, unsure whether the question required an answer. Andy ploughed ahead regardless. "I don't appreciate that kind of attitude," he said, slapping his driving gloves against his palm. "We'll be escorting them off your property shortly. A judge will decide if they're coming back."

"Can I speak with them?" Katherine asked.

"I don't know…can you?" Andy replied. Katherine ignored the grade-school taunt, marveling again at the man's awkwardness. She pushed past him and walked outside, headed for the foreman. The rest of his men and the other cops stared at their boots as she approached. The man met her gaze evenly, but said nothing. She handed him back the permit. "You don't even know who you're working for," she said icily. "All you do is destroy things."

Still he said nothing. Instead, he jerked his head slightly, and the men headed for their trucks. At last, the foreman took a few steps back and swung up into the cab of the drilling rig. He revved the thunderous engine several times, then turned to tug on his seat belt. He reached for the gearshift but then seemed to think better of it. He locked eyes with Katherine and raised his arm. Lest it be confused with a wave or salute, his wrist swiveled and his middle finger slowly extended in her direction.

"See what I mean?" Andy's dull, flat voice startled her a second time. He was standing right behind her. "Such low quality, these people. No respect. I'll have to cite him. Disturbing the peace."

Katherine almost laughed. "Thanks Andy," she replied. "I mean, Officer Harris."

He looked at her dismissively. "Don't thank me," he responded. "Better get a good attorney. I'm citing you too."

"For what?" Katherine asked, flummoxed.

"For that," Andy said simply. He pointed at two satellite trucks near the ranch entrance. "Those imbeciles" – he said the word slowly, dipping each syllable in disgust – "have been running around out here during your touching family strategy session. The cowboys manning the barricades made it sound like the storming of the Bastille."

Katherine tried her best to mask her delight. She could not believe their luck. Jackie would be proud. Now, she thought, there is just one other person who needs to say a few words. *The icing on the public relations cake.* She walked away from Andy and stepped inside the farmhouse. She was relieved to find Jill needed little convincing. She hung back during the brief interview, which included her dad standing supportively at Jill's side. Afterward, she hugged them both and said she would be in touch that evening. They were tired and worried, but still relieved that things had not gotten any worse.

Andy's squad car squawked at her as she made her way across the parking lot "Thanks for blocking us in with the news circus," he said as he pulled up. "Appreciate that..."

Katherine, for the umpteenth time, was unsure how to respond. She opted for gratitude. Surely that was a safe route. "Officer Harris, thank –"

"No. No thanks are required," he said brusquely, cutting her off. "We're heading out. Would you like a police escort back to town?"

Katherine was alarmed by the offer. "Why? Am I in danger?" she asked, studying his face for clues. "Is there something I should know?"

Andy cracked a small smile. "Well, it sounded back there like the whole world was against you. Like even going outside might be a bad idea. It's hard to know sometimes..."

"Thank you for your concern, officer," Katherine replied, enjoying the opportunity to cut him off in return. "I'm going to stay here for a few more minutes." She thought about the Network and now Wellsey and Deep Jungle and shuddered. *You have no idea what we're dealing with.*

"Suit yourself. Keep an eye out for that citation." His car's wheels spun in the gravel. It peeled away in a cloud of dust. The other squad cars followed.

Katherine shook her head. How had Jackie ever dated him? She understood the appeal of the whole law-and-order thing, but not when it came packaged with zero empathy and a world of sarcasm. *You dodged a bullet, there, Jacks,* she thought. Definitely not a keeper. She walked over to her car and stood there, taking deep breaths to slow everything down. *I just want to listen to this sweet music.* The reporters were fine-tuning their leads before going live. A young woman in a purple blouse was staring intensely into a camera mounted on a tripod. She was gripping a microphone so tightly her knuckles were white. "On most days, Bunscombe Ranch is a quiet, peaceful place," she started off. Her tone was bright and chirpy. Jarringly inappropriate for the story, Katherine thought. But whatever – the story is getting out. That's all we care about. "Today, this nationally renowned horse stable and training facility was engulfed in conflict and uncertainty," the woman continued. "A quick response by county police averted what otherwise could have been a bloody encounter. Tonight, we bring you comprehensive Channel nine coverage of this remarkable confrontation…" She stalked away from the camera, berating herself under her breath for some imagined infraction or hint of a regional accent. Katherine could see now how young the reporter was, no more than a few months out of school. That last bit – the bloody encounter part – was a little over the top, she thought, but overall, I'll take it. You cannot beat local news. They love a good David and Goliath story. Even they can't screw this one up.

She got into her car and drove carefully past the news trucks and out onto the state road. Her eyes followed the curves of the asphalt, but her thoughts was already far out ahead. They were going to need office space. Lucille might as well move to Grand Junction for a while. Jackie needed to surface pronto. And if those trucks returned to the ranch, they needed to be ready…a tail and a PI would help with that. Fully occupied, Katherine did not notice the dark-green SUV several cars back. When she stopped to get gas in Fruita, she did not see it pull in across the street. By the time she got home, her to-do list was a mile long. Scanning her street for suspicious vehicles was not on it. Minutes after she closed the front door and started making calls, the SUV drove slowly past, turned around, and parked nearby.

They followed the clerk to a bank of massive steel elevators, leaving behind a land of fine leather furniture, backlit oil paintings, and burnished wood. They descended several floors. When the doors opened, they followed her down a long white hallway, which led to stairs and more hallways. At a seeming dead end, the clerk asked them to wait. She placed her palm on the wall and peered into a small black hole at eye level.

Derek looked over at Anna and raised his eyebrows. "Your brother," he whispered. "He didn't mess around."

Anna shrugged. "Only the finest. That was his thing. Stashing stuff at a local bank would never have occurred to him." In front of them, a low humming sound started up, followed by clicks as gears moved and tumblers disengaged. A hairline fracture appeared in the wall. Seconds later, an entire panel slid silently out of view.

The clerk stepped aside. "Please, take your time," she said with a broad, plastic smile. "I'll be outside if you need anything."

Derek followed Anna into the inner sanctum, raising his hands to shield his eyes from the dazzling white light bathing the circular room. Safe deposit boxes extended from floor to ceiling in all directions. Some were smaller than cigar boxes; others were good-size lockers. They walked around a long, high table in the middle of the room, seeking out the lower digits. The lack of chairs sent a clear message.

It's a Tuesday, he thought. I'm supposed to be at the store. Fix bikes, tell some stories, maybe grab a beer afterward with the guys. That's my day. Instead, it's 10 a.m. and I'm in Chicago. My wife is the daughter of one of the greatest guerilla fighters of the twentieth century. We're chasing down mysteries left behind by her murdered brother, while a psychopath in the nation's capital is licking his wounds while plotting an energy revolution and our imminent demise. It was a lot to take in.

"What number are we looking for again?" he asked, running his fingers along the cool white tiles. If only these babies could talk, he thought, staring at the silent rows of copper locks. We have to be surrounded by millions of dollars in valuables, he figured. Untold treasures, artwork, bullion, bearer bonds…the whole trip felt surreal, like something out an action movie, except he wasn't sure what role he was playing.

"Over here," Anna called out. She was across the room, staring at a row of boxes. Derek walked over and slid his arms around her.

He kissed her several times. "I'm right here with you," he said simply. Anna slid the key in the lock. It turned easily. She pulled out a long, thin box. "It's light," she said in a strange, distant voice, and carried it over to the table. Derek watched as she carefully lifted the lid. She reached in and pulled out a single, crisp white envelope. She untucked the back flap and pulled out a folded sheet of paper. She opened it with trembling hands and they both stared down at several paragraphs of black ink.

Pepi.

My hope is that the past, or at least curiosity, has carried the day. My hands have always been dirty enough to find you. Anna asks me sometimes if I think you are alive. I never liked uncertainty. So here we are.

Marquez wrote of una muerte anunciada. I know you were more of a Fuentes man. You create options, openings, possibilities. Somehow, my work has always led to borders, limits, gates, boundaries. The people I worked for do not forget. You know of whom I speak. I was young, but there is no excuse. This day has been a long time coming.

After me, they will come for them, as they did once before. I thought the Network had been destroyed. I was wrong. One serpent remains, and he grows stronger every day. My only saving grace is that I kept them safe. Now I ask you to do the same. If not for me or Anna, for your grandson. They never need know.

For me, there is not much else to tell. I was never one for the big struggle. I know I fell short of your ideals. Winning and money were enough. But Anna is different. Her life is a tribute to what you and Mami fought for. Her life, and Paul's life to come – and the valley – are worth fighting for.

We have both made many choices. I regret only a few. Mami, perhaps most of all. But you never came, and so here we are. What you need to know is below. The account details are to fund what needs to be done. Better late than never.

Luis

Derek's head swam. Luis once worked for the Network? He could not remember the man ever letting anything slip, ever saying something strange or out of place. But neither had he once doubted them, he realized. Her brother had questioned their ideas and plans, their timing and equipment, but never once mocked the idea that they were facing down a massive, untouchable crime syndicate. *Because he knew what we were up against.* Derek had found the man unbearable. He remembered his disdain, his arrogance, his casual, brutal dismissiveness. When they first met, Luis had uncoiled from his chair like a snake. "You know nothing about me, and next to nothing about my sister," he hissed. "Leave your conjectures out of this…" But one thing was indisputable. Without his help, they would never have survived. He looked over at Anna, expecting to see tears of anger or frustration. Instead, her eyes were shining. "I knew he was in there!" she said emphatically. "Every time I drove to Sandoval Hills, part of me hoped to find the boy I grew up with." She held up the paper and shook it. "You see what this gives us, right? Motive. And not just one. Two. Fortinbras killed my brother because he betrayed the Network *and* he because he was a loose end."

"Easy there. Please slow down," Derek said gently. "I'm trying to keep up. We can't just go to the cops with this letter, right? John Wellsey no longer exists; there's no smoking gun. His new self owns everyone, anyway. Plus, aren't we the other loose end here? Haven't we always been?"

Anna crumpled the paper in her fist. "Let's flip this thing on its head," she said grimly. "Let's make Fortinbras the loose end." She picked up the envelope and turned it upside down. Another key slid out. She dangled it in front of him. "Let's see what my brother left us to work with."

Derek didn't answer immediately. Something else was nagging at him. "Your brother, he left this for Pepi…" he said slowly, feeling his way forward. "Not us. Why?"

Anna shrugged. "My father's the assassin, remember?"

"Yeah, an assassin who abandoned his family and never looked back," Derek countered, feeling increasingly unsettled. "A man who sent us here instead of coming himself. Sounds like a..." He managed to hold his tongue just in time. We never asked for any of this, he thought. We've already been through so much. Now we're just supposed to saddle up and go save the world again? I don't know what I was expecting coming here, but everything is getting way too real, way too fast...

Anna's face softened. "It's a lot, I know," she said quietly. "You know what I was thinking just now?"

"What?" He was trying to keep an open mind, but a thousand details were fighting for his attention. What about getting the BMX park off the ground? What about pulling off the next Bookcliffs Challenge? Life isn't slowing down any...

"That if I turned that key, I could never turn back," Anna continued, bringing him back. "Part of me wanted to turn around and walk right out of here. With you, back to our lives."

"Why didn't you?"

Anna sighed. "Because I realized our lives turned that key a long time ago," she replied. "Part of me wishes things were different. That we were different people, living different lives. But this is who I am. I understand now. Trouble didn't just follow Katherine, Jackie, and Ry out west. My brother was already living on borrowed time. I don't think he ever forgave Pepi for leaving us. It was like he flipped a switch. He was our father...and then he was gone. This is my brother's final attempt to bring him back."

"But he's not coming, is he?"

Anna's eyes narrowed. "I don't know. After Ry's phone call, Pepi sent a message in Manaus. Then he sent us the key...to give us a choice." She reached for his hands. "You didn't ask for any of this. But you did ask for me to be in your life...I'm a woman with a lot to be thankful for. And I intend to fight for it. *Our way*, whatever we decide that is going to be."

Derek shook his head. "I sound like such a whiner," he replied. "And I feel like a fool. I'm sorry. Part of me somehow thought it would be all peaches and ice cream after the Network went down in the desert. I figured one nasty mess was enough for this lifetime. I want this to end."

Anna met his gaze evenly. "It will," she replied, "on our terms." Then she smiled. "Are you saying you wished I came in another flavor?"

Derek smiled sheepishly. He shook his head. "With you is where I want to be," he replied. "Always. You know that. This is all just a little overwhelming."

"It's a lot more than that," Anna replied. "Trust me when I say I would like nothing more than to ride off into the sunset with you."

Derek looked deeply into the eyes of the woman he loved. "I'm going to hold you to that, somewhere down the line," he said. "After...all this." He looked at the second key. Anna was right. There was no turning back. They had made their choice. It was time to open the other box and get back on an airplane.

Jackie waved away her friend's concerns. "You sound like my mother!" she said, feigning shock and horror. "I'm more worried about you to be honest." She was, too. Katherine looked exhausted. Her skin was pale and her eyes were bloodshot. Mascara could not hide the bags under her eyes.

"But Jacks, seriously, why didn't she take you to a hospital?" Katherine asked. "You've never had fainting spells like that before."

Jackie laughed, marveling at the double standard. "Don't you remember a certain hunk of a man rescuing you on the streets of Washington several years ago?" she asked, incredulous. "That seems to have worked out just fine."

Katherine blushed. "I suppose," she conceded. "But you've been out of contact for days. I mean, a ton has happened. We've got a lot to catch up on."

Tell me about it, Jackie thought. That's exactly why I went off the reservation, she wanted to say. I needed a break from crisis, calamity, legal proceedings, stress of all kinds. Most of all, I needed a break from uncertainty. There's a lot to be said for taking some time out. Especially if there is a special someone involved…"I've got some news to share as well, you know," she followed up. She could not help but smile. Even thinking about Liz for a moment made her heart race. "Liz and I have been…together the past week. She didn't take me to the ER because she wanted to take care of me. And she's been doing a wonderful job."

Katherine looked lost at sea for a moment. "You mean…together together?" she asked finally.

Jackie giggled. "Yes!" she shouted happily. There was so much to tell. They had walked, bowled, skated, eaten, biked, run, shopped, and held hands across Grand Junction. Jackie had been the tour guide at first, but Liz was a quick study. Late one afternoon, she whisked Jackie out of town for a romantic picnic in the National Monument. As shadows filled the red rock canyons and stars pinpricked the sky overhead, they talked about their families and their hopes and dreams, eating takeout and downing glasses of red wine. They may well have spent the night out there, were it not for the startling thunder of bighorn sheep clashing their horns together on a nearby ridge. Instead, they headed back to town for another memorable night in bed.

"Sounds amazing," Katherine chimed in. A tired smile tugged at the edges of her mouth. Her eyes were glassy and distant. "Tell me more about Liz. What's she like?"

"Funny, sexy, brilliant…you know, the usual?" Jackie giggled some more. "Did I mention she's amazing?" She knew she had fallen hard for her. Was head over heels in fact. It was the best part of a relationship. She wasn't much good at the details that came later. But these early days were pure magic – the hunger in a glance, the crackling electricity in the lightest of touches. This is where I want to live, she thought. Right here, in the moment. I don't want to come down from this cloud. She could see Katherine had both feet firmly planted on the ground, however. Her friend was doing her best to humor her, but it only went so far. The minute I ask her about the past week, Jackie thought, I'll be right back where I started. Tense, unhappy, sad. *I can guess where things stand. Nowhere good.* So she didn't ask.

At first, the revolutionary idea worked pretty well, while they sipped on herbal teas and talked about the kids' summer camp. But things eventually started to fall apart. Katherine stopped making eye contact, then started drumming her fingers on the arm of her chair. I know what she sees, Jackie thought, resenting what she saw in her friend's eyes. But I'm not a petulant child, or an ostrich with my head buried in the sand. *I know what's what.* I just don't want to be a part of *this* for a while. I've been on this merry-go-round before. I never signed up for a mortgage and kids. And I *have* been sitting behind a desk way too long. "I'm going to get caught up on everything at the powwow tonight anyway, right?" she responded when Katherine tried bringing things up. "Let's talk about you. How are you doing? How's Ry?"

Katherine flinched. "I can't really separate those things," she replied. She looked like she had more to say, but looked away. "Things are not great," she said finally.

Fair enough, Jackie thought. We might as well be on different planets. An awkward silence fell between them. She felt no desire to fill it. She wanted to get up, walk out the front door and driverunsprintfly across town to find Liz. She needed another long drag. Another hit of that magical lightness, that floating feeling, that freedom. She needed to see Liz smile and watch the sparkles in her eyes dance. They're for me, she thought, tingling with excitement all over again. *Time to go.* She reached for her bag.

"You will be there, right?" Katherine asked. Anxiety strained her voice. "Tonight?"

Jackie sighed. "Yeah, sure," she replied dismissively. "Can't wait." She got up to leave. She saw Katherine was staring at her, waiting for her to say something else. You have to be kidding, she thought. "I'll be coming solo," she said quietly. *Duh.* I wouldn't bring Liz into our little cabal if my life depended on it, she thought. That would be cruel and unusual punishment. *Any other unreasonable requests?* She blew out of the house as fast as she could, before she could say something she might regret. She sent a quick couple of texts while sitting in her car and hit the road. When she pulled up outside the hospital, Liz was waiting. Her heart leapt. "Well, hello there," she called out. "Good day?"

"It is now!" Liz replied, opening the door. She reached over to hug her.

"I've only got a couple hours tonight," Jackie said reluctantly, pulling back. "Although you could stay over at my place..."

"No worries," Liz said with a shrug. "I should probably do some work. Plenty to catch up on. Got time for dinner? We could go back to that hole in the wall over on Fifth."

It was an inspired idea. After a couple of drinks, Jackie could feel the day starting to get back on track. Liz, as usual, was incandescent – the warmth of her smile alone made her feel like she was the only person in the crowded happy hour. Still, sitting alone just for a few minutes after Liz went to the ladies' room was enough to bring the worries back. The evening ahead loomed, dark and heavy. I just want to live my life, she brooded. To wake up in the morning and live in the moment. Is that so much to ask?

She felt a soft touch on her wrist and looked up, surprised. "Hey there," Liz said gently, "if something's going on, you can tell me about it, you know."

Jackie wanted to curl into a ball and disappear. Am I that transparent, she wondered. Are my emotions always out there for the world to see? "I'm sorry," she replied. "I don't mean to be so distracted…"

"And I don't mean to be blathering on about small stuff," Liz replied. "Tell you what, next round is on me. I'll be right back." She returned with two jack and cokes. Jackie took a long sip and then another. She savored the kick of the alcohol as it cascaded down her throat. She looked across the table at her girlfriend, fighting back tears. If I can't talk to her, what's the point of being together, she wondered. *I've never felt this way about anyone.* The thought came out of nowhere, and struck her with the force of a hammer. She gasped.

"You okay there? Can't hold your liquor?" Liz asked with a smile.

"I'm going to be," Jackie said softly. She knocked back the rest of her drink. Then the floodgates opened.

Just to make sure, Liz shook the powder in and stirred. The miracles of modern science never cease, she thought, watching the tiny crystals spin. She stood there like a proud parent long after they had dissolved. The thrill had never gone away. This particular concoction took her way back. It was still one of the most useful potions in her arsenal. The early iterations had left people with blurred vision and a pounding headache. Useful for intimidation, perhaps, but not much else. This version left a person feeling invigorated and refreshed. It was also undetectable. Jackie would be out until morning, and then ready to start the day with a bounce in her step. *Unless plans change.*

Cough medicine and vodka mixed with rat poison had been enough to save her own life. The cocktail had gotten her out of the basement. She flirted with the guard, said she would give him a high he wouldn't soon forget, if he would just let her work some magic. He drank the stuff down, groaned and stumbled around, eyes wide, foam flecking his chin. He crashed to the ground inches from her, his face red and swollen, his tongue lolling from his mouth. As she reached for his keys, she heard the bidding upstairs start again. She knew she was the main event. Earlier, the buyers had sat in the shadows, watching the pathetic parade. Most of the girls, brown skinned and local, would be farmed out to other cities, drugged into oblivion and chained to beds until they slit their own wrists or a client beat them to death. The parade halted when she stepped into the light. "Uma princesa de ouro!" the auctioneer boomed. A tall blond anglo girl would fetch a high price. A nice side benefit of a robbery gone wrong. The response had been oddly respectful – quiet murmurs and nodding heads, as if they were sampling a rare wine. She turned slowly in the spotlight, spent the precious moments casing the place. They were in a large house, still under construction. Tyvek wrap surrounded the windows. Rooms had been framed in; fountains of wires and sections of PVC pipe jutted from the ceiling. The floor was bare wood, gritty with drywall dust. Smart choice, she thought. They were unlikely to be disturbed…no risk of nosy neighbors. We could be in any new housing development near the city. Then they were sent back, shuffling awkwardly down the stairs in ankle chains. One simple fact stood out. The main entrance to the house was only a few feet from the basement stairs. There was no front door.

"Vendido!" The auctioneer's final cry rattled the floorboards. Liz looked up, startled. She had thought there would be more time to free the others. She looked around at the crouched bodies and wild eyes. "Quick. Use these," she whispered, handing the keys to the nearest girl. Then she scrabbled up the staircase and tried the door handle. It squeaked loudly but opened. She slipped out, glancing down the hallway. Glasses were raised in a toast. No one looked in her direction. She crept outside, looking for any signs of life. There were none. Rows of identical houses stretched in either direction, mute witnesses to her escape. She picked a direction and ran. The gravel road ended in a cul-de-sac and she took off across the sodden grass, passing stacks of lumber, hulking loaders, and gravel piles. She made it to a nearby park, stumbling barefoot across the unfinished cobblestones as a thunderstorm moved in overhead. No one heard her screams when they came for her. The men calmly wrenched her arms behind her back and marched her to a waiting van.

The door slid open. A stranger smiled warmly at her and told the men to let go. "Please," he said, gesturing at the empty row behind him. "My name is Bruno." She stepped up into the van and the door slid shut behind her. She turned down a towel and stared straight ahead, shivering. The man said nothing for a long time. Flickering glances revealed a vision straight out of a fashion magazine. Tight brown curls, perfect stubble, strong cheekbones, warm brown eyes.

"You are…good with materials." His statement caught her off guard. *What the hell?* She nodded cautiously. "Chemistry, you mean?" she asked. When he didn't respond, she offered a little more. "Changing things around, making new stuff, yeah, that's what I do." She blew through her first science kits as a kid, turned to cannibalizing the materials for other purposes. Melting holes in metal. Dyeing clothes and pets. Burning designs into lawns and trees. Making it rain. Then she hit up her parents, both chemists, for supplies. She painted on a broad canvas – Rio's sewers, ports, tunnels, and beaches. Wherever raw materials presented themselves. When her parents balked, science lab became her after-school base of operations. Once she got hold of the supply catalog and convinced the teacher she needed an assistant, the keys to the kingdom were hers.

"We have a job," the man finally responded. "You know who we are?" Liz could guess. Comando Vermelho ran the city's underworld. Going to one of their funk parties was a common dare among the expat kids from her prep school. Gunrunning and drugs were their bread and butter. Human trafficking is also apparently part of their portfolio, she thought. She looked at him. "It's not much of a choice, is it?" she asked.

The man shrugged. "You have nothing left. You help us. We help you." Fragmented memories cut through her consciousness like shards of glass. The morning sun's rays stretching across the living room. Her parents talking quietly in their bedroom. Standing by the counter in her pajamas, making some oatmeal, sprinkling in raisins and brown sugar. A Saturday morning like any other…until that knock on the door.

Liz watched the man carefully. Something about his casualness was setting off alarm bells for her. He knows things about me, she realized. He knows – or thinks he knows – how this is all going to play out. "Do I know you from somewhere?" she asked. "Have we met before?"

"We were looking for someone special," the man replied, staring past her. "Everyone we ask says the best is not in the university labs, is not working for big pharmaceutical companies, like your parents. Some others did not believe you were the one. A child. But I never doubted..."

The man's words faded into the background as she struggled to make sense of what he was saying. *Like my parents?* She bent over in horror as the pieces knit together. *There was no burglary.* She curled into a ball and started to howl like a wild animal – deep, primal shrieks rocked her body. Before she could come across the seat and rip the man's face off, he reached over and expertly jabbed a syringe into her thigh. Liz felt a surge of euphoria almost immediately, and fought it with every fiber of her being. No luck. She gasped for air, riding high on a tide of chemical happiness. Andandamide, if she had to guess. But there were other strands in the mix too. A neuromuscular blocker for one; she could not move. At the same time, her vision and hearing felt sharper. And already the euphoria was transitioning into a sense of warmth and well-being. The speed of the transition was remarkable.

"There are others like you," the man was saying in a mild, matter-of-fact tone, as if nothing was out of place. "Working for us. With us, I mean. You will achieve your true potential now." He reached over and patted her shoulder. "It is a new day," he said. "A painful one for you. The end of one life. The start of another. You are safe now. And congratulations. Today was a test. You passed."

Liz stared at him, incredulous. She thought back to the ingredients on hand in the basement. The lives of a dozen girls and the death of a guard were nothing more than the backdrop for an audition? In that moment, before the chemicals carried her off to a deep, dark, dreamless sleep, she made herself a promise. By the time she met Fortinbras, she had moved up the food chain and kept it. She learned from every chemist in the organization, and kept some simple rules along the way. No explosives work. No addictive substances. She specialized in untraceable changes to organic matter. If others realized how dangerous she had become, they were unable to stop her. Bruno the fixer was the last to go down, after Fortinbras made her an offer she could not refuse. Bruno's death – in suspicious circumstances on enemy turf – helped spark a gang war that raged across Rio for weeks. Fortinbras helped her disappear, and she helped him get his energy revolution off the ground.

She laughed the first time she heard his speech. Bigger and better things, she thought, aim for the stars, blah blah blah – I've heard it before. But he backed it up. Doors opened. She was fast tracked to a doctorate at the University of São Paulo. Everything had to be official, above board, legit, he told her. And he left her alone. No more minders. No more quotas. Colleagues and equals, as he promised. With a mission to change the world this time around. If she still had a conscience, it would have made her all warm and fuzzy inside. As it was, she found it a clinically interesting proposition.

Then came this, she thought, reaching for her phone. A detour would be a kind description. The hastily arranged placement at the hospital, completely out of the blue. A cover held together with staples and duct tape. All while still keeping secrets. I understand alone, she wanted to tell him. I understand no family. I understand reinvention, obliterating your own history along the way. *You want me to put myself on the line, you had better let me in.*

Her hopes for any kind of breakthrough were quickly smashed. Most of his responses were grunts. She almost threw her phone across the room in frustration. "Dammit! Why can't I get a straight answer? Who are these people?" she shouted. "I'm done playing house. I was supposed to be out of here by now, remember?"

A long silence replaced the grunts. "You're right, of course," Fortinbras finally replied. "I haven't lied to you... I may have left out some things along the way."

Liz stared at her nails and waited. He was used to others diving in to fill silences. No more games, she thought. No more scampering along behind, waiting for scraps of information like some starved animal. It's my ass on the line out here, and I'm working in the dark.

"So that's it?" he asked. She could hear his temper starting to stir, like a coiled rattlesnake getting ready to strike. "You just clam up, until I take you on a trip down memory lane?"

"I think you'll find the detour worth your time," she hissed back. "I'll be able to do a decent job if I have some clue why I'm here." She could picture him pacing back and forth in his office, simmering. When he finally spoke, though, his tone surprised her. "This is...*personal*," he said quietly. "And embarrassing. That's why I don't like talking about it. It has nothing to do with trust. Understand?"

"It's a start." Liz held firm. You're not getting off that easy, she thought. It was feet to the fire time. "Tell me."

More silence. When Fortinbras finally opened up, there was a sadness in his voice she had not heard before. "In a previous life, I worked at a law firm in Washington," he said. "I was a hotshot attorney. Or thought I was, anyway. I worked with a guy named Luis Garcia." Liz recognized the name. Jackie had mentioned him on the drive home. He was related to one of them. Now dead. Murdered, according to her lover.

"We were both young go-getters, cutting our teeth at the same time, gunning to make junior partner before we hit thirty," Fortinbras continued. "But Luis seemed to have the wind at his back. He brought in all kinds of clients, and big money. He made it look easy. No one realized until it was too late. He was dirty. The clients were all fronts for some of the world's most sophisticated crime syndicates. When I finally uncovered the tip of the iceberg and confronted him, he tried to blackmail me. Said I was in just as deep as he was. My name was on everything. He was right. I took it to the partners anyway. They backed me up. We threw him – and his clients – out after a boardroom vote." Fortinbras paused. "I'm sorry," he said, his voice cracking. "Those were scary times. Every time I heard a door slam or a car backfire or even an elevator chime, I thought they were coming for me. Payback."

"And…did they?" Liz asked, breathless.

"Not for years. He bided his time," Fortinbras admitted, begrudging respect in his voice. "He went on to be a high-flying defense attorney, a genius move. He could take in all of that dirty money right out in the open, no questions asked. I made the mistake of thinking that was how it would end. He would do his thing, and I would do mine, and we would never speak again." He abruptly stopped talking. She could hear him muttering and pouring himself a drink. Whatever it takes, she thought, pleasantly surprised. Get loose. Set those memories free. "The bastard turned state's evidence," Fortinbras growled when he picked up his phone again. "The feds had something on him, and he led them to us. Put us on a silver platter. It was brilliant. He pinned everything on the firm, had a paper trail to prove it, said he was the one who had jumped ship at the first hint of corruption, that we had hounded him for years, threatened his life…"

"What happened?"

"He won," Fortinbras replied, gritting his teeth. "He destroyed the firm. Federal agents kicked down doors. People went to jail. And I was a fucking fugitive, on the run. I went to ground…for a long time."

Liz was nodding her head. "I believe you," she said quietly. We are finally getting somewhere, she reflected. Now I have a thousand new questions. *I need a drink myself.*

Fortinbras read her mind. "Let me guess. How does my past

relate to your gig?" he asked. "They seem like regular people, right?"

"Except they're hell-bent on coming after you," she observed. "What gives?"

"The man I was before – his name, his past, his entire life – he no longer exists," Fortinbras responded. "Luis told them who I am. He used his own family and friends against me, in ways a person cannot forget…or forgive. Now they think I killed him. *Payback.*"

Liz let several long moments pass before asking the obvious question. "Well…did you?"

"No!" Fortinbras shouted. "Don't get me wrong, I didn't shed a tear. I would have liked to throttle him to death with my own hands. But that man had a lot of enemies. I was at the end of a long line."

Liz hesitated but decided to push it further. "They think you're a monster," she said finally.

"That's good to hear!" Fortinbras snorted. "Luis is having his last laugh, reaching out from beyond the grave. They've been trying to frame me for months."

"And?"

"And? AND?" His temper crackled back to life. "And nothing!"

Liz smiled, savoring the moment. She had found the edge. *I had to know this was for real.* Now it was time to step back. There was no need to jump into the abyss, no need for lasting damage. "Forgive me," she said innocently. "I meant, what happens next?"

"You want me to spell it out?" Fortinbras huffed, pinning her ears back. "You'll forgive me if I want some payback of my own!

They may seem like average joes, living their lives. But I'm not making that mistake again. Bygones are never bygones. I want to ruin their precious valley. I want to make them feel like hunted animals. Have them feel like I felt for so long. That's why you're there – I need to know when to hit them, and hit them so it hurts."

Truer words were never spoken, Liz thought. I'm always on board with a little well-deserved revenge. Things were starting to make more sense. She could hear him breathing hard. Her own pulse was fluttering. No two ways about it, she thought, power and vision are the best aphrodisiacs going. A rush of adrenalin made her gasp. *I can't get enough.* She heard him pour himself another drink. "I have been more than forthcoming," he said softly. "Your turn."

Liz took a deep breath. She made sure Jackie was still out of commission, then sat back down in the living room. "They think our pussyfooting around in the valley is all Deep Jungle," she started out. "The stunt out at the ranch pushed them into overdrive. Dealing with that is taking up a lot of their time. They're working with an attorney named Lucille. She's flying into Denver tomorrow."

Fortinbras grunted. "Good. What else?"

"Two of them flew to Chicago for the day. Came back with stuff with your name on it."

She heard him stop pacing. "What?" he asked. He sounded genuinely surprised.

"I don't know yet. I –"

"What do you mean, you don't know?" The temper was coming

around again.

"I didn't get inside tonight, for God's sake," she replied quickly. "I gave Jackie a ride to their meeting, remember? All I know is two of them went to a bank. They had a key to a safety deposit box." So much for our heart to heart, she thought. It was back to business as usual.

"We need eyes on that stuff. Fast."

"Understood. Will do." She kept her sarcasm to herself. Anything else, she wondered. Dance on a pinhead? Swim the Atlantic? *He makes it sound like they'll just hand it all over.*

"That's more like it," Fortinbras replied, oblivious. "Anything else?"

Liz was about to sign off when she remembered the SUV. "I think I was followed earlier," she said. "I lost the tail in traffic. Do you think they're keeping an eye on me?"

"Count on it," Fortinbras declared, turning serious. "Anything is possible with these people. Don't trust them for a second. But don't lose sleep over it either. They are no match for you."

Liz blushed. You old so and so, she thought. Maybe we do have a shot at something. I just have to get out of here in one piece. *There's no bigger turn-on than coming out on top.*

It was a delicate balance, he reflected. He reached over to turn off the electronic jamming gear, cursing as he did so. He hated needing her like this. Expendability was right up there with loyalty and silence in what he most looked for in people. People with no history to trip them up and few if any ties asking questions down the line. Liz fit that bill. He had seen to it, after all. She was too good to pass up. Still, bills had a way of coming due. He could no longer dismiss the voice in his head. It was getting louder, more insistent. She was like him. Which meant she would want what he wanted. Correction, he thought. *She does want what I want.* He could hear something else in her voice as well. Something he could use, at least for a while. There was a lot of ground still to cover. He felt reasonably confident he had the balance right. There was enough truth mixed in with the lies to make everything plausible. I *am* pissed, he thought. And I do want to wipe those irritating gadflys off the face of the Earth. He found it plausible they had hired a PI. "It won't help," he muttered. Following Liz around was a dead end. Above all, he was counting on them not sharing anything with her. It was too risky for them to expand their small, pointless circle of trust, no matter how much her lovestruck partner might want them to. *Every day they don't let her in, the more my creative imaginings look more like the gospel truth.* Liz didn't need to get any closer. Jackie was already gushing information like a fountain. That was more than enough.

A new possibility stopped him cold. He thought back to his trip up into Sandoval Hills, to the last moments of Luis' life. There had been no pleading, no begging. The man said nothing, in fact. He simply sat there in his office chair, watching as the intruder set up the crime scene. Finally, as Fortinbras turned to pick up the gun, he spoke. "Tell me. Is it the man himself behind the mask?" he asked defiantly. "Or did he send someone?"

My turn to be silent, Fortinbras thought. I'm not parading myself in front of your security cameras. But he did lean in close and lift the edge of his balaclava, so Luis could know he was no coward. That was when he saw it. A sparkle in the man's eyes. A knowing grin completely out of place at one's own execution. As if the hunted was actually the hunter. As if the jaws of a trap had just sprung shut. In the moment, it had driven Fortinbras crazy. He stepped back, grabbed the gun and fired. Even in death, as the body slumped sideways, the smile did not fade.

What did he do? What did he leave behind? In his mind's eye, Fortinbras saw a corpse digging its way to the surface, scrabbling to pull itself upright. Torn flesh hung in ribbons from bones and tendons. Scores of worms weaved their way through the decay; beetles scuttled away in all directions. When its head turned, he saw its face was ghoulishly white but untouched, unblemished. Luis' sparkling eyes stared back at him. His mocking smile curled into an enormous grin. His mouth opened, revealing black teeth and writhing maggots. Booming laughter cascaded across the graveyard.

Fortinbras racked his brain, trying to think of any overlooked possibilities. All possible paper trails led back to John Wellsey, not to the head of the Aponix Corporation. He had made sure of it, quietly and methodically. All loose ends had been taken care of. He poured himself another drink, willing himself to relax. You always thought you were the smart one, he seethed, raising a glass to the corpse. But look who's still standing. Look who's on the verge of changing the world forever. Get back to your dirt nap. And don't bother me again.

~

Part III

~

Hidden Away

A different time and place, and she would have smiled. It felt like something out of that groundhog movie. Here she was, again, standing on the same concourse. She looked around. People were milling around, lining up for coffee, searching their bags for boarding passes, herding children toward bathrooms. Just like yesterday. She looked up at the list of departures. There was their early morning flight to Chicago. She scanned the huge board, suddenly desperate to find her flight. The airport's PA system put her at ease. "Flight 6291 to Portland, Oregon, is now boarding at Gate B21," intoned a robotic female voice. "All passengers, please make your way to Gate B21…"

She sighed. Portland was just the beginning. She had never heard of the town. It was on the coast, several hours' drive from anywhere. That was all she knew. She could have taken a puddle jumper, but had no interest getting on a plane that small. The plan was simple enough – the note had been easy to memorize. An address. At the bottom, curt orders – "Go immediately. Tell no one. Burn this" – with a strange postscript: "if the time comes, hit the ground." The note and a slim manila folder were the only things in the second safe deposit box. The folder was tantalizing but useless. More law firm files. These ones confirmed that John Wellsey and Luis Garcia worked together. Anna had stared at their signatures for a long time. Part of her refused to believe that her brother had ever been part of such evil.

The drive was easy enough. Several hours south on the interstate – she stopped for bad coffee and a breakfast sandwich that tasted like a salt mine – and then took small roads west. They curved through miles of forest and then out across farmland. It was beautiful country – lush and green compared to the valley's dusty red hues. Then she was there. The rental car crested a final hill and coasted down the town's main street. The place had a funky, new age kind of vibe – she passed a body art place, a vinyl store, several coffee shops, something called Sunflower Granola Haven, and a tiny health food store. "Kom in for fresh Kombucha!" read a sign out front. She saw the street number in the store window and realized she had gone too far. Whoever lives here is hiding in plain sight, she noted. She pulled into an empty space and put money in the meter. She looked around, trying her best to ferret out anything suspicious. Nothing looked out of place. It seemed like an ordinary day in a small town on the Oregon coast. She walked back to find the address. She found it – a glass door with "249" stenciled in black – between an old movie house and a laundromat. She tried the door; it opened. She climbed the creaky wooden stairs, which led to a short, narrow hallway and a single door. She stared at the peephole in the door. *Only one way to find out who's on the other side.*

After she knocked, she heard footsteps on a linoleum floor. A minute passed. Then bolts slid back. The door opened slightly – a thick metal chain strung tight across the opening. A woman's face, small and round, appeared in the gap. "He said you would come. Wait, por favor,'" she said simply, then disappeared. When she returned, she passed Anna a photograph. "He said to show you this." Her voice was quiet but firm. Anna could make out a slight accent. As she looked at a faded, folded picture of her and her brother, she realized the woman was trying to make her feel safe.

"Muchas gracias. Soy su hermana," she responded, trying to do the same for her. "Te dijo eso?"

A warm smile crossed the woman's face. "No! He say no ask questions," she said, reaching to unlatch the chain. "Por favor...venga."

Anna found herself sitting in a tiny apartment with tight hallways and worn floors. The furniture was sparse – she was sitting on a threadbare two-seater on one side of the room; a beat-up table and chairs was across the way – but the walls were a riot of color: unicorns, rainbows, intergalactic space cruisers, ocean beaches. The woman laughed when she saw Anna checking out the drawings and paintings. "Mi niños," she said. "All they do is daydream."

"Someone else has the green thumb?" Anna asked, gesturing around at the bookshelves and windowsills. Ferns, vines, and other plants cascaded off every available inch of space. The midday sun made the place feel like a greenhouse. The woman shook her head. "Not me. Que es mi marido. I tell him I don't want to live in the rainforest, but he no listen…"

Anna smiled and nodded. Watching the woman busy herself in the kitchen, it felt like visiting her old neighbor Francine – stopping by for coffee and staying for the afternoon. She was beginning to relax, could feel her nervousness and trepidation melting away, releasing tense fingers and loosening locked-up muscles. She sat back on the couch and took a deep breath. The woman came in with a pitcher of ice tea and a plate of cookies. "Please. Help yourself," she said, sliding the tray onto the black chipboard coffee table between them. The woman walked around the table and sat next to her.

Anna found herself staring at a pile of golden, honey-drizzled pastries. She reached for one and bit into a crisp, buttery, sweet puff of goodness. If this is a trap, there are worse ways to go, she thought. "Orejas," the woman said brightly. "You call them elephant ears, I think? They are a little taste of home, so I make them…" Curled around at the top and bottom, they did look a little like that, Anna thought, trying to identify the woman's accent at the same time. "Where is home?" she asked finally, unable to place it.

"Venezuela…" she said quietly. "But that was before." She looked away. "Lo siento. I don't mean to sound ungrateful. Thanks to your brother, this is home now. Without him, I don't know what we would have done. We are citizens thanks to him. My husband, he has a good job. My children, they like their school. We never even knew his name, you know. Your brother?"

"Luis," Anna replied. "It was Luis." She tried her best to look calm and poised. Inside, she was increasingly bewildered. Why am I here, bothering this sweet woman, she wondered. What possible connection could she have to us? *Why did my brother send me here?*

"I see questions in your eyes," the woman said, a sad smile on her face. "No sé nada de ti. But I understand enough. And I am sorry for your loss."

Anna sat bolt upright. She stared at the woman, eyes wide. "How do you know?" she asked. "What else do you know?"

"Nothing." The woman shrugged. "He say that. He say there would be a visitor one day, after he was…gone. The woman in the picture. Just one, and that would be all. Our debt would be paid."

"What debt?" Anna asked, nonplussed. She found it hard to believe Luis would ever hold anything over the heads of an immigrant family.

The woman ignored the question. She leaned over and reached into the plants next to the couch. "He say we should not talk long," she said. "He say to give you this and explain." She pulled out a small, worn package and handed it to Anna. A big bold heading at the top splashed "*Retratos de Una Obsesión.*" She turned it over slowly. Apart from the Spanish words, it looked like a thousand one-hour photo envelopes from back in the day. A windswept elderly couple held hands on a beach at sunset. Children soared high on a swing set.

A perfectly coiffed man proposed to a dazzling brunette tableside in a fine restaurant.

"The men made us keep records," the woman said. "We stored them in back of a camera shop, in the envelopes, in case anyone came around."

"Records for what?" Anna asked. "What men?"

"Open it. Por favor." The woman's tone had changed. "There were many like him. They came in. We took care of them after. Then they left."

Like him. The woman's words were like an electric shock. Anna's fingers tore at the flap and she shook the envelope open over her lap; a handful of Polaroids fell out. She flipped one over and froze. There was John Wellsey, plain as day. Eyes closed, hair slicked back. Dashed red lines crisscrossed his cheeks and forehead. The headshot was taken on what looked like an operating table. She looked at another one. The same backdrop, but now the patient's head was a swath of bandages, with a small opening for his nose.

She looked at a third and her jaw dropped. A man was lying on a low cot hooked to a portable IV, one leg hanging over the side. The walls were stained dark with mold; the floor was filthy. But the most horrifying sight, even at a distance, was his face. The bandages were gone. A large, puffy mound of flesh lay there, shot through with angry, dark red veins that connected to ragged patches of blackened skin. Anything recognizable – eyes, nose, mouth – was lost inside the hideous swelling. "No es fácil de ver, yo sé," the woman said quietly.

"Recovery did not go well. He was there a long time."

Anna stared at the scrawled black writing below each image. Different dates and then the same eight digits. 88352129. A patient number, if she had to guess. "You took these pictures?" she whispered, struggling for breath.

"Si," the woman replied. "Insurance, the men say. Before and after shots for every client." Anna had trouble believing anyone would pay to have their head turned into a ruined, infected mess. It was the end of the line, she realized. His last resort. Once, he had been hunted. Once, he had been desperate. "What were you doing there?" she asked, unable to look at the Polaroid any longer.

"I was a nurse."

"In God's name, why?" Anna wondered aloud.

The woman looked away again. "One day, men come to the hospital where I work," she said. "They say if I no go with them, they kill us all. So I did what they asked."

"I am so sorry." Anna looked down, trying to imagine the woman's nightmare, her powerlessness, the never-ending threat hanging over her family. As she did, she realized one of the Polaroids had fallen to the floor. She picked it up; it was another shot of the man lying in the room. *Wait.* Something was radically different. Same room. Same body. *Different face.* There was still some swelling, but there was no doubt. She was looking at the man running the Aponix Corporation. A man with one name. *Fortinbras.* She scanned the patient number. It was identical. The image was from months later.

"Soldiers came for him just after that was taken," the woman said, pointing at the photograph. "I heard them downstairs, kicking down doors. I helped him escape, and then I ran too." She looked at Anna apologetically. "Lo siento. I did not know who he was. I still don't."

Anna entertained the tantalizing possibility for a moment – Wellsey on the run, trapped at the end of an alley, barbed wire fencing at his back, as men with machine guns and body armor moved in. How did he escape, she wondered. How did he survive? How the hell did he crawl back into the world? She would make sure to ask him those questions one day, she thought. *During visitation hours at his prison.* She looked at the woman for a long time. It seemed too good to be true – the photos brought Wellsey and Fortinbras together, linked him directly the legal malfeasance in the other safe deposit box, gave them a real chance against him for the first time. "Is this for real?" she asked, unable to hold back. "No catches? I want to trust you, but…"

The woman shrugged. "Do you have a choice? No lo hicimos. My family was starving. We were in hiding, afraid for our lives. One day, I knew they would come for us. Your brother got there first, and he say something terrible. He say if that man ever remembered that I help him, things would be very different. Your brother, he made us disappear. Not new faces, but new lives. He helped us start again. He say without his help, there was no hiding from that man. I believed him."

I would do well to heed that advice, Anna thought. *We need to move fast. We need to move soon. To do that, I need to break this woman's heart.* It didn't sound like Luis had told her the complete truth. Her ordeal was not over yet; she would have to testify. "I don't know how to say this, but —"

The woman fluttered her hands in the air, cutting her off. "No. I know what you are thinking. This is it. Your brother and I work something out." She reached into the plants again. This time, she pulled out a thumb drive. "This is as far as we go. My signed affidavit is on there. I'm not stepping into a courtroom."

Anna's thoughts swirled. A sworn statement was worth something, but wouldn't hold a candle to the woman testifying in person. *We need her.* But before she could say anything, the woman had stood up and was gesturing for her to leave. "Time is up," she said simply, avoiding eye contact. "Te deseo lo mejor."

"I never even learned your name," Anna said, trying to keep the conversation going. "Would you consider —"

"No, mi querida," the woman replied, guiding her to the front door. "No names. The burden is yours now. I did what your brother asked. You have what you need."

As the door closed, Anna realized the woman was right. Her brother had sent her a thousand miles so she could vouch for the only living witness. This is what we have to work with, she thought, making her way down the stairs. *If we do this right, it will bring him to his knees.* She stepped outside with a bounce in her step, oblivious to a tall man passing by. He crashed into her, nearly knocking her down. He caught her with one arm. As he did so, she felt him jam a piece of paper roughly into her hand. He pulled his ball cap low over his face and walked on without saying anything. It was over in an instant.

Hands shaking, she opened the note. "The man in the car was following you. He is not anymore," it read. "Leave immediately. You are safe." Anna looked up, panicked. She scanned the cars parked nearby. Most were empty. Kids were getting into a minivan. A dog was sitting in the backseat of an old Volvo, panting. *There.* A man was sitting behind the wheel of a red sedan, alone. His head was tilted back, as if he was sleeping. The angle was all wrong, however; his neck had to be broken.

Anna fumbled for her keys and felt in her bag to make sure the envelope and thumb drive were still there. She took a few tentative steps and then ran for the car, locking the doors and slamming the keys into the ignition. She peeled out into the street and did a sharp U-turn. She was several miles out of town, driving like the wind, before she thought of the woman and her family. *Oh God, no.* She called Derek. "The police department in Coos Bay," she shouted. "Call them! Tell them there is a disturbance at that address. Tell them it's life or death, that a family is at risk. I'll explain later."

The drive back to the airport was a blur. She spent most of it looking in her rearview mirror. No one made any moves. She accelerated for several miles, then slowed down for a few more. No one was keeping pace with her. Gas was getting low but she figured there was just enough to pull into the rental lot. I'm not stopping, she thought. *I'll coast in on fumes if I have to.* No one on the airport bus or at the terminal seemed to pay her any mind. Check-in and security were uneventful. She found a seat in a corner near her gate and was finally able to breathe. No chance of getting blindsided over here, she thought. A good, clear field of vision. I'll scream bloody murder if anyone comes near me. When her pulse finally stopped racing, she reached for her phone and called Derek back. "Please tell me the woman is okay," she pleaded when he picked up. "Please tell me the police got there in time."

"I'm not quite sure how to tell you this," Derek said gently. "They forced their way in when no one answered. No one lives there, hon. The landlord told the cops he rents the place out as a short-term vacation rental, but no one has stayed there for some time. Now tell me, what is going on?"

Anna's head swam. *Everything was a cover. I was supposed to walk away with a head full of false memories, so there was no trace to follow.* When she had left, she had the weird feeling that if she came back later, a stranger would have answered the door. Reality was stranger still. Did the woman even have a family, she wondered. Had they died back in Venezuela? *Where does she go now?* She tried to focus on the only things that mattered – what the woman had given her. *But it still feels like the floor could fall away at any minute.*

"Anna, are you there?" Derek asked. She could hear the deep concern in his voice.

"Sorry…yes," she replied. "I'm okay. We have what we need. But I think we're in danger. All of us. We need to get everyone together. Lucille too. Safety in numbers. Try not to scare anyone. Katherine and Ry should bring their kids. Jackie should bring Liz. Any family and loved ones. Understand?"

"Yes," Derek responded quickly. "Where?"

Anna paused. She loved his answer. No doubting, no questions. Just understanding and action. "We need to meet somewhere different, somewhere out of the way," she said. "Somewhere no one can listen in. Somewhere we can see people coming. Somewhere familiar only to us."

There was silence on the other end as Derek took it all in. "And you?" he asked finally. "What about you?"

"My plane leaves in an hour," Anna said, scanning the gate area again. "I'm fine, really. Can you meet me at the airport?"

"Sure thing," Derek replied. "I'll be waiting. I'll talk to Katherine and we'll figure out a meet-up point. Paul and Sam can pick people up. Don't worry about anything here. We'll be in good shape by the time you touch down."

Anna wanted to reach down the phone and hug him. "Derek, I think we've got him," she whispered. "This is for real."

Liz had just walked in the door when Jackie called. She barely had time to reach Fortinbras after they spoke. She heard a car screech to a stop out in the driveway. "One of them, Anna, went to Oregon *today* –," she was saying.

"I know that!" Fortinbras shouted impatiently. "We had a man there. But it's been hours. He hasn't checked in. What did she tell you?"

"She said a cloud over their lives is about to lift. But in the meantime, none of them are safe until Anna gets to the feds," Liz replied, ignoring the slight for now. Who else do we have on the ground, she wondered. *Please tell me there's a squad of armed men in the house next door.* "Two of them are driving around picking people up as a precaution. Including me, thanks to Jackie. They just –"

"Fine, fine," Fortinbras snorted, cutting her off again. "Let them run around like chickens with their heads cut off. More documents, I'd bet."

"It's not paper. There's a witness. A woman. A signed affidavit. Photographs." For a long time, there was no response. "What do you want me to do?" Liz followed up, feeling increasingly frantic. "They're about to knock on my door."

"Listen carefully," Fortinbras replied. His voice had turned strangely deep and hypnotic. It was unrecognizable. "Go with them. Slow them down as much as you can. I will be there soon."

Liz froze. "You're coming… *here?*" she asked.

"Me and some of my closest friends," Fortinbras replied. "But we may not get there in time," he continued. He did not wait for her to answer. "You have to get your hands on that stuff. Use any means necessary. *Any.* We'll take care of the cleanup. Do you understand?"

"Not a problem." Liz mentally repacked the overnight bag she was about to throw together. The tools of her trade traveled light. "I've got to go." As she spoke, she heard footsteps outside. The bell rang. When she opened the door, Sam was standing there. "Uh, hi, Liz," he stammered, looking at the ground. "Jackie said she called? She said you would be ready?"

"Oh, hey there," she replied, flipping her hair. She flashed the most brilliant smile she could manage. "I just got off the phone with her. We're taking a trip?"

"Just a short one…to a safe place nearby. I know this must all sound crazy."

"Should I be worried?" Liz asked, firing up the delaying tactics. "I mean, what is this all about?"

Sam shrugged apologetically. "I'm sorry," he replied. "I can't really explain, not now anyway. I hate to say trust me, but…trust me?"

Liz did her best to look worried and cautious but still calm, secure in his mighty protective powers. *Wherever we're going, I'm going to need as many allies as I can get.* "Please, come in," she said. "I need a few minutes. Make yourself at home."

"Sure thing," Sam replied. "We need to get Lucille on the way. Paul's picking up the others."

Nice TMI, Liz thought. *Keep it coming.* This is a man I can trust to spill the beans. She was surprised. If the attorney was on the list, they were scooping up everyone. That meant all and any close friends and family would be part of the rodeo. She was going to have to err on the side of taking out a good-size contingent. She smiled. *I'll need a bigger bag.* She headed upstairs and closed the door. She sat on her bed and took a moment, imagined walking out to meet the cavalry after it went down. It would be a pleasure. *Things have been taken care of here, boys. No need for your guns and grenades. There's been a tragic group suicide. Who knows why these things happen?* She stood up and headed to her closet. She hauled out a good-size carry-on and went to work.

She checked her watch when the first mild calls of protest started downstairs. Almost an hour had gone by. *Nice.* "I'll be down soon!" she shouted. Every little bit counts, she thought. Two basic rules of mind games – take away regularity, and take away rest. Another twenty minutes slid by. This time, there was a knock on her door. "Liz, we really have to go," Sam said, pleading.

"Be right there!" she called out, zipping the bag shut.

After a hunt for keys that were not lost and cleanup of several glasses that did not need breaking, she was about out of ammunition. "Good to go!" she said brightly. "Thank you for being so patient." Sam blushed despite his obvious irritation. Good to see the crush is still in full swing, she thought. Relieved and released, he headed for the front door as if sprung from a catapult. His car was running and pulled up by the curb when she walked outside.

Cue phase two, she decided as they pulled away. There wasn't much time to pump him for information. "Sam, I'm starting to get a little freaked out," she said, chewing on a nail. "No offense, but I hardly even know you. When people are in danger, they don't drive off to a secret location. They go for help, right? Can't we just go to the police?"

"We just...*can't*," Sam replied. He glanced nervously at her. "Has Jackie told you anything?"

Liz shook her head. "We've only been dating a little while," she said, playing the wounded dove. "I barely know you guys, and then there are secret meetings, and I'm somehow part of things because of my trip to Brazil? Everyone knows more than I do."

"Maybe it's better that way?" Sam offered. He turned onto the highway, headed for downtown.

"Now I really am getting freaked out," she replied, adding a shrill wobble to her words. "No one knows where I am. I don't have time off at work," she continued. She watched the resistance start to crumble in his eyes. *Time for tears to push it over the top.* "What is going on?" she sobbed.

Sam put a hand on her shoulder, tried to comfort her. The tears kept falling until finally, he relented. "I'll tell you what I know," he said. "Please...just stop crying?"

Liz dabbed her eyes with a tissue. "Thank you," she gushed.

"Before I ever met them, Katherine, Ry, and Jackie came out here from the east coast." Sam offered. "They were trying to escape their old lives and start again. They met Derek and I, and Anna and Paul, and we all got mixed up together. Katherine and Jackie had worked for a dirty law firm. The firm looked clean but really fronted for a global crime syndicate? Anyway, it came out west, looking for a foothold in meth and gunrunning and God only knows what else. They came across us by accident, I think…" Sam paused. He looked over as if to say, are you with me so far?

Liz glanced at him and then looked back at the road – the exit was coming up. They had five minutes, maybe less. "I'm good," she replied, a little too quickly. "Really. It feels like I've been dropped into a James Bond movie, but apart from that…"

Sam smiled thinly. "I told you it was crazy stuff. Well, it got crazier. We had coded files that threatened to expose all of the firm's operations. They came after us in the middle of the Bookcliffs Challenge. Derek was blown off his bike in an explosion and almost died. But we got the files to the feds, and then it turned into an all-out war. A friend betrayed us. The women almost didn't make it. Our friend Cobie died. Afterward, the FBI, the ATF, and the military hushed the whole thing up, said it was desert training exercises for a terrorist attack. They rolled up everyone back east too, put a bow on it, said we were free and clear. But one guy survived. He killed Anna's brother, and now he's hunting us down. We're a loose end in his grand plans."

"Who is he?" Liz asked, genuinely anxious. She watched the blocks pass, willing pedestrians to step out and traffic lights to turn red. She knew the office they had rented was somewhere around here. Minutes were turning to seconds. *We're just getting to the good stuff.*

"Why can't anyone stop him?"

"He's a ghost," Sam replied. "He vanished into thin air in the desert. He has a new name, a new face, a new life. But we've finally got something on him. Anna found a witness, someone who can tie his identities together. We need to stay together, and stay safe until she gets back later tonight. This man, he has ears and eyes everywhere. He owns people. He can't know…"

Oops, she thought. *Too late.* A wicked smile crossed her lips, flickering and vanishing beneath her poker face with Sam none the wiser. She tuned him out for a moment, thinking back over what he had to say. Someone was telling tall tales. Fortinbras was playing fast and loose with the facts, as she had suspected. But she understood collateral damage. Everyone was playing their roles. This group of plucky heroes was fighting on until the boot came down, as it had to. For Fortinbras to live, they had to die. *Fair enough.* In any case, the truth seemed mostly beside the point now. *I just need to know enough to hold a good hand at the table.* My job is simple, she thought. I'm staying several steps ahead of everyone else. She tuned back in as the car pulled up outside their new office. "Derek is taking care of everything else," Sam was saying. "That's why we're meeting up with him at the ranch." A pained look crossed his face. Thank you once again, Liz thought. You are a regular jukebox of information. *Just hit play, sit back, and relax.* Hiding out in the valley was a good call. After all, where else did this motley crew have to go?

"Okay if I wait here?" she asked. "And are you sure she's here?

Isn't it getting kind of late?"

"Yeah, Lucille's pretty much been sleeping in there since she arrived," Sam replied. "She's pissed."

Introductions were brief and perfunctory. Liz offered her the front seat. Lucille declined and sat in the back. The older woman looked like she had swallowed a hive of angry bees. Watching her in the side mirror, Liz could see her staring daggers out into the night. Her lips were pursed in a small, tight circle. She balanced a laptop bag and a stack of folders and papers on her lap. "I still don't see why I need to come with you," she grumbled. "Derek's a sweet talker and all, but I can take care of myself. Ain't nobody coming to break down my door."

"It's not just for protection, Lucille," Sam replied as they pulled away. "We need to stick together. Once Anna gets here and shares what she's got…speaking of which, have you had any luck?" Liz saw Lucille's neck muscles tighten. "No," she said emphatically. You mean *not here*, Liz thought. Not with a stranger in the car. The attorney's tone made for a quiet car ride. Liz watched out the window as the city's lights faded behind them. She checked her phone several miles later and was relieved to see cell service wasn't going to be a problem. So this is it, she thought, looking out at flickering shadows, dirt driveways, and battered mailboxes. Their precious valley. They have no idea that fighting back is making everything a thousand times worse for everyone else.

Finally, they turned into one of the driveways. Liz caught a glimpse of a horse on a carved wooden sign and then they were plunging through forest. Ahead, she saw they were racing toward some kind of bright light, which made no sense. As they got closer, the intensity was almost blinding; Sam slowed the car to a crawl. In an instant, the light shifted sideways like a lighthouse beacon and lit up several empty corrals. There was a tap on the windshield. Everyone jumped. A figure was standing next to the car. Sam squinted and then slapped his hands on the wheel. "Jesus! You scared us half to death," he called out, lowering his window.

"Sorry about that...welcome!" the figure replied, leaning in. It was Derek. He smiled grimly and nodded at Liz and Lucille. "Welcome to Fort Knox. We've got a full house. Come on in."

They pulled past a makeshift checkpoint made out of straw bales and splintered delivery pallets and parked. Liz got out and walked around the dusty lot, taking it all in. She was impressed. Someone had rented a trailer loaded with generators and gas cans. Tall men in cowboy gear were maneuvering them around and carting them off toward several large structures next to a fenced track behind her. A couple of the generators were already up and running, powering portable floodlights that had the entire area awash in the sterile white light that had wiped out their eyesight on the way in. Other men were standing around in small groups, talking and holding what looked to be hunting rifles. She saw Derek making his way over to them.

"Are we headed in there?" she asked him, looking at the ranch house behind the checkpoint.

"Nice decoy, eh?" he asked, smiling. "We left the lights on, tried to make it look welcoming. You're Liz, right? We met briefly at that city council meeting..."

Nicely done, once again. Liz nodded, marveling at the warmth of his smile and his easygoing charm. She realized with a start that the man standing next to her was an Olympic hero, a man she had watched on television over the years, a mountain biking legend. Not an adversary to be taken lightly, she reminded herself. Just in time, she remembered to slide her frightened deer facade in place. "I'm scared, Derek," she whispered, wincing slightly. "I don't understand any of this. Sam said some crazy man is after us but we can't go to the police?"

Derek's reassuring smile did not waver. "Yeah, I'm sorry about this," he replied. "It's precautionary stuff. But we can't be too careful. You're safest here with us."

Liz looked away. "I hope so," she said softly. "What happens next?"

Derek gestured over at the buildings behind her. "You'll find folks in the horse barns," he said. "Jill and Carl are sorting everyone out. Jill owns this spread. Carl is Katherine's dad. And a pretty good cowboy in his own right these days."

"Alright!" she replied bravely. Her eyes went wide, as she pretended to struggle to take everything in. "See you in there later?"

Derek nodded. "Thanks for coming, Liz," he replied. "Jackie thinks the world of you."

And I think of her as a means to an end, Liz thought. Still, she blushed despite herself. The man was a dreamboat. Eye candy was an unexpected side benefit of the gig. She turned to find her bag and headed for the barns with Sam and Lucille. As they got closer, she realized they were more like castles – huge wood beams and trusses stretched overhead, towering over the landscape. The cavernous double-doors of the nearest barn had been thrown wide open. Inside, an elderly couple was standing behind a large wooden table, handing out sleeping bags, bottles of water, and flashlights. The stocky, red-haired woman had a quick, brilliant smile, and appeared to have everything well in hand. The man – stocky as well, but shy and quiet where she was outgoing – was like an extension of her, darting off to find things at her request.

After a warm welcome, directions to the bathroom, and an explanation from Jill that the barn's usual occupants had moved to the far end, Carl led the three of them past some empty horse stalls to join the group. Liz was pleasantly surprised. Straw bales had been arranged in a circle in the center of the barn – a huge square area with massive, rough-hewn floorboards underfoot and open all the way up to the pitched roof overhead. Ry and Katherine were sitting with their kids over to one side. Paul and a young woman, presumably his girlfriend, were near them as well. On the far side, Jackie was sitting by herself. *No neighbors or family friends, then.* Even with Derek and Anna joining them, and the elderly dynamos out front, it was a baker's dozen. That made things more manageable. She scanned the room for food. Another good sign. People had not eaten yet. Ingestion was a preferred pathway, if possible. Airborne pathogens in a drafty barn could be seriously unpredictable. Lastly, the air was warm and close. *Bonus.* With the sweet smell of straw and hay hanging heavy in the air, faintly tinged by the acrid bite of manure and urine, people looked slow, tired, lethargic. *Out of sorts, and out of place. I couldn't have asked for a better setup.*

She made sure to make a beeline for Jackie, hug her and then try to disappear into the background. That was the flipside of a small group – as the newest arrival, she knew she could stick out like a sore thumb if she wasn't careful. She did her best to make small talk with Jackie while her brain worked on dosing, timing, and other variables. Jackie seemed relieved when she told her Sam had filled her in on the drive. "I'm still scared and confused," she said quietly. "But I trust you and your friends. It sounds like you've been through hell and back." Tears filled Jackie's eyes. "I can't believe it. You understand!" she whispered. "You are the best!" They hugged some more.

Liz was so busy multitasking, she didn't realize Derek had joined the group until he opened his mouth. "Make yourselves comfortable," he said. "We're in for a long night. Anna's plane was diverted to Sacramento with mechanical problems. She called. Everything is okay. They're due to take off in a couple of hours. I'm driving to Denver now to get her. So it'll be almost morning before she's here. In the meantime, the most important thing we can do is rest. I'm sorry."

Liz watched the group's reactions as Derek walked back outside. Some slumped over on their hay bales and shook their heads. Others groaned and stared off into space. The kids went back to their screens. Her own response was easy to manage because it was genuine – disappointment, shot through with jealousy and begrudging respect. Fortinbras had her in place, in case. But he was calling the shots. And job one was buying himself enough time to get on the ground. Mission accomplished. It made no sense for her to move forward without Anna there. *But that doesn't mean I'm going to sit here and spin my wheels.* She was paying close attention to Katherine and Ry across the way. They hadn't batted an eyelid at the news, and were now whispering furiously to each other. Next to her, Lucille's poker face had not cracked either. *Interesting.* The attorney stood up, scowled, and said to no one in particular: "I'm going to find some space to work in this henhouse." She ambled off down one of the barn's dimly lit corridors.

Liz looked at Jackie and shrugged. "Guess I wouldn't mind checking this place out," she said. "You okay?" Jackie nodded and said she was going to try closing her eyes. "Good thinking," Liz replied. "I'm too keyed up to sit still." She patted a pocket, making sure the patches she needed were there, and stood up. She made sure to walk down a different corridor. Soon, she was lost in an equestrian maze. She passed dozens of empty horse stalls, feed bins, and then more horse stalls. Down the far end, she could hear low whinnies, nickers, and snorts. She realized the cluster of buildings was actually a single, interconnected super-barn. A sudden flutter of wings near her head made her leap back and squat in a defensive crouch. She looked up to find a white barn owl peering down at her from a new perch, swiveling its head to take her in. Don't worry, she thought, relieved. You're not the prey I'm after.

There was no sign of Lucille, so she tried a new direction. At least it was something different. Racing pictures hung on the walls. Shelves groaned under trophies and worn leather saddles. Memorabilia was everywhere – turnstiles and seats from torn down tracks, saddle cloths and jockey racing silks, framed race day cards from decades past, even a restored betting window, the faded Benning Raceway letters barely legible on the worn wood. They have their own equestrian museum, she thought. How nice for them. Then, something else, much more interesting: a series of small, square rooms. Could be offices, she realized. Down the far end, a light was on. *Bingo.*

She slid like a shadow into the office next door, felt around for a chair, and sat in the darkness, waiting. Lucille coughed, shuffled papers, muttered to herself, typed on her laptop. What are you working on, she wondered. *What do you know?* Fortinbras had never mentioned her, but after what Liz had seen in her eyes, she knew enough. The woman was a problem, and tougher than the rest of them. She was a stubborn old bulldog and she had something clamped in her teeth. Her glances earlier left no doubt about one other thing – she had little time or trust for the newest member of the gang.

The attorney's phone buzzed. "Yes, that's what I needed," she said impatiently. "Uh-huh. Okay. Got it." She hung up. "Yes!" she hissed quietly. "Got you, you son of a bitch. Peel away all the layers and it's not Deep Jungle out here. It's you...everywhere we turn. Now what are you doing fracking up the valley?" More typing and muttering followed.

Liz stayed put for a moment, weighing her options. If things went wrong, she would be toast, but Fortinbras could roll on. If Lucille stayed on the scene, she was going to cause endless problems. It didn't sound like she'd had a chance to share her news...yet. The bitch could be writing an email, she realized. That did it. She checked to make sure there were no other shadows haunting the offices. They were alone. There would not be a better opportunity. She palmed one of the patches and stood up.

"Hey there," she said brightly, stepping into Lucille's makeshift office. The attorney looked back at her, startled. She frowned as Liz pulled the door closed. "Working late?" she asked, looking over Lucille's shoulder. The cursor was flashing in some legal database search box. *Excellent.* "I overheard your call," she continued. "I have to say, that's good work. Still, it did take months, didn't it? Time no one really has..." As she spoke, she moved fast, slamming the patch on the back of the attorney's neck before she could react.

"What the hell?" Lucille tried to pull away, understanding blossoming in her eyes. Liz leaned in heavily on her chair, trapping her against the desk. "I —" The attorney's jaw locked up in mid-sentence.

"Wow. That was fast, wasn't it?" Liz asked, releasing the pressure on the chair. "I know, you're thinking you'll shout for help. Get up and knock me over. No time for either, I'm afraid. Can you feel your heart racing? Your pulse fluttering? Your face is turning purple, Lucille. You're struggling to breathe. It won't be long now, I promise. I'll be over here, going through your stuff. Goodbye."

Liz pulled out a pair of plastic gloves and went into overdrive. She riffled through papers in a stack of manila folders on the desk, pulling anything that mentioned Aponix. She removed all handwritten notes as well. She counted seconds under her breath. A solid minute early, though, she felt the swivel chair begin to slide past her, and was unable to stop it. Lucille's body crashed to the floor. In the quiet of the barn, it sounded like a small rhinoceros had gone down. *Damn it!* She stood up, fighting a surge of panic. The dosage must have been off. More likely, the woman had been a steak dinner away from a coronary. She stared at Lucille's laptop. Had anyone seen her with the computer, she wondered, trying to remember. It was a small one, easily lost among a stack of files...*there's no time!* She grabbed it, threw it together with the files, and ran out into the hallway. *No one yet.* She scanned the walls of memorabilia, looking for anywhere she could stash them. One of the bookshelves had fancy, curly-cue edging running along its top edge. *Good enough.* Liz ran over and flung the materials up there. They vanished from sight and landed with a small, satisfying thud.

The moment did not last long; another oversight – *sweet Jesus, the patch* – propelled her back into Lucille's office. She tore it off the body and looked around frantically for other loose ends. Slow down, she told herself. See everything. Breathe. No one is coming. She remembered to tug off her gloves and stuff them in a pocket. *Okay. That's better.* Lucille had fallen nicely, sprawling across the office floor. The look of surprise on her face would take care of any doubters. The woman had just suffered an enormous heart attack. An autopsy would reach the same conclusion. *This is going to work out after all.* It was time to call for help. She ran down the hallway, screaming.

He hit the water fountain again. There wasn't much else to do. Walking around an empty airport in the wee hours of the morning had quickly lost its appeal. I should have brought my bike, he thought. The place was big enough to pull off some quality maneuvers. He nodded at a group of night janitors and started another lap of the concourse, keeping an eye on the runways. Finally, lights pierced the night sky. He watched as the jet touched down and taxied out of sight. Twenty minutes later, Anna was the first person to walk out of the arrivals gate. Any relief he felt at seeing her quickly evaporated. She was shaking like a leaf.

"He's coming. He's right behind us," she said, struggling to make eye contact. "Somewhere up in that sky, there's a jet and he's on it."

"What?" Derek asked, horrified. "How could you possibly know that?"

"Because *he called me*. Just now, after we landed," Anna replied. "He said he was glad our mechanical problems were nothing serious. He thanked us for gathering everyone in one place. Said it made their job a lot easier."

"Anna, look at me!" Derek demanded, disturbed by the distant, vacant look in her eyes. He held her face in his hands. "You said it yourself. We're going to get him. You got what we needed. And we've got safety in numbers. We camp out at the ranch and call in the feds."

There was no sign she heard him. "Derek, he said he was sorry about Lucille, that he hated to lose her," she said, her breath hitching in great, gulping gasps. "What does that mean?" She fell into his arms and started to sob. "What does that even mean?"

Derek staggered backward, struggling to make sense of the words himself. Lucille had been in the barn with the others. She had looked annoyed and cranky, but that was business as usual, right? We've trusted her with everything, he realized. We've been an open book. The thoughts were familiar. *We've been here before*. The face of his best friend Jake spun into his mind. *Lead FBI agent for our protection, and he gave us up out there in the desert. It's what this guy does. He turns our strongest link into his own back door.* If Lucille was an informant, that meant —

"He gave us a choice," Anna said quietly, interrupting his thoughts. "Go back to the ranch, and everyone dies. If we so much as think about calling someone for help, everyone dies. Or…you and I bring him what I have, time and place TBD, and it ends with us."

Derek shook his head in amazement. Get a load of this guy, he thought. Mixing threats and offers as if he had a shred of credibility. Wellsey was clearly enjoying himself. *Playing God and thinking he can get away with it.* "I've heard this story before," he said finally. "We wrote our own ending last time, remember? Let's keep this simple. We drive back to Grand Junction. We make a copy of the stuff you brought back. I'll leave a package at the bike shop with instructions in case I don't turn up again. And then we hightail it out to the ranch and circle the wagons. We're all in this together. If he thinks he can just roll in there and wipe us out, he's badly mistaken."

Anna nodded wearily. "Deal," she replied. "Let's get on the road." Before her exhausted eyes closed, she managed to walk him through her day. He drove and listened, stunned. It sounded like something out of a spy novel; he couldn't believe he had just let her get on a plane and fly into such turbulence. "From now on, I'm putting you in bubble wrap," he joked awkwardly, feeling guilty. He glanced over at the photographs and affidavit, and could see they were showstoppers. "No wonder he's coming," he said grimly. "These will end him."

Out of all of the madness of her day, though, one detail nagged at him long after Anna had fallen asleep. The dead man was no mystery. But who was the guy who had protected her? Where had he come from? *I didn't think anyone had our backs.* No savior came to mind. He promised himself he would not let her out of his sight again. His mind quieted as the car's headlights bored into the darkness and the miles flew past, lulling him with the smooth thrum of the road. Sometime later, grinding metal and breaking glass jarred him out of it; he looked in his rearview mirror and saw two cars locked together, sliding off into the median. It looked like a nasty collision. He shook his head several times, willing himself awake. The timing of the crash had been fortuitous; his heavy lids had been moments away from closing. *We should be debris on the side of the highway right now.* He stopped at a twenty-four-hour copy shop and took care of the package, then ran over to a convenience store to caffeinate himself. He drove downtown and left the copies in an envelope next to the register in the bike shop. All the while, Anna slept on. By the time he turned onto the valley road, dawn was tugging at the sky to the east. This is going to be a day like no other, he thought. *This is the day we finally end this.* He stared at his phone for a long time, reluctant to give up the last few moments of peace and quiet. Finally, he made the call.

Ry picked up almost immediately. "Derek, we didn't want to bother you," he said, sounding frazzled, "something terrible has –"

"We know about Lucille," Derek cut in. "There's no time to explain. You didn't…"

Ry sighed. "No. We're holding the fort and waiting for you," he replied, sounding dejected. "We've done nothing about it. The others didn't like it. They're sleeping now."

"I'm sorry, Ry. I can only imagine," Derek replied. *Everyone there still thinks she's on our side.* "Look, we're coming in hot – Wellsey is somewhere in Colorado and we've got what we need to blow him out of the water. We're about ten minutes away."

"Understood," Ry answered, shifting gears as best he could. "Same plan?"

"Yes! The minute we get there, the minute we're all safe and accounted for, we make the calls," he replied. "Five different agencies. Five different contacts. He can't control all of them. Then we sit tight and wait for the cavalry." He left the rest unspoken. *After they get there, maybe then we can think about Lucille.*

When they hung up, Derek felt relieved. He found it hard to believe. He had half-expected Ry to drop in a code word, letting him know they had been compromised. That the defenses hadn't held. That some key detail had been overlooked. Something. He sounded stressed, exhausted, anxious. But not like someone was holding a gun to his head. *They're safe and we're still safe.* Now we just need to get there, he thought. He watched the road like a hawk, waiting for roadblocks to erupt from the asphalt, a corrupt cop to pull out from a cottonwood grove, zombies to leap over the horse fencing racing past the window. He was long past being surprised by anything. Instead, the last few miles rolled by. The morning sun glinted off a nearby pond. Cows buried their heads in a food trough. The

Bookcliffs and the Grand Mesa stood tall in the distance, framing the valley with their ancient ridges. Soon enough, the sign for Bunscombe Ranch came up on the left. They turned in, passed the checkpoint and parked. As he walked around the car, vines did not sprout from the ground and tie him down. Hungry dinosaurs did not step from the forest. Anna snapped awake when she understood where they were. "Let's get inside," she said urgently, fumbling for her seat belt. "Let's finish this."

They ran past the sentries and into the barn. They found the group mostly awake, rubbing eyes, stretching sore muscles, brushing off straw. The kids were the only ones still out. Smiles and sighs of relief were contagious as everyone laid eyes on Anna. "You did it," Katherine said quietly, coming over to hug her. "Can you show us?"

Anna nodded. After more hugs, and squeezing Paul extra tightly, she pulled out the photographs and the affidavit. She walked them through everything as fast as she could. Then it was Derek's turn to break the news about Lucille.

"There's no way," Paul protested. "She always worked tirelessly for us."

"Yeah, that's bullshit," Jackie agreed, shaking her head as she walked over. "There's no way."

"I know. I don't want to believe it either," Derek replied. "I don't know what to say. She was working for him."

"It's time to bring Wellsey to justice," Anna said firmly, trying to refocus the group. "For us, for my brother, for the thousands of others he has brutalized." Everyone nodded solemnly.

"Let's do this," Sam said. "Five phones, five calls. Let's find him a jail cell." They went to work, watching each other to see who would make contact first. Jackie was the first to hang up, reporting that she had hit a recording instead of a hotline. "What gives?" she asked. "How could the FBI not answer?" Paul was next. "ATF's line is down, too," he said. Ry looked up. "Same thing here." Derek paced back and forth; his phone was still ringing. Finally, he heard a faint click on the line. "We are unable to connect your call at this time," droned a robotic female voice. "Please try your call again later…"

Derek realized with a jolt what was going on. "Quick, try another number, any number!" he shouted, jabbing 911 into his own phone. The line rang and rang. Then there was another faint click, and the robot started her mindless patter once again. He glanced around and saw the looks on the others' faces. He didn't need to ask. He's turning our strengths into weaknesses, he realized. *Strength in numbers means nothing if we can't communicate. And we can't be safe in here if we don't have eyes out there…* He didn't get much further. Ry's phone was ringing. "Unlisted number," he said quietly. "It's him."

Here we go, Derek thought. *I knew it wasn't going to be that easy.*

Shaking Things Loose

"I'm not one to get misty eyed, but it has been a long time, Mr. Austin," the voice said. "We weren't able to find each other in the desert."

A real shame, Ry thought. *If we had, we wouldn't be here.* He grimaced nonetheless, unable to stop the voice from snaking deep into his brain. In an instant, he was back there, staring out across Washington's skyline, trying to reach Katherine with the news that would change everything. Then only fragments of memory remained, as everything went horribly wrong. A flock of pigeons exploding into flight behind him. Men bursting out onto the rooftop, fanning out to surround him. Behind them, watching, the man in an expensive suit. A man who said little, even as they held him over the edge and let him go, as he clawed at the air and sky and clouds and the ground flew up to claim him –

"Mr. Austin, are you there?" the voice inquired, breaking his fall. "Phone service can be so...*uneven* these days." Ry still did not respond. Finally, he cursed quietly and flicked at his phone. "You're on speaker," he growled. "We have unfinished business. Leave the others out of this."

"Oh come now," the voice purred. "All for one and one for all, isn't that more your speed?"

No one answered him. Most of the group – Sam, Paul, Jackie, Katherine, Derek, Anna, and Liz – huddled together around Ry's phone.

"On to business then," the voice barked. "I approve. The time for fun and games has passed. Although you've done well. Evading my men. Taking out Lucille –"

"We didn't take out anyone, asshole!" Sam shouted. "She had a heart attack."

"I don't know who that is talking and I don't really care," the voice hissed. "I was trying to be polite."

"We're way past that, Wellsey," Derek called out, trying to get a rise out of him.

"If I run into someone with that name, I'll be sure to pass along your message," the voice replied, unperturbed. "My name is Fortinbras. You have some things that belong to me. I need them back. You need your lives. So I think we can work something out."

"We heard your ultimatum the first time," Anna said quietly. "The answer is still no."

A wave of digital laughter echoed from the speakerphone. "That offer is no longer on the table," the voice followed up. "New day, new rules. You may find the new terms less to your liking."

"Why would we ever agree to *any* terms with you, asshole?" Sam shouted. "We have everything we need right here!"

"The man makes a good point," the voice said drily. "I have a feeling that's going to change. You guys hold steady out there at beautiful Bunscombe Ranch, and I'll check back in a few." The line went dead. The group looked at each other, confusion, anger and fear swirling in their eyes. "Wellsey makes no idle threats," Derek said urgently. "We have to take it seriously. I'll let the sentries know. You guys, check out the rest of the barn, make sure there's nothing strange."

That's a nice way of putting it, Ry thought, looking over at his friend. We're talking about explosives, bombs, poison gas...hell, there could be soldiers hidden away in a structure this massive. Still, he didn't bat an eyelid. "A couple of us should stay here, with the kids," he said calmly. "Everyone else, come with me!" Down the first hallway, he found a stack of hay rakes, and passed them out. Poke every bay of hay, look behind every barn door," he called out. "And let's stick together. We all know what happens in horror movies when people split up."

They searched for a good half hour, and came up with nothing but a rusty car battery and a collection of hammers, saws, and wrenches. The only thing out of the ordinary was the horses in the pens down the far end. They seemed spooked, stomping their hooves, occasionally rearing high in the air. Foam dripped from the mouths of the colts. Ry and his crew had no idea what to make of it. "Let's head back," he said finally. "There's nothing here."

When they reported back, Derek nodded grimly. "The sentries are on high alert," he said. "But nothing's going on out there either."

*Yet...*Ry thought, finishing his friend's sentence. He looked up. Jill, Carl, and several ranch hands were carrying in plates and trays groaning with sausages, scrambled eggs and pancakes. It was an amazing sight. "Coffee and syrup's coming," Jill said with a smile. "That little kitchen of mine is in overdrive." He saw the kids were up now too. He made plates for them and sat next with them and Katherine while they ate. Around him, everyone fell on the food like animals. He poked at his plate, but wasn't hungry. "We're sitting ducks," Katherine whispered. He nodded. "I agree. Any other ideas?"

"Maybe we could send someone out to the road, or ask Jill about other ways to get off the property," she offered. "Someone could slip away?"

"It may come to that," Ry replied. "But that means risking lives. Sitting put may be the best option we have." He checked his watch. The minutes were crawling past. He got up to help the kids find a bathroom and then played hide and seek with them, trying to pass the time. Derek walked over to say he had tried calling 911 again but the robot lady was still there – all frequencies remained jammed.

Ry dug his phone out of his pocket to try his own luck. He stared at the device for a long moment. The screen was dark, but different parts of its innards were lighting up for brief instants, as if a lightning storm was raging inside. When he tried to dial, everything worked as normal. And by the time the robot voice greeted him, the light storm had died down. Was Wellsey launching some kind of electronic warfare, he wondered. He already has us all in one place, cut off from the outside world. Why mess with our electronics? It didn't seem like the main event. *Everything we have on him is analog.*

He was about to say something to Derek when he saw a strange movement out of the corner of his eye. He didn't hear the roar. He just stared at a widening crack in a thick support beam. *It shouldn't be doing that.* "Earthquake!" he shouted. Everything started shaking. People fell sideways. Plates, food, bags, tools flew in all directions, turned into lethal debris in an instant. There wasn't time to get outside. There were no doorways to huddle under. He looked up and realized entire sections of the roof were shifting from side to side. His eyes fell on the table that the farmhands had moved over to serve breakfast. It looked solid. "Over there!" he shouted at the group, pointing at it while looking around frantically for Nora and Jonah. He saw them emerge, straw-covered, from hiding places nearby. They were rooted to the ground, terrified. He raced over as best he could, scooped them up, one under each arm, and headed for the table. They crashed to the ground after a few feet and carried on on their hands and knees. Ry saw the others converging as well, scrabbling, swaying, staggering, stumbling to hoped-for safety. Wordlessly, they packed in like sardines, two and three deep. He held the kids close, whispering that everything would be okay. "Close your eyes," he told them. "Think about your favorite place. Imagine you're there. Right now. The sun is shining. People are having fun…"

While he spoke, he looked around, praying Katherine had made it under the shelter. All he could make out were objects, jittering, sliding and crashing around, brought to life in a sudden, lethal dance. He watched a feed bucket launch itself at a horse stall so violently that it shattered. A hay rake shot past, skittering across the floor until its tines buried themselves deep in a beam. Somewhere high above them, a high-pitched creak kicked up. Ry realized it was the sound of wood under tremendous strain. Moments later, there was a loud snap, sharp and sudden, followed by the terrifying whistling of a large object in freefall. Instinctively, he placed his body on top of the children and braced for impact. A deafening *boom* just inches away drove wood splinters into his neck. Table legs bent inward and the tabletop pressed down on his back. He gasped for breath as dirt and dust filled the air. He pushed Jonah and Nora out from under him as best he could, not knowing if he was sending them into greater danger. It wasn't until he clawed his way out and hugged them close that he realized the ground had stopped moving.

He turned around slowly, afraid of what he might find. Through the haze, he could make out others pulling themselves free from under the table. Something large and gray lay on top of it. He reached out and touched the sharp, broken edge of a metal blade. It was a fan. One of the barn's massive overhead air circulators had broken loose and hurtled to the floor. Ry peered closer, looking at the tangle of wood, wires, and metal. Somehow, just barely, the table had held. Around them, beams were warped and split, bent at crazy angles.

Overhead, sunlight was pouring through huge, ragged holes in the roof. But the barn still stood. He asked Liz if the kids could stay with her for a moment, and then stepped over piles of fallen shingles, looking for Katherine. Moments later, she found him. "You saved us!" she cried, wrapping her arms around him. He hugged her tightly, pressing his face into her soft, warm hair. "Thank God you're alright," he murmured. "Let's help the others."

They tried their best. Incredibly, everyone had made it under the table. Now, dazed and covered in dust, they were walking around, testing joints, wiggling fingers, brushing off their hair and clothes. Ry came across Jill and Carl sitting off to one side, saw the tears in her eyes as she looked around the ruins. "We're going to check on the horses," she said softly. "We'll be back." He found Katherine with Anna and Derek – they were both shaken up but okay. "I don't mean to scare anyone," he said quietly, "but what if that was the beginning? What if his men are outside, waiting for survivors?" Eerily, as if on cue, Anna's phone started to buzz. "Here we go…" she muttered. She put the caller on speaker.

"Do I have your attention?" the voice crowed. "Some wastewater injections into a few wells and *voilà*, rock and roll. I've always loved science. Power at your fingertips."

No one said anything. Around them, the dust continued to settle.

"I'll take your silence as a big, fat white flag," the voice continued. "Here are the new terms. Drive to the Kriegler

Enterprises facility near the Bookcliffs. All of you. Immediately. I believe Anna's been out his way before. Contact no one. Do not stop. Come unarmed."

They looked at each other, stunned. It could not be a coincidence. Deep Jungle had kept their wheels spinning for months, blinded them to the real conspiracy unfolding in the valley. Wellsey had been lining them up in his crosshairs for months.

"What about the children?" Anna croaked.

"All of you!" the voice snapped. "Was I not enunciating clearly? Every last man, woman, and child. Bodies too. Got it?"

"We understand," Ry replied quietly, desperately trying to think of any way to slow down a runaway train. Looking at the others' faces, no one was having any luck.

"For any heroes sitting around the campfire sharpening your daggers, remember something," the voice hissed. "It was small, localized. We have thousands of wells across that valley. And a lot of wastewater. I think Anna can attest to that. Earthquakes are bad. Toxic flooding is worse. You're doing the right thing. Think of the greater good. You have sixty minutes. The clock is ticking." The line went dead.

Carl rejoined the group. He threw a bolt gun into a corner in disgust. "They're all gone," he said quietly. "We had to put the horses down…and now it's our turn, is that right? I only caught the end of what he was saying." Paul and Sam turned to talk to him. Something in Carl's tone made Ry think of his failed attempts to calm the doomed animals. Their wild eyes, their panicked movements. *They knew this was coming. They could sense it.* Wellsey seemed the same way. His timing was impeccable. Ry looked around at his friends. They all looked petrified. None of them had calculating master plans in their eyes. How am I supposed to spot a mole, he wondered. I failed at it twice before. We all failed with Lucille. The thought stopped him cold. Wait a second. He *still* has someone on the inside? His mind started to race. *Liz had found Lucille. She told us what happened.* He looked over at her, appalled. She was smiling and talking with Jonah and Nora. But her hands were hidden beside her lap.

Staring at her, revulsion gave way to a small, dirty glimmer of hope. Perhaps we still have a card or two left to play, he thought. *Assuming Wellsey values his lieutenant.* He mumbled something to the group about needing a moment, and could he talk to Derek briefly? He got his friend off to one side and spoke quickly, while trying to look as untroubled as possible. "Lucille was no traitor," he whispered. "She must have found something. Something worth killing for." He nodded over at Liz. "Notice how Wellsey has perfect timing? That's because she's his eyes and ears. She's texting…right now!"

Derek's eyes flickered in her direction. His face was ashen. "Here's what we need to do," he said hurriedly. "Ask Katherine to take Jackie outside. Say you'll explain later. You buzz by and grab your kids. I'll take care of Liz."

Ry nodded. "Whatever happens, don't let her text him," he

replied. "We can impersonate her for a while. Buy us some time." Coming up with the plan was one thing. Talking to Katherine was easy enough. By the time he turned to walk over to Liz, though, his palms were sweaty and his heart was pounding. He wanted to tackle the intruder before she could text another word. Instead, he tried to sound casual. "Hey Liz, thanks so much for keeping an eye on these monsters," he said as he approached. "I think everyone is okay. Are you alright?"

Liz looked up at him and smiled weakly. "Pretty shaken up, to be honest," she replied. "And s-c-a-r-e-d by what I overheard. Are we going to do what he says?"

Ry sighed. "I'm not sure," he responded, choosing his words carefully. "I don't know that we have much choice. Anyway, we'll figure it out together in a second. I just want to get these guys out of the way."

Liz nodded. "Sounds good," she replied coolly. "They're great kids, you know?"

Ry choked out a thanks, outraged by her duplicity. Thanks for the compliment, he thought. They're great kids you've put in harm's way. He figured he was looking at another sociopath. It was the only possible explanation. *These two deserve each other.* Furious, he wanted to knock her out of commission. Instead, he ruffled Jonah's hair and picked up Nora. "Let's go, team!" he said with a cheerfulness he did not feel. "Mama's outside."

Stepping out of the barn only made him angrier. Jill and Carl's farmhouse was a blackened, smoldering ruin. Cars lay on their sides and roofs; several had smashed together and come to rest in a bed of broken glass. Pieces of fencing and shards from utility poles lay everywhere, scattered like the broken toys of a giant. The fact that everyone had survived such devastation was a miracle. He noticed the ranch hands were working their way through the horse paddocks around the track. He watched as one of them steadied a shotgun and pulled the trigger. The sudden, loud report reminded him that the animals had paid the heaviest price.

Derek poked his head outside. "We're in business," he shouted to Ry. "She's out of action." He tossed him her phone. Ry looked over at Jackie. *Shit. Cat's out of the bag.* He ran over to catch her before she could run inside. "Jackie, look at me," he said, grabbing her arms. "I have bad news. Liz has been using…all of us. She's working with Wellsey. She killed Lucille."

Jackie stared at him as if he had lost his mind. She struggled to escape from his grip. "What are you talking about?" she asked, her voice trembling. "Let go! Liz is not our enemy. Trust me. I know her."

"No, you don't. None of us do," Ry replied forcefully. "But she's not who you think she is." He let her go and held up Liz's phone, scrolling through recent texts: ATTNY SITUATION RESOLVED – TREMORS STARTED – CALL NOW – NO

CASUALTIES.

Jackie's eyes went wide. "I've been living with an assassin…my God, what have I done?" she whispered. "I confided in her…I've been so blind…I've put us all at risk."

"It's not your fault," Ry said quietly. "None of us knew. And we've caught her. She can't hurt anyone else now." He heard footsteps and turned to find Anna jogging over to join them. "Guys, we've got to move," she said quickly. "Derek just brought everyone else up to speed. The clock is ticking."

"We're actually going to do what he says?" Katherine asked, incredulous. She hugged Nora and Jonah close. She looked at Ry, sure he would back her up. "Tell her it's madness!"

Ry's shoulders fell. "We have to at least make him think we're doing what he wants," he replied. "He won't hesitate. He'll do this" – he gestured around them – "to the entire valley, and follow it up with a toxic tidal wave."

"He'll do that anyway!" Katherine replied.

"We have to face him one way or another," Anna offered. "Either we let him destroy the valley first, or we fight back. I don't want him hunting us down, one by one. We need to stand up to him together."

"And we can at least put some more time on the clock," Ry followed up. "To give the feds and the police enough time to reach us." MORE TIME. TREE BLOCKING ROAD, he texted. Wellsey's response – UNDERSTOOD – was almost instantaneous.

At least we have his attention, Ry thought. He felt his own phone vibrate in his pocket. When he checked it, there was no sign of a call, but the laser light show had kicked in again. Soon enough, it faded. *Bizarre.*

Any further discussion was cut short; the rest of the group had walked out to join them. Liz stumbled forward next to Paul. She had been gagged and her hands were tightly bound behind her back. Jackie walked over and punched her in the face. Tears poured down Jackie's cheeks. "How could you?" she gasped. "How dare you!" Liz shook off the blow and stared straight ahead.

"Let's get the ranch hands in the lead and rear cars," Derek was saying to Paul, Sam, and Carl. "Get the kids settled so they don't see anything. I wrapped Lucille in a horse blanket. I suggest we put Liz in a trunk as well. You wouldn't believe what I just found in her bag. Unmarked vials full of liquids. Powders in plastic bottles. Enough syringes to stock a hospital ward. I'm guessing she was Wellsey's Plan B." His tone was grim and harsh. He was a man ready for battle.

The group marched away from the ruined barn, headed for the cars. Ry used a crowbar to tear out spider-webbed windshields while the ranch hands rocked several vehicles back onto their tires. It was going to be quite the convoy. Most of the cars started easily – a couple took some coaxing. As they pulled out, they heard emergency air sirens in the distance. It was a tantalizing reminder. Safety and the outside world were not that far away. Paul and Sam would take a car and head south to make the calls. Wellsey can't find out about their detour, Ry thought. Then there was the delicate part – getting him away from the triggers before he realized others were closing in. He figured Liz's fake texts would buy them an hour or so. They would drive slowly and pull over to make sure Paul and Sam caught back up. It was risky. If Wellsey had men out on the road, the game was up. But he had a sense their adversary was a little cocky, feeling like he had this thing all rolled up. *He thinks he has eyes on the inside. He's saving the rest of his chips for the main event.*

Finally, they pulled out, moving slowly, looking for threats. All seemed quiet as they headed north. Behind them, Paul and Sam hit the gas in a mostly intact Mustang. Ry had chosen a small, badly dented SUV. Jackie was sitting beside him, doing her best to put on a brave face for the kids. "Windshields are overrated," she pointed out. "Just look at this natural air conditioning." Katherine was in the back with the Jonah and Nora. He looked at their tired, scared faces. I am not driving my family to their deaths, he told himself. We're doing the best we can.

He tried to keep his eyes on the car in front, but the landscape crawling past made it difficult. Fallen trees lay in piles, stacked in some places like kindling. A busted transformer hanging over the road rained down sparks on the convoy. Cows and horses wandered past, freed from splintered pens and ungated fields. Raw ridges of earth and rock rose up on either side – he realized with a start that the road had shifted sideways as a result. He revved the engine and pulled over a huge, buckled knot of asphalt. Red lights lit up in front of him and he hit the brakes. Going nowhere fast is just fine, he thought. He reached for Liz's phone and hammered out another text. CONVOY MOVING. SLOW. ROAD IN BAD SHAPE. Wellsey responded with a terse OK. Ry looked up to see ranch hands herding reluctant goats off into the grass. A few minutes later, the convoy lurched forward again.

Katherine fought the urge to commandeer the vehicle and drive away, the accelerator pinned to the floor. She understood the plan, and hated it. She watched the tortured, broken landscape slip past and cursed Wellsey's name. Lucille was dead. Jackie's out-of-nowhere girlfriend had betrayed them. The entire valley was in danger. Once again, they were living a nightmare. *And now we're driving right into his open arms.* She tried reminding herself that they just needed to buy some time. Until help arrives. The words were cold comfort. Wellsey was liable to shoot them on sight. By turns he was calm and calculating, then off the handle. If only he had caught a stray bullet out in the desert, she thought. This might all have been different.

Up front, Ry gripped the wheel tightly. He put down his window and stuck his head out, straining to see ahead. "Shit, shit, shit," he muttered under his breath. As they pulled closer, Katherine could see it now as well. A huge silver tanker had jackknifed in the middle of the road. The driver was inspecting his rig – he looked dazed but was otherwise in one piece. She remembered Anna's descriptions of the silver cylinders pulling past her when she had driven out on her fact-finding trip. And in a heartbeat, she knew why her husband was anxiously checking the rearview mirror every few seconds. That driver had a CB. Anything out of the ordinary – a car racing to join the convoy, say – might merit a quick check-in with the boss. "Stop," she said coolly. "I can buy us a couple of minutes."

Ry looked back at her warily. "Don't worry," she said reassuringly. "I'll play dumb and see if he needs anything. Tell the others to open their trunks to block the view. It's the best we can do." Ry nodded. "Good thinking," he replied, his brow furrowed. "We might even get a hostage out of it…" Katherine shook her head at the insanity of the situation. In the alternate universe we're now living in, she thought, this is what passes for logical thought. The car slowed. She told Jonah and Nora she would be right back, and got out of the SUV.

"Everything alright?" she called out as she approached. The man turned to look at her, then went back to what he was doing. He was checking a tangle of curled red hoses that connected the cab to the tanker.

"Damned if I know," he replied, cleaning off his hands with a rag. "Even if I could get her moving, the brake lines are shot." He squinted at her, then looked at idling vehicles. "Is there something I don't know about?" he asked. "Shouldn't you be headed south?"

Katherine could pick up no hint of malice in his words or body language. He seemed like a regular guy – ball cap, worn jeans, weatherbeaten face – marooned in a strange land. If he was part of Wellsey's team, he deserved an Oscar, she thought. "We've got friends up there," she replied finally, shrugging. "Need a ride?" she followed up, trying to sound casual.

Before he could answer, the radio crackled in the cab. "I'll be right back," he said, turning as he spoke. He covered the ground quickly and swung up into the cab. Katherine took the moment to check on the convoy. She had to smile despite the situation. Behind her, several of the convoy vehicles had pulled up next to each other. All of their trunks were up, creating a multi-colored shield of battered metal. Quick-thinking ranch hands had busted out snacks and sodas from the food supplies. They were pulling off an impromptu tailgate, looking distinctly unconcerned. She checked her watch. Ten minutes had passed. If Paul and Sam didn't show up soon...

She heard footsteps and turned around. The driver had again covered ground quickly – now he was standing close to her, hands on his hips, head cocked to one side, leaning in. "I need to stay with my rig," he said. The easygoing smile was gone. His lively eyes were now dull and flat. "You best get to those friends of yours."

Katherine nodded, unnerved by the sudden change in his manner. She had planned to make more small talk, ask if he needed help – anything to buy precious seconds and minutes – but there was no longer a need to keep up pretenses. If it had not been so before, it was now. The man had orders from Wellsey. She turned and headed for the SUV. As she walked back, the ranch hands pulled down the trunks. She almost cried out, knowing the grim face behind her would call in anything suspicious in a heartbeat. Instead, she almost shouted with joy. There was a battered red Mustang idling back there. She could see Paul and Sam's faces. Take that, psycho, she thought, savoring the small victory. *You may have your plans. But we can improvise on a knife's edge.*

Ry hugged her when she got back to the SUV. "Sorry," he said, cracking a small smile. "I waited as long as I could. I figured Liz would get in touch. So I had to. Plus, as you may have noticed," he added, jerking his thumb behind him, "the Mustang showed up."

"I figured. Consorting with the enemy." She smiled and kissed him. "What did they say?" she asked eagerly.

Ry managed another small smile. "It's good news," he replied. "They got through, made the calls. Help is on the way."

Katherine's heart leapt. As the convoy juddered back into motion, hugging Jonah and Nora close, she allowed herself a small moment of hope. *Crisis averted.* Passing the damaged tanker, however, her heart sank again; they were jumping from the frying pan into the fire. Ahead, the road stretched to the Bookcliffs in the distance, straight as an arrow. Trees and fence posts were still upright here. They were leaving the destruction zone behind. And they were back on Wellsey's clock. A mile passed. Then another. She could not keep her eyes off the declining numbers on the state highway posts. In between, she monitored the receding asphalt for flashing red-and-blue lights, scanned the skies for helicopter blades.

"They'll come," Ry said gently, reading her mind. "But not yet. They'll be tracking the convoy. They know not to come over the horizon until we get there. Wellsey's as good as his word, you know that. If he gets so much as a whiff we're not playing by his rules, the entire valley pays the price."

She leaned forward to whisper in his ear. "I don't like playing games with our lives," she said quietly.

Ry turned to look at her. "My love, I give you my word," he replied. "The moment he lets down his guard, the moment he gets carried away with delusions of grandeur, I will end him. The rooftop may be years ago, but it feels like yesterday. Wellsey has a lot of debts to pay." His words kept alive the embers of hope in her heart as they left the highway behind. Lulled by the hypnotic thrum of the SUV's tires on the crushed stone, Jonah and Nora burrowed in close to her and fell asleep. Moments later, emotionally exhausted, she closed her eyes as well.

When she awoke, it was to an abrasive, crackling sound that set her teeth on edge. It sounded like someone was scraping metal across a microphone. She realized with a start that they were not moving. She could not see much through the dust-covered windows – the vague outlines of a contractor trailer loomed off to one side. She looked around the inside of the SUV, panicked. Next to her, Nora and Jonah were starting to stir. Up front, Ry and Jackie were facing straight ahead.

"The clock has started," Ry said, speaking calmly and quietly.

"The agencies will be coming for us. Our job is to buy time. Minutes, maybe an hour? We do what Wellsey says. Do everything as slowly as possible. No talking. Everyone understand?"

Katherine and Jackie nodded. Outside, the terrible noise started up again. Katherine realized it was a loudspeaker crackling to life. "Exit your vehicles!" a voice was barking. "Guards are coming around. Throw your keys and phones in their trash bags."

So, she thought, the moment of truth has arrived. She felt strangely calm. She leaned forward and planted a kiss on the top of Ry's head. "I love you," she said quietly. She looked at Jackie and told her the same thing. Jackie met her gaze and mouthed the words back to her, tears in her eyes. Then they did as they were told. Katherine held the children close and opened her door. They stepped out of the SUV, squinting in the bright sunlight. She tried to take in as much of their surroundings as possible, waiting for her eyes to adjust.

There was not much to see. The convoy had pulled into a dirt lot hemmed in on two sides by tired, worn-looking contractor trailers. Well rigs and dancing methane flames towered in the background. All of the cars and SUVs had pulled in as a group, so only the rear vehicles had any chance at escape. The one open side, to the west, was hemmed in by a towering barbed-wire fence. Behind that, the ground stretched away to the edge of the horror that Anna had described. The ocean of pollutants dominated the landscape, a massive black eye punched into the earth. There were vehicles over there too; men were walking around carrying wooden crates.

Movement in the corner of her eye instinctively made her turn. She realized a dozen masked men in flak jackets and camo fatigues were stationed around the perimeter of the lot. Two of them were walking toward them, tugging open black trash bags.

After Katherine tossed her stuff in the bag, she and the kids found Ry and made their way to the front of the convoy. Everyone was doing the same, milling around nervously, waiting for the loudspeaker to crunch syllables into a screeching mess of feedback once more. Minutes passed. The guards returned to their positions. Nothing else happened. "So far, so good," she whispered to Ry.

Ry nodded. "Yeah, Wellsey's got quite the God complex. My bet is he wants us feeling small, alone, and helpless before he takes the stage in all his glory. Should be quite the entrance," he said sarcastically. "The longer he takes, the better."

Katherine looked around while they waited. They were standing in a space about the size of their backyard, bordered by car headlights, trailer siding, and the rock wall that finished off the enclosure. She hadn't paid it much attention before, assuming the trailers were placed next to it for security reasons. On closer inspection, she realized it was not stone or natural at all – it was some kind of dark, burnished metal. She stepped back, trying to get a better sense of what she was looking at. The looming structure was the size of a small house, with a dome on top that jutted into the sky. Otherwise, its smooth skin revealed nothing – there were no windows, no stairs, no entrance. As she stared into its opacity, parallel lines suddenly began to scythe through the dark metal. She cried out in surprise and stepped back, pointing. The lines were perfectly parallel, about seven feet apart. A moment later, they stopped. Katherine looked over at Ry. She knew what was coming next. "You called it," she said quietly. She didn't need to watch the next set of lines appear. When a slight gasp went up from the crowd, she had no need to turn around.

Instead, it was the voice that did it. Seeing that familiar stranger on television was one thing. But hearing him open his mouth just a few feet away was too much. His low, nasal whine had not changed one bit. She spun around and there he was. Short, squat Wellsey, standing proudly in his space-age portal.

"Thank you for coming," he said, an impish smile on his manufactured face. "You're going to be part of history."

The sheet of metal whispered past his face. Fortinbras stared up into the electric blue sky. A pale sliver of silver moon hung low on the horizon. A slight breeze tugged at his shirt. It was a beautiful, perfect day for the dress rehearsal. Finally, irresistibly, he looked down upon his guests. You followed my yellow brick road, he thought. You passed through my fields of destruction. He could sense the fear, track the uncertainty in their eyes. But mostly, there was resistance and anger out there. *You've come looking for the man threatening your hearts and minds, for the stranger calling your courage into question. Welcome to my personal Oz.* Such a sweet beginning, he thought, holding onto the moment. When hope remains. When self-control is still a choice. When humanity insists on masking its true nature.

It was time for the tour. A technician inside flipped a switch. Stairs unfolded below him. "Please," he said simply, "come up. See the future." No one in the crowd moved. Predictably, the biking hero was the first to respond. "No more games! We brought what you wanted!" he shouted, brandishing a backpack. "Then we all walk away."

"Indulge me!" he shot back. "Human history is about to change. We can settle everything else after you check it out. And in any case, what choice do you have?" he asked, gesturing at the armed guards. He thought about saying no one would get hurt, but that seemed a bridge too far. "You'll have to trust me," he offered instead. "You have what I want, and I hold your lives in my hands."

People began shuffling toward the steps. Fortinbras saw the hope in some of their eyes as they stepped past him. Reading minds continued to be child's play. This time, it went something like – *wandering around this maniac's play toy is buying time for our rescue. Do what he says and stay alive.* Fair enough, he thought. Hopelessly misguided, but understandable. Ahead of them, steam was pouring out of vents in the orb. He thought back to the kid and smiled. Thanks to him and so many others, the design had been perfected. Operations were completely silent. Capacity had quintupled. And the limits of the conveyor belt had been overcome. Now the entire floor tilted to deliver heavy loads.

He headed for one of the platforms overhead while the technicians started giving the tour. He watched the group shuffle reluctantly over to the dark orb. "Go ahead, touch it!" he called out, unable to resist. "Such beauty…such power! Within months, the orbs will be all over the planet. Converting any material into energy, transforming natural resources at almost no cost! We can leave behind the crash course we set for our planet during the Industrial Revolution. Mother Earth will be able get up off her knees!" He realized he was getting carried away and stepped back, leaving the technicians to finish giving the tours. Still, he was struck by his own generosity. The great and powerful Oz had done far less for his benighted subjects. Here you are, behind the curtain, he wanted to say. He felt himself tearing up. Wrapping up the loose ends of the past here, inside the promise of the future was beyond poetic. Perhaps one day, he thought, I'll write a memoir detailing how I changed human history. Unlike Tesla and Marconi, I will live to see the glory of my genius. I will stand astride this planet like a colossus. But let's not get ahead of ourselves, he reminded himself. These fine people need to understand we're not in Kansas anymore. And this time, the man behind the curtain is not going anywhere.

The technicians herded the group back outside. He could hear the raised voices and shouts. "We're not cattle!" someone was saying. "You can't treat us like this!" It was time to start stripping away the hope, to lay bare the basic truths of the situation.

"Actually, I can," he said, stepping back into the doorway. "I can do pretty much whatever I want." The view pleased him even more now. During the visitors' brief time inside, his men had slung a ring of chain-link fencing around where they had been standing. The metal circle was tight enough that it was standing room only down there. He could see growing anxiety had replaced much of the initial outrage.

"The old ways of doing business, of powering the world through pollution and contamination, are on the way out," he continued. "We are about to topple some of the world's largest companies. But to do so, we need to send a final message, to push things over the edge. We cannot afford to live this way any longer. Today, we bury the old world. It's inefficient. It's pathetic. It's corrupt. It's downright dangerous. In a few minutes' time, the basin behind you will accidentally rupture. By tomorrow, the toxins will have reached the Colorado River. Alaska's North Slope was the tragic opening chapter. Today is the last moment of darkness before dawn."

It was like striking a match. A group of young men near the front exploded into motion, sprinting toward the stairs, hatred slashed across their faces. "You're not messing with the valley!" one of them shouted, fist in the air. They made it part of the way up before a hail of tranquilizer pellets brought them down.

"Anyone else?" Fortinbras inquired nonchalantly as some of the guards stepped inside the fence. He stepped to one side as they started pulling the bodies up the stairs. "I appreciate all this attachment to Grand Valley. It seems like a nice enough place," he continued. "But really, we need to see the big picture, don't you think? This is the cost of doing business. Kriegler Enterprises will be wiped out by the cleanup. In the long run, your valley is a rounding error in creating a better world."

There was full-blown fear out there now, he was pleased to note. But still way too much resistance for his liking. The main players were standing together in a tight cluster, looking at him while whispering urgently to each other. "Tick tock, tick tock, am I right?" he asked them. "Where are those pesky feds? Shouldn't *someone* be here by now?" He was almost ready for panic now. *Almost*, he told himself, savoring the knife's edge. *There is no going back.*

One of the women – Anna, if his memory served – spoke up next. "You promised that if we came with our files, you wouldn't destroy the valley," she said, spitting out the words with venom. Fortinbras smiled. "Think back, dear lady," he replied. "I did no such thing. I simply stated that if you didn't get here quickly, I would be forced to do so." Next to her, the bike hero was looking agitated. He was dying to say something. Soon enough, your wish will come true, he thought.

"We made copies," Derek blurted out finally. "If our friends don't hear from us, they go public with everything."

Fortinbras waved away his concerns. "I presume you're talking about the package at the bike store?" he asked, a wicked smile on his face. "It's the strangest thing. The place will be firebombed shortly.

Arson. No one knew the famous owner had made such enemies. But after his death, new details will come to light that explain everything…you get the idea." He enjoyed watched their faces flinch as his words knocked out another pillar of their resistance. He was enjoying the game now. Pretty soon, they would have no reason to exist. He was pretty sure which card they would play next. They didn't have many left. The pleas for the children would come last.

It was his old adversary who offered Liz up on a platter. "We have her," Ry said simply. "Let us go and we'll tell you where she is."

Ding ding ding, we have a winner, Fortinbras thought, smiling. They have gone with the traitor in their midst for one thousand dollars, just as I predicted, please Alex. Sadly, the host will find there is no clue or answer on the little blue screen. *Double jeopardy means nothing in my courtroom.* "You'll have her to thank for the tranquilizers later on," he said quietly. "She's always done her job well." The extracurriculars were the problem. It had taken her longer than most, but she had still gone there. *Probed the past. Tried to befriend me. Acted as my equal.* There was nowhere to go from there but up. Best for everyone to nip that in the bud, he thought sadly. She was talented, no doubt. But not irreplaceable. And now of course, the queen of chemistry knew too much.

"Even if you could produce her," he continued, "I think you would find her value has dropped precipitously." He looked over at the trailers, pleased. The windows were open. "Talk about a disappointment. I had to move heaven and earth to bring her onboard. Or certainly put people in the ground, anyway. Loving parents. A sibling. But she's had only one eye on the job for some time now. Served her purpose and all that...not unlike you, I suppose. It's time for her to join her family."

The group were watching him warily, aware that he was no longer speaking for their benefit. No one responded, and Fortinbras plowed ahead. "Anyway, I have a pretty good idea where she is," he noted drily. "We took the liberty of searching your vehicles while you were taking the nickel tour." He nodded to one of the guards. The chiseled soldier went over to the trailer to his right and yanked out their proposed hostage. When he saw Liz, his anger surged, washing away any regret. He had made the right decision. "Did you enjoy my speech?" he needled. Judging from tears running down her bruised cheeks, his salvos had hit their target. "I made you, remember? Having thoughts of your own isn't a crime. *But not on my time.* Throw her in with the others!"

Inside the pen, Liz retreated to one side, alone. "Would you do me one last favor?" he asked her. "Tell them what else is in the trailer?" She raised her head and met his gaze for a long time, staring daggers at him, saying nothing. Finally, she spit in his direction and looked away. He ignored the gesture. "It is so difficult to get good help these days," he said, returning his attention to the group. Things were looking up. The anger and resistance was gone. Confusion and bewilderment reigned. "This brings us back to the matter of the cavalry," he said, preparing to cut through the last strands of hope holding them together. "No need to mince words. They're not coming. They never were. Those touchingly urgent calls were routed here, to the communications center in that trailer. Don't be shy. Walk over and look in those windows." Fortinbras waited. No one took him up on it. He watched as hope fled from their eyes. "Never mind," he said, shaking his head. "Take my word for it. There's a lot of gear in there. And even if someone decided to come up this way, that truck you passed was a stroke of good luck. Another sign this is all meant to be. My driver will tell them to stay back. The tanker's contents are unstable. They could explode at any moment."

"Why do all this? Why not just kill us?" asked one of the other women.

Fortinbras smiled, slightly surprised by her audacity. *You, my dear, have been played like a violin*, he thought. *If I were you, I would never open my mouth again.* "Because I wanted you to *know*," he replied, slightly exasperated. "To understand. And to witness this moment. You are the past. But you will help power the future. Today, I am reborn! I cleanse myself of all those years of subjugation and pain. You are the only remaining links…" He spread his arms wide as he spoke. He closed his eyes, savoring the rare chance to speak freely. "Today," he continued, "the slate shall be wiped clean."

"You expect us to march into your fancy baking oven?" Ry asked incredulously, breaking into his moment. "Like a bunch of robots?"

"The choice is yours. There is always a choice," Fortinbras

snapped, returning reluctantly to mundanity. Why did people always struggle against the inevitable? Why did life insist on veering into messiness and chaos? He opened his eyes.

Ry was staring at him, hands on his hips. "The alternative being…you let us go?" he asked. "We come together and sing kumbaya? What?"

Fortinbras shrugged. "You watch each other get knocked out and dragged away, one by one, not knowing when your own time is up," he replied. "Either way, you can see my generosity. There will be no pain. No need for suffering like mine any more. That is the promise I'm bringing to the world."

"You are one sorry son of a bitch," Ry replied. "I don't need to check with the others. We speak with one voice. Go fuck yourself!"

"I figured. So be it. You can't help some people," Fortinbras replied, disappointed. He would have enjoyed some begging. He motioned to the guards and turned to walk inside. The prospect of watching their lives end en masse in the orb put a spring in his step. He had not made it far, however, when a phone's ring stopped him cold. He poked his head back outside, and gestured for the guards to hold up. The phone rang again. It was coming from one of the garbage bags. *That's not possible.* He went down the stairs himself and tore at the bag, oblivious to anything else. Phones and keys scattered on the ground. He grabbed the vibrating slab of glass and plastic and headed back up the stairs.

"I told you to leave her alone," a voice hissed when Fortinbras picked up.

"What are you talking about?" he asked, his heart pounding. *Why am I talking to a ghost?* "We did what you asked," he continued, trying not to stammer. "Cleaned up down there. Everything has been taken care of. No more testing."

"I have no time for this. Free my daughter, you son of a bitch. You talk too much."

The head of one of the guards nearby split open like a ripe melon. The body fell to the ground, pumping blood out across the dirt. Fortinbras stumbled backward into the facility, horrified. *The ghost is here? What the hell is he talking about?* He scanned the landscape, frantically searching for intruders.

"Games demean people," the voice growled. "I can see her in my scope. Stop hiding. Tear down the fence and let them go. Tell the guards to put all weapons in a pile and join you."

Fortinbras peered down at the group. He was astonished. *One of them is his daughter?* He shot back through the grainy video in his mind, realizing he had missed other signs as well. The tails. The death in Oregon. The crash on the highway. All way beyond the means of this crowd. They're just who they say they are, he thought caustically. *A bunch of dupes with a hidden sugar daddy.* He shifted seamlessly into crisis mode, pushing the intelligence failures to the back burner. This was an opportunity too good to pass up. Wiping the slate clean had looked pretty damn good. Extorting and then killing off the head of the world's most dangerous, near-invisible private army as well?

Possibly even coopting the brigade? Close to priceless.

First things first, he thought, his hands trembling in anticipation. *I need to get my hands on her.* He mumbled a response to the old man while running the numbers. He figured he had around thirty men, counting the ones in the trailers. He doubted the old man had that kind of firepower this far from home. *Besides, get everyone out of the open, and they have to come in here on our terms.* He muted the phone and called out to the guards. "Bring me the women," he shouted. "The rest of you, take cover."

As the men approached the group, another two went down in a red mist, shot in the chest. Both lay unmoving on the ground. Outside the fence, men were pouring out of the trailers. They may be fish in a barrel, Fortinbras thought, but there are a lot of them. Too many to stop —

"Time's up," the voice whispered in his ear. Fortinbras heard a sudden whistling sound in the distance. Something very fast screamed closer. Before he could move or think, one of the trailers blew apart in a hail of flame, torn metal, and burnt flesh. The force of the shockwave blew him backward into the facility, knocking him off his feet. He scrabbled around in the sudden, smoke-filled darkness for the phone, ready to scream epithets at his hidden enemy. Coward, he wanted to shout. Do you want everyone dead? Unable to find it, he staggered to the doorway; he found nothing there but swirling black-and-gray smoke. The sun was reduced to a dirty silhouette in the background. Screams of pain and calls for help pierced the burnt air.

Fortinbras took a tentative step downward, hoping the air would be clearer closer to the ground. That was as far as he made it. A blur of motion exploded into his midriff, knocking him back into the facility once more. Before he could move, someone's knee slammed down on his chest. They grabbed a fistful of his hair and pulled. He screamed. They slammed his head against a metal floor grate, making a sickeningly wet thud as bone cracked and flesh tore. The world went black.

When he came to, Fortinbras was enveloped by a glorious warmth that eclipsed the massive throbbing in his skull. It lasted a moment. Then he realized what it was. His eyes flew open. His breathing took off. He was lying on his side. His face rested on the ridged grill plates next to the orb. He tried moving his arms and legs. They did not respond.

Sometime later, he heard footsteps. "Welcome back! I took the liberty of escorting everyone else out," a voice said. "They were kind enough to leave everything running." The voice was familiar. A pair of dirty boots appeared in front of him. Liz squatted down to make eye contact. She placed one of the guards' handguns on the floor next to his face. "Your hands are not bound. Your legs are free to move. But you'll never use them again. You lied to me about a lot of things, Fort, but I won't lie to you." She dangled a small empty syringe in front of him. "I always carry this close to my heart. For special cases." She stood up and took a step back. "If this baby is everything you say it is..." Her voice trailed off. She shook her head. "To get so close, I can't imagine..."

He started blinking frantically, trying to communicate a thousand stories, a million moments. Intense effort to open his mouth yielded a small, plaintive wail. It died at her feet.

"I had a correction for the record. You didn't make me, Fort," she continued, ignoring him. "You made me different. But I can still feel. I miss my sister. My parents did not deserve to die. I don't try to escape the past like you do. It makes me stronger. I think that's why I'm standing here. What do you think?"

Another flurry of blinking. A series of bleats. Fortinbras stared into the blackness only a foot away. He was sweating profusely now.

"You're no different than Bruno, you know. Another fixer. Nothing more," Liz followed up. "Any regrets?" she asked, squatting down again. "Once for no. Twice for yes."

He blinked once.

"Me neither," Liz replied, walking away. "You're coming out as compost, Fort. First time you'll actually help make the world a better place. I'd say thanks, but..."

Her voice trailed off. The room fell silent. Fortinbras could do nothing but count the seconds until the platform started to tilt. He strained against it ferociously, willing his living prison cell into motion. Not so much as a muscle fiber twitched. His body slumped forward, then slid the rest of the way, finally catching on the lip of orb. The metal wall cranked up and up behind him until his body finally tipped in. He slid to the bottom like a marooned fish, his face inches from the drains that would eventually take away his remains. He heard a faint whump of air as the orb's entry panel settled in place above him.

It was hot and getting hotter. Sweat was pouring off him. The metal began to burn his skin. For several more moments though, he was still able to formulate thoughts. He had always wondered about the moment of conversion. The idea gave him an erotic thrill, pushed him into asphyxiation play with his whores. Only a few subjects had gone in alive. But it seemed like a gift beyond measure, to swim in an electric ocean, to look up at an infinite sky as your life force poured out into the world, pure energy seeking out other forces in the universe. As his skin began to split, blister and crackle, he realized his fate was different. With the orb on its current setting, he would slowly cook to death. He would be alive for hours. Then he descended into agony.

Epilogue

Anna remembered fragments. The certainty of what was coming. Then, only swirling smoke and dirt as the world came apart. At some point, someone knelt beside her, held her hand, kissed her on the forehead. His words were a whisper. "You're safe now. Your friends will live." A forest of men in black boots and fatigues followed. Rumbling vehicles. Hints of blue sky. Last of all, a stretcher in an ambulance, an IV bag swinging overhead. A familiar face leaning in, a rough tug at her clothes. The woman's lips were moving, but the words made no sense. Anna realized she was losing consciousness. She tried to reach for the woman but could not move. She stared up at the woman's strange, tight smile and cold violet eyes, terrified. Then a deep, restful darkness like she had never known swept her away.

The proceedings, when they finally started, were brisk whirlwinds of questions, objections, rulings, and reframed statements, broken into twenty-minute chunks so she could rest. Their questions deserved better answers. But the ones Anna gave Derek and the others were no different. She had no choice. The note Liz had stuffed in her pocket made that painfully clear.

"I'm not sure."

"I don't know."

"I don't remember."

She lived elsewhere now, in anticipation of what was to come. Cleanup. Transfer of Aponix technology to an international energy organization. Real, tangible things that could be counted on. Proceeds from the Bookcliffs Challenge would help people in the valley rebuild their lives. Deep Jungle had pulled out, citing "recent events and long-term uncertainty." The BMX park would open in the fall. Missing Lucille's service was the only regret she allowed herself. Looking back any further threatened everything.

We all walk away, the note read. Or none of us do.

*****

ABOUT THE AUTHOR

Jasmine Winterson is the author of several novels. She lives in Charlottesville, Virginia.

If you enjoyed *Power Play*, check out *Roost* and the other books in Ms. Winterson's *Uncertain Ground* series, available at:

www.amazon.com/Jasmine-Winterson/e/B008XMMTTW.

www.ingramcontent.com/pod-product-compliance
Lightning Source LLC
Chambersburg PA
CBHW032145190626
46814CB00005BA/1839